BlackAmber Books
BRIXTON ROCK

Alex Wheatle, of Jamaican origin, was born in South London. He is a founder member of the Crucial Rocker sound system, for whom he has written lyrics for performances. Alex is now working with Book Trust to introduce literature to the dispossessed; to this end he organises and holds workshops in prisons and young adult institutions. His fiction includes *The Seven Sisters*, *East of Acre Lane* (re-issued by Harper Perennial), *Checkers* (co- written with Mark Parkham) and, most recently, *Island Sounds* (Allison & Busby).

Praise for BRIXTON ROCK

If you are not thrilled by the book and moved to tears,
then you have no right to call yourself a book lover.
A powerful first novel...an extremely explosive story.
The Borough News

Its great virtue is to articulate a world that rarely
finds a sympathetic voice even in fiction.
Caribbean Beat

Wheatle's choice of chapter headings reads like
a classic late seventies' reggae collection...with
knowing reference to Marley lyrics.
Echoes Magazine

Brixton Rock

Alex Wheatle

BLACKAMBER BOOKS

Arcadia Books Ltd
139 Highlever Road
London W10 6PH

www.arcadiabooks.com

First published by BlackAmber Books 1999
This revised seventh impression published by BlackAmber, an imprint of Arcadia
Books 2010

ISBN 978-1-901969-15-3

Typeset in 10/13 Plantin
Printed and bound by CPI Group (UK) Ltd, Croydon, CR0 4YY

Arcadia Books gratefully acknowledges the financial support of Arts Council
England.

Arcadia Books supports PEN, the fellowship of writers who work together to
promote literature and its understanding. English PEN upholds writers' freedoms
in Britain and around the world, challenging political and cultural limits on free
expression.
To find out more, visit www.englishpen.org or contact
English PEN, 6-8 Amwell Street, London EC1R 1UQ

Arcadia Books distributors are as follows:

in the UK and elsewhere in Europe:
Turnaround Publishers Services
Unit 3, Olympia Trading Estate
Coburg Road
London N22 6TZ

in the USA and Canada:
Dufour Editions
PO Box 7
Chester Springs
PA, 19425

in Australia:
The Scribo Group Pty Ltd
18 Rodborough Road
Frenchs Forest 2086

in New Zealand:
Addenda
Box 78224
Grey Lynn
Auckland

in South Africa:
Jacana Media (Pty) Ltd
PO Box 291784,
Melville 2109
Johannesburg

Arcadia Books is the *Sunday Times* Small Publisher of the Year

ACKNOWLEDGEMENTS

My respect and gratitude goes out to Raymond Stevenson of THK. Love to Joan Deitch, my first fan. I raise a glass to Mark and Mike and the rest of the 'Out of Reality' writers' group. Stirring thanks to Sharon and Claudia whose contributions have proved invaluable. Special mention to Carl Vidol, my former flatmate. Also, I can't forget my former sound-system spars, the T.K. Posse. Lastly, but not least, special mention to my brethrens and sistrens whom I befriended when I grew up.

Motherless children, if no one loves you in this world, make a start and love yourself.

This novel is dedicated
to Beverley
with all my love

Solitary

Early December, 1979

Brenton Brown looked around at the cell walls: they were covered in a dank grime that seemed to ooze from between the cracks in the grey breezeblock. A vile smell hung in the chilly air and Brenton guessed at, but could not look upon, its source - an upturned plastic bucket - working on the assumption that if he did so he might never shit again.

Wearily, he went over and peered through the tiny hatch-like window in the cell door to see if he could detect any signs of movement, but there was nothing except for a deserted passage.

Brenton flicked his eyes up at a small misted window set high in the opposite wall. This was where all those bastards in the Home said I'd end up, he recalled with a defiant grin, and he now admitted they were right.

Just below the window he could see where a pissed-off inmate had etched his feelings in biro. He read out the writing on the wall laboriously: *We, the oppressed, far outnumber our oppressor. If we unite and rise up as one, then no shitstem could ever control us.*

Half an hour later he was still eye-drilling the inscription when the sound of footsteps and the rattling of bunched keys disturbed him. Maybe all jailers rattled their keys on purpose, he thought, to remind inmates of where they were. He decided there was no way he would let the beast know of the tribulation that was clubbing his heart. He would repel any intimidation; the police wouldn't scare him!

The door's tiny flap slid open, but Brenton turned his body away to show his contempt of whoever stood outside.

"Brenton Brown?" an unseen voice bellowed out. Then receiving no reply: "Brenton Brown! I've got your food and drink!"

Brenton glimpsed a rectangle of uniform through the flap. "I don't want no beast food. Did you piss in the tea, or what?" he rebuked angrily, and added a frosty: "Stuff your food."

He knew he was being needlessly raspish - after all, the bloke was only doing his job - but the young Brixtonian didn't care. No one ever cared about him, so why should he make life easy for a beastman?

The officer, clutching a tray laden with a full English breakfast, plastic cutlery, white napkin and a hot mugful of tea, shook his head and retreated back along the hallway, looking forward to the end of his shift.

Brenton counted his footsteps until they faded away, then stretched out on the concrete bench, the blurred image of the graffiti remaining just visible through his half-closed lashes.

Just as his body was armchairing into a much-needed sleep, a new voice boomed out: "Rise and shine, you fucking young lunatic!"

For a short second Brenton wondered where he was, but recollection came as his eyes focused on a uniformed middle-aged man below average height and stocky appearance standing about four feet from him. He was clean-shaven, with thinning hair, but his features were riddled with marks like small craters. Brenton thought he must have suffered from serious acne in his younger days. He had a 'don't mess with me' face and the three white stripes on his arm revealed that he was a sergeant.

"You're in a lot of trouble, my lad. We can't have you young people stabbing each other just because of a bit of name-calling, now can we?"

Brenton noticed another, younger-looking officer looming by the cell door. He looked like a man who would be more comfortable working as a bingo caller for the old greybacks.

Vexed by his prisoner's lack of response, the sergeant instructed: "Follow me, young man. I've some questions I'd like you to answer."

Brenton let himself be storm-trooped from the cell into the empty passage. He could hear the clicking of a distant typewriter and as the thick, brown doors flashed by he noticed they had various names and crimes chalked on them.

After three turns, the trio reached the interview room where Brenton was faced by a bare wooden table and two chairs set opposite each other.

"Sit down," the sergeant ordered.

Feeling he must keep up his 'bad bwai' pose, the captive parked himself on one of the chairs, his legs oaring out in front, and insolently tapped his feet in an attempt to irritate the senior officer. His adolescent face curled into a half smirk.

The younger PC closed the door and remained standing by it with his hands behind his back like one of those bellhops outside a flashy hotel, while the sergeant wolf-prowled about, forwards then back. Brenton knew this was the cue for the 'Why' questions, and he wasn't disappointed, because after a few laps of the room the sergeant demanded: "Well, are you going to tell me what happened tonight, or what? I mean, how did this little incident get going? Did the other one start it? Did he provoke you? Maybe it was over some girl?"

Brenton silently replayed the answers to these questions in the cinema of his memory. This guy had insulted him in a pool club, a fight broke out and the opposition opted for the asset of a snooker cue. With the prospect of a cracked skull in view, Brenton had decided to defend himself with one of those squarish beer mugs; he'd smashed it hard into the bastard's leg. Simple, really, but he decided to answer the sergeant's question in rude-bwai style.

"'Cos I didn't like the way the guy looked at me," he said truculently.

The police sergeant was taken aback at this smack-in-the-face reply. "Is that it?" he asked. "Some guy gave you a funny look, so you decided to carve him?" Suddenly he bawled: "Who the fuck do you think you are, Brown? Do you think I was born yesterday? Something must've happened!"

After lowering his voice a little he added: "Now come on, sonny. I don't think you'd have assaulted someone for no reason. Was he trying to nick your money, or what?"

Brenton was annoyed by the shouting. He'll have to do better than that to scare me, he thought, and to prove the point he decided to compete in the shouting match. "No, that is *not* it!" he bellowed. "I don't like the idea of some guy beating my brains out with a fucking snooker cue! What do you want me to do? Sit there and say, 'Thanks a lot, mate, hit me with your snooker stick and I won't do fuck all about it'? Well, fuck you, man, I ain't lying down for nobody."

The verbal fork in the eardrum stunned the sergeant. He wondered why Brenton wasn't fretful, apprehensive or remorseful like most youths whom he interviewed.

"Well, this isn't a bunch of roses for me either," he said grumpily. "So for Christ's sake can we get on with it so we can all go home?"

Brenton looked up to the ceiling, feigning sympathy as the officer continued: "Now, Brown, perhaps you'll calm down and tell me your address. I've only got your name and I need more than that. You do understand, don't you?"

Feeling he had won some sort of victory, Brenton was ready to co-operate. He was gasping for a snout so he asked: "Got a cancer stick?"

With an air of impatience, the sergeant produced a packet of cigarettes, but before he offered one he said somewhat brusquely: "Address first, then you get one of these."

Brenton's face was impassive. "I ain't got no parents, man," he revealed quietly. "I'm a half-breed bastard of sixteen and I live in a

4

council hostel for kids coming out of care. I suppose you can call the duty social worker at Lambeth - they're used to picking me out of the shit."

The sergeant glanced at his colleague with a frustrated expression on his face. Sixteen? Thank Christ they hadn't taken a statement yet. The court'd have him for breakfast for interviewing a minor without a chaperone. Still, it was no fault of his - the kid shouldn't have been nicked on licensed premises.

As he pondered what to do, he took stock of Brenton's appearance. He noted the semi-Afro uncombed hair, the light-brown and blemished face below that was so full of satanic resentment, and the huge hands that seemed to be hewn from brown coal. Then his gaze shifted to the knitted pullover that barely covered Brenton's muscular torso and the strong, snooker-table legs that filled his bloodstained jeans down to a pair of trainers that were mud-splattered and ready for the old-trainers' graveyard.

"We'll have to call the Social in, then we'll get this ironed out," the sergeant said, giving up the embargo on the cancer sticks. Brenton lit one and watched the smoke as it corkscrewed towards the ceiling like a ghostly cobra. As he did so a feeling of fatigue suddenly dropped over him. He realised that he just wanted to get the questioning and statement over - this wasn't fun any more.

He was marched back to his cell to await a member of the social services who would act as chaperone during the interview then escort him back to his hostel. Alone in his cell once more, he re-parked himself on the refrigerated slab for about the running time of three reggae albums and began to regret his bad-bwai attitude to the pig with the swill. To take his mind from his hunger, he stared at the graffiti on the wall and whispered the words to himself: "We, the oppressed, far outnumber our oppressor. If we unite and rise up as one, then no shitstem could ever control us."

The sound of heavy footsteps again; keys rattling in his lock.

As the thick cell door slowly swung open he recognised the scraggy-looking, bespectacled man who stood there with an 'I don't need this' look on his face. "Getting quite a habit, isn't it?" he said. "This time you've been charged with causing an affray, apparently."

Brenton didn't bother to argue with the social worker, but wondered what 'affray' meant as he was led from his cell.

After giving and signing his statement, he followed the duty officer out into the street and winced as the cold hand of the breeze slapped and boxed the fight wounds on his face.

Mr Sumner, one of Lambeth social services duty officers, secretly thought that Brenton Brown was nothing more than a hooligan, but he dared not say as much as he shepherded him into the car. He didn't want a scene. Only last week some black juvenile whom he was escorting to Blue Star House called him 'a four-eyed, devil-bone sucking paedophile' in Brixton High Street, and it had proven very embarrassing.

The pair got in the vehicle with Brenton furiously rubbing his hands in an attempt to get warm. Mr Sumner turned the ignition key then directed an angry look at the shivering youth. "Will there ever be a day when you might just walk away from trouble? Why can't you stop to think about your actions? The trouble with you, Brenton, is that you're always playing the hero. Well, let me tell you something, young man. There are more dead heroes than live ones."

Aware only of his praying stomach and the lack of food within it, Brenton ignored the social worker and groaned: "I'm starving, man. Can't you stop at a chip shop or something? I ain't had nothing to yam for hours."

The duty officer was irritated because Brenton treated his sermon like a teenaged audience handles an ageing stripper, so he rebuked: "It's a pity your hunger can't be matched by remorse or regret. You haven't even said sorry to me for the trouble you've caused."

Brenton felt as though he had heard this particular speech a million times before, or maybe seventeen times, he'd lost count. He continued to peer out the window as the social wanker resumed his lecture. "You just don't seem to have any respect for authority. You're nearly as bad as those Arabs who stormed that American embassy the other day - where was it, in Tripoli? No respect, that's their trouble - and yours."

Brenton fought a quick battle for the control of his tongue in case he put his supper in jeopardy. Moments later, Mr Sumner parked his car outside a fish and chip shop. He gave Brenton a pound note then warned: "Don't be too long or I'll leave you here." His fears were unfounded because before the traffic lights had changed twice, Brenton had returned clutching a bag of hot, wrapped food.

Contented now, Brenton assaulted his pie and chips as if he would be sentenced to death if he didn't finish the lot within twenty seconds. He clocked the traffic flow by his window, recognising the ugly streets of Camberwell, South London. Then, having devoured his dinner, he rolled the oily paper into a ball and hurled it through the window into the chilly night air, where it landed at the feet of a bemused pedestrian. Mr Sumner was disgusted, but he said nothing because they were already drawing up outside Brenton's hostel on Camberwell Grove.

The hostel was a small terraced building that was supposed to accommodate four teenagers who had just left various children's homes run by the council. At present, there were only two boys living there because the project was still in the experimental stage. The council had installed a social worker to keep an eye on things; if the need arose, he would counsel the teenagers and maybe sleep there overnight. The downstairs front room was kept for his office, while the upper rooms were designated as the residents' living quarters.

As Brenton searched in his pockets for his keys, the door was opened from within by Mr Lewis, the social worker in charge of the hostel. A tall man in his early thirties he, too, wore glasses, which gave him an intelligent air. He had a heavy frame without being muscular and his long black hair squatted on his shoulders like a greasy black cat. His appearance suggested that he attended many an anti-National Front march, but Brenton still thought of him as just another social wanker.

He brushed past Mr Lewis without greeting him and strutted along the hallway towards the kitchen, where he filled a coffee mug full of orange squash. He heard Mr Lewis thank Mr Sumner for contacting him and escorting their wayward charge home, then the door closed and Mr Lewis's steps padded along the hallway.

"It's nearly one in the morning," he said sternly. "I'll be busy a while yet finishing the paperwork you've caused, so we'll discuss this little matter in the morning. You got that?"

Brenton nodded, relieved that he wouldn't have to suffer any Lewis lyrics tonight, and when the social worker had retired to his office he heaved himself to his feet and went up the dimly lit stairs to his room.

A latchkey opened the door. After switching on the light, Brenton kicked off his trainers and collapsed on his single, unmade bed. He closed his eyes for a few seconds, then opened them so he could look around.

A large brown wardrobe placed opposite the door dominated his small room. A chest of drawers stood beneath a dusty window, a black laundry bag resting against it overflowing with dirty clothes. Odd socks littered the tired blue carpet. A few toiletries were in evidence on the dressing table, along with some cassette tapes and a sprinkling of roll-up papers that cried out to be employed. Others sat temptingly beside a large glass ashtray that had been kidnapped from a pub.

It was cold in the room on this December night; Christmas was just around the corner. Brenton was visited by a sudden sense of isolation and bitterness. He wondered whether he had any brothers or sisters; maybe an aunt or uncle; then his mind rewound to his childhood spent in a children's home. He recalled the Christmas period when the more fortunate kids would spend the holidays with their families. He himself had had nowhere to go and no family to go to. It had been soul-destroying.

The only thing he knew about his parents was that his mother was black and his father was a white man. Ironic then, that Brenton was only ever called 'black bastard'. He felt strongly that his parents were the cause of all his misery – and wished he had never been born.

Still dressed in the bloodstained jeans and brown pullover, Brenton struggled to find a comfortable sleeping position. Sellotaped to the back of his bedroom door was a large poster of the late film star, James Dean. Peering deep into the actor's eyes, Brenton whispered to him, "I've had a shit day, James," then fell into a restless doze.

CHAPTER ONE

My Conversation

Brenton didn't get out of bed until the middle of the next day. Still wearing his bloodstained battle-armour, he prised open his drawers, took out a crumpled white towel, then ambled across the landing to the bathroom. His movements alerted his hostel-mate, Floyd, who poked his head through his doorway and scanned Brenton for any sign of a 'don't talk to me' mood. Satisfied, he asked: "Brenton, what-a-gwarn last night? Someone told me you bust up Terry Flynn. What did you do to him? That Flynn is supposed to be a bad man."

Brenton had the hot-water tap running and was already stripped to the waist. He pondered for a couple of seconds then smiled, Mona Lisa-like. "Well, Floyd," he replied, "that bad-card Flynn was running and cussing me down in Pop's Pool Club down Kennington. Anyway, fight bruk out and he comes to me with a fucking cue, so I picked up a beer mug and smashed it on his leg. I don't care about rep, man."

Floyd emerged from his bedroom onto the small landing to face his pal. He was slightly taller than Brenton, caramel-skinned, with a handsome, mischievous face. In contrast to his hostel-mate he appeared well groomed, with a young sprouting of facial hair. Brenton had bought him a Bic razor recently; a gift for when he had just kissed his seventeenth birthday goodbye.

Brenton lathered his chest with a soap-gorged flannel then resumed his tale. "Before I knew it, the filth come and fling me inside a meat wagon. They took me to Borough pig pen; the one near London Bridge."

Floyd couldn't help but admire his front. As for Brenton, he thought his hostel-mate was some sort of sweet bwai; never wanting to get his digits dirty in someone else's bath-water, but he respected Floyd's Brixtonian wit and smooth, melted coconut chat.

Drip-drying, Brenton made his way back to his room swabbing himself as he went. Floyd followed him and said, "I t'ink Lewis is waiting downstairs for you."

From Floyd's voice, you could guess he had spent most of his childhood in the watchfulness of a West Indian influence, but if you heard Brenton speak without seeing him in the flesh, you would have taken him for a white, cockney teenager.

Brenton finished drying himself and changed into a fresh pair of pale blue jeans; then he pulled on his brown jumper over a punctured, sad T-shirt. He wasn't ready to face Mr Lewis just yet. Instead, he bull-frogged down the stairs and into the kitchen where he grabbed the corn-flakes packet from a cupboard and an unwashed cereal bowl and mug from the sink. He ran the crockery under the tap and just as he was thinking crossly how Floyd never washed up his dishes, Mr Lewis snailed in from his room.

"Morning, Brenton," he said tersely. "You obviously slept better than I did."

"Well, you didn't have to spend hours in a cell, did you?" Brenton shot back, unwilling to have anyone suggest they'd had a worse yesterday than him.

Mr Lewis bore the pale, drained look of an old man who has recently been exhausted by a young, energetic lover. He stepped back into his office, ordering: "When you finish your breakfast, come and see me. I want to talk to you about last night."

When it couldn't be avoided any longer, Brenton trooped reluctantly into Mr Lewis's room, wondering why his wallpaper was a more eye-catching pattern than the dreary woodchip paper that covered the rest of the house.

Mr Lewis sat behind a desk, nervously drumming his fingers on its scratched and scarred surface. At the far end of the room was an unmade fold-up bed, and beside it two Burgundy-coloured armchairs facing a black and white portable television balanced perilously on a cardboard box. A mass of Lambeth Council headed notepaper, with various other leaflets and envelopes covered Mr Lewis's desk.

Brenton elected to keep standing. "Got a snout?" he asked, spotting the packet of ten on the desk.

Mr Lewis couldn't really say no so he offered one. Then, after lighting a match, he burst out: "When are you going to get wise to this macho kick, Brenton? You can't keep fighting everybody who insults or threatens you. Get this into your skull; if you don't find a way of subduing that temper of yours, the law of the land will!"

Brenton scratched behind his right ear then caressed a pimple on his chin. A shaft of sunlight that glared from the window seemed to have a magnetic effect on his eyes.

"In my opinion, you can make a go of life," Lewis continued more quietly. "You're intelligent enough, but you have to learn right from wrong."

Brenton drew tensely on his cigarette. "There's no way I'm going to let any man take libs with me," he said eventually. "I ain't backing down no matter who it is; Terry bloody Flynn or even King bloody Kong. If someone troubles me they're not getting away with it. I don't look for strife, you know that, but it sort of follows me about."

Mr Lewis pushed an overflowing ashtray towards the youth; aware that he would have his work cut out to persuade Brenton Brown to take a more restrained attitude. "Look," he counselled. "It doesn't have to be like that. Walk away before the argument starts. The way you're going on, you'll end up in jail; and it'll probably only be me who'll come and visit you."

"Who says I'll want to see you if I'm in bloody jail?" Part of what the social wanker said was true, all right – there, he admitted it – but he still wanted to give a bad-bwai reply.

"Come on, Brenton, no matter what you might think I'm here to advise you and help you the best way I can. But I can't do it if you won't let me."

Brenton was listening intently now, but he still avoided eye contact with the social worker because he knew his countenance had a guilty look about it. "You don't know what it's like, man," he lamented. "You can read all the books you want, but that won't make a difference, 'cos you don't actually know what it really feels like to live my shit of a life. You understand me?"

He paused to reach out for the cigarette packet and matches while Mr Lewis waited, thinking there was a large hint of truth in that last remark.

Brenton lit up again, and stared out of the window aimlessly, then continued in a despairing tone: "I wish I'd never been born. If there is a God, He's got a sick sense of humour to give me the mother like the bitch I've got. Floyd might fight with his old man but he's still got aunts, uncles and cousins. What have I got? Fuck all, that's what."

A cocktail of bitterness and adrenaline flushed through his body, and his voice, when he raised it again, was full of pain. "Why did she give me up, eh? I was too bloody young to have done fuck-all wrong, so was it something else about me – a bit of me she couldn't put up with? I mean, she hasn't tried to contact me since she threw me away – the bitch – has she? So what the fuck was it?" His emotions were ready to overflow. He seemed incapable of keeping his feet still, while his hands waved about to signal his frustration.

Mr Lewis didn't quite know what to do or say. He just concentrated on keeping calm and appearing relaxed. His heart reached out to the troubled teenager, but he couldn't think of anything appropriate to say. University had proven unable to prepare him for these moments.

Brenton raged on, almost shouting: "I'm just a half-breed bastard. I'm a fucking half-breed bastard. You hear me?"

He threw himself on the chair opposite the social worker and lowered his head into his hands. Mr Lewis watched him pityingly. For a few seconds everything was still while he sensed Brenton's weeping pain, then he finally found his tongue. In a soft voice he encouraged: "Tears are nothing to be ashamed of. It's just a way of letting pent-up feelings out of your system. I think this has been boiling up for quite a time."

As Mr Lewis paused, Brenton rubbed his eyes until all traces of tears were dispersed. He was now suffering from acute embarrassment. He tried to say something, but no sounds came out. Feeling dreadfully self-conscious, Mr Lewis lit up another cigarette and thought that maybe he should have chosen a different career. While he smoked he gazed at Brenton's stormy face. "You all right now?" he said eventually, his tone gentle.

"Yeah."

Gaining confidence, Mr Lewis continued: "How can I help you, Brenton? Tell me."

Brenton pondered this for a few seconds. "I want to see my mother," he admitted quietly. "I've got a load of questions I want to ask her. I'm just curious about her. I wanna know what she looks like and I need some explanations for my own peace of mind."

"Have any of your former social workers ever made contact with her, or tried to get in touch?" Mr Lewis asked.

"When I was in the Home I didn't want to see my mother, but now I do. Social workers asked me if I'd like to try and find her, but I always thought it was up to her to find me. Since then I've changed my mind."

"If that's what you want," Mr Lewis said thoughtfully as Brenton prepared to leave the room, "I'll do all I can to find her, starting off with Area Three Office where they keep your files. There must be something in there that can give us a clue as to her whereabouts. But be warned. These episodes rarely get a storybook ending. Reality doesn't work like that."

Brenton was just closing the door behind himself when he said: "I know."

CHAPTER TWO
Judge Not

The magistrate looked as if he should be joining the queue at the Post Office for his pension. What wise thinking could come from this moss-growing tool of so-called Truths and Rights? He seemed to be hibernating, only glancing up when he spoke.

Brenton felt intolerably uncomfortable in the blazer and slacks Mr Lewis had loaned him, and notwithstanding his sweet-bwai attire, he still oozed a ragamuffin appearance, mainly due to his hair, which he refused to comb in spite of his social worker's pleas. He gave the impression of one that had aspired to become a dreadlocked rastaman, but had harboured second thoughts and left his hair in a state of tangled confusion.

He looked around the courtroom, taking note of all the unsmiling faces. It was like a competition to see who could pull the most serious expression.

Brenton had pleaded guilty to the charge of causing an affray, and all he wanted to know now was whether the magistrate would send him to a government house or not. He watched the ponderous proceedings, curious about how much dough the magistrate received at the end of the month for sleeping on the job.

Mr Lewis had attended the hearing a short while ago. To Brenton's surprise he had presented the court with a sympathetic character reference that had made the youth smirk and think, What a liar!

The lawyers fought their verbal battles, then the time eventually came when the magistrate passed sentence; Brenton received a one year suspended detention term. His face burned when the magistrate proceeded to lecture him, saying that he did not want to see him in court again, and that if he did so, Brenton would receive a much harsher sentence. In his reply, Brenton assured the magistrate that he would seek a job and that in future he would not retaliate when faced with provocation.

Back outside, Brenton found himself joining Mr Lewis on the steps of the courthouse. The social worker looked him up and down for a few seconds then stated: "You know what? I agree with the magistrate. I don't want to see you in this damned place again either. Besides, as he says - you won't be walking down these steps to freedom if you're nicked again."

When they reached the car Brenton declined the offer of a lift home, saying he preferred to 'hol' a bus' and check a spar he hadn't seen for a while. That was his first intention anyway, but as he passed an off-licence he couldn't resist the tonsil-pleasing delights of strong lager.

Using the cash Mr Lewis had given him for his bus fare, he bought a can and opted for the long trod to Brockwell Park, but as he emerged from the shop an Asian man stopped in his tracks and stared at him. Brenton scowled as he opened the brew with a hiss. "What the fuck you looking at?"

The Asian man soon retreated, not daring to look behind.

It was a crisp day. The smell of heavy-vehicle engines skanked in the air and Brenton felt the breeze on his brown face as he strolled past Kings College Hospital on Denmark Hill. As he trudged on he could see illuminated Christmas trees in the front windows of a few houses and he thought how Christmas didn't cater for the likes of him. A while later, when he was ambling down Herne Hill, he passed a church that had a large poster at its entrance. It read: *Don't forget the real meaning of Christmas. Come to church where we rejoice in the true meaning.* At that

Brenton kissed his teeth and sauntered on, hands thrust deep in his pockets.

When Brenton reached the park he saw a brace of schoolboys fishing with pole-extended nets in a condom and crisp packet-filled lake, searching for any life forms in the soiled water. Brenton sat down on a bench nearby. It was a peaceful spot where someone could relax their tormented mind.

In the last couple of days he had heard some rumours concerning him and Terry Flynn. Flynn and his posse, as the ghetto press would have it, were headhunting Brenton to exact some sort of revenge. The thought of this baked fear into his mind, but he refused to display his consternation. The youths who knew Brenton well thought of him as being an ice-man, but he had his fears like anyone else. Also, he dreaded the fact that he would now be looking over his shoulder everywhere he roamed as a consequence of his beer-mug versus snooker-cue clash.

He remembered the first time he laid eyes on Terry Flynn. It was just after he arrived in Lambeth, freshly brainwashed from the children's home. Following a stroll in Brixton, some reggae-toasting guy wearing a Sherlock Holmes hat pressed a card into his hand. On it was the address of a forthcoming blues party not five minutes walk from the hostel.

He arrived at 9:00 p.m. and wondered where everybody was, but a kindly girl told him he was a few albums early and that things would start to warm up about midnight.

Midnight came, and feeling the need to be refreshed, Brenton made his way through the growing throng to a makeshift bar that was set up at the entrance to the kitchen.

En route he accidentally trod on someone's foot. He looked up, muttering an apology, and beheld a mean, bearded face wearing a beret and hoovering a spliff. The face glared at him like he was a slave who had refused a chore, then growled: "Watch weh you ah go, bwai."

"I said sorry."

"Don't mek me see you again, you liccle half-breed, you."

Without hesitation, Brenton punched his tormentor smack on his jaw and made for the front door where he fled into the still, inky night. He learned later that the man he had boxed was this Johnny Too Bad deal called Terry Flynn.

Viewing their recent fisticuffs in retrospect, Brenton was certain of one thing: he sure as hell wouldn't like to visit the park in a wheelchair with a ratchet-designed face.

For the time being, though, he revelled in the ghetto youths' excited talk about how he had sent Terry Flynn to the bone-juggler's. He was aware that his fifteen minutes of fame had put him in some danger, but he reacted to it with a grin and thought of the camping trip Mr Lewis was hoping to organise; now the prospect of rain and no TV was fact becoming an attractive option.

Thinking time over, Brenton got to his feet then began to trek through the park, hands in pockets, shoulders hunched, head high. He passed two elderly women and imagined them in the still of the night being chased by Terry Flynn through a decaying housing estate. He recalled moodily how earlier in the morning Mr Lewis had advised him to go to the Job Centre, but he knew it would be a total waste of time. What employer would give him a job? Besides, filling in an application form was always upsetting because of the question *Next of kin?* He was always at a loss about how to answer this apparently simple question, and he hated the sympathetic looks on the faces behind the counter when he explained why he couldn't.

CHAPTER THREE
Catch a fire

It was the last Saturday night before Christmas and Brenton was lying on his bed trying to work out how he would budget his meagre government brass throughout the raving festival. How would he ever afford all the double-priced cab fares for the coming parties and dances? Something else troubled him, too – the glaring countenance of Terry Flynn...but a slap on the door diverted his thoughts.

"Hey, Brenton, you awake?" asked his hostel-mate Floyd, knowing full well that he was.

"What if I am?"

Grinning, Floyd strutted into the room. "I've got a pair of legbacks in my room and a few cans of Special Brew, so I need you to kind of match up the situation," he boasted. "Come on – slap a smile on your boat and follow me."

Brenton stood up slowly, grinding his right temple with his palm and unwilling to show too much enthusiasm. He fielded for a box of snouts on the dressing table and fingered inside for a screwed-up ball of betting shop paper. Opening the wrapper, he exposed a sprinkling of cannabis. As he followed his spar out of his room he uttered mischievously: "Well, you've got the liquor and I've got the good grass."

Floyd smiled his anticipation. He guessed that his friend spent nearly as much dough on herbal items as he did on food with his G-cheque.

The happy duo entered Floyd's room where a battered suitcase thumped out Dennis Brown's *Money in My Pocket* from the top of the dressing table. Brenton acknowledged the two girls, who were nodding their heads in time to the bass, then seated himself beside them on the bed.

Floyd, still standing up, made the introductions. "This is Brenton – the guy who crucially dealt with Terry Flynn." After gesturing with his hands he added, "Brenton, sitting next to you is Sharon, the facety one, and next to her is quiet Carol, who don't say shit, she's so quiet."

Looking aggrieved, Sharon voiced: "Who are you calling facety?" She nudged Brenton sitting beside her. "You all right – don't listen to what he says."

Carol leaned forward and faced the uncomfortable-looking Brenton. She greeted him softly. "All right? How do you manage to live with someone like him?" She concluded her question with a thumb jerked in the direction of Floyd, who was smiling.

It would take a fool not to find Sharon attractive. Her hair was pulled back in a short ponytail that revealed her clear brown complexion, and her countenance bore the confidence of a newscaster. She appeared very smart in her green suede jacket and black skirt, and the ensemble showed off her Olympic-swimmer build – a build that still pip-squeaked femininity through the medium of her almond-shaped eyes and full lips.

Carol was slimmer and taller than her friend. She also had the darkest complexion in the room. A relaxed, permed hairstyle and piercing eyes made her a fine challenge to all the sweet bwais and bad bwais alike, and this challenge was made more tempting by the matching black sweater and skirt she wore under her unbuttoned beige trenchcoat.

"Give me a brew, Floyd," Brenton ordered to hide his shyness.

Looking contented, Floyd grabbed a lager off the dressing table while Brenton pastried his joint. The girls watched him, clearly fascinated.

"So what are you doing in a sex maniac's bedroom?" he asked. "You're taking a risk coming here – Floyd's a pervert. He goes walking and talking in the park wearing nutten but his sticksman coat, flashing his small t'ing to old white ladies."

Sharon rocked back laughing out loud, while her pal grinned with embarrassment because of the rudeness of the remark. Carol, although self-conscious, was magnetised by Brenton. She liked the look of his solid physique.

Not minding that Sharon was laughing at him, Floyd handed out beers all round. Brenton head-butted his shyness through the window marked 'Fuck off' and, looking at Sharon, enquired: "So where did you meet Floyd, then?"

"At Bali Hai, two weeks ago. Carol and me were enjoying ourselves at the club, dancing and t'ing, then I buck up on Floyd. He asked me that if I don't want to dance with him he would go home and think about being a monk. I mean, what a load of nonsense! Anyway, he looked like he had nuff refusal from a whole 'eap of gal, so I danced with him 'cos I felt sorry for the poor bwai."

Brenton and Carol sniggered, making Floyd suffer the red lash of embarrassment. Despite what she had just said, Sharon liked Floyd's roguish looks and trickster personality, but she wasn't prepared to tell him so, not just yet. The guy's ego was big enough without her feeding it.

Sharon watched the ruffled Floyd sip his beer then nagged him: "You're supposed to be taking us raving tonight. What's 'appening?"

Floyd parked his beer on the dressing table while thinking up a retort and he caught Brenton's smile; his friend was enjoying his discomfiture.

"That party we're supposed to go to was cancelled," he admitted. "I think my source's mother didn't like the fact that a party was being arranged in her yard, and she didn't know a damn."

A look of disbelief swarmed over Sharon as she glanced at Carol, who was peacocking herself by flattening the creases in her skirt.

Raising his palms to make the internationally known gesture of 'it's not my fault', Floyd attempted to defend himself. "My budget ain't big enough for us to go to a club like Nations, and I don't know of any other parties, so, er, do you want another brew?"

Brenton laughed aloud while Sharon remained dumbfounded. Carol, show-boating her irritation, gave a rebuke. "So I've got dressed up for nutten?"

By now Brenton had finished gift-wrapping his spliff so he christened it with a Vista while Carol watched.

Time mooched by and with the cocktail of alcohol and cannabis the foursome slowly relaxed; talking and laughing more and more. Inhibitions were binned as they giggled at the most trivial things. Sharon and Carol's attempt to construct a spliff was greeted with uncontrollable laughter from the two young men.

Soon it was approaching two o'clock in the morning and everyone had metaphorical weights pulling down their eyelids. But Floyd, the only one of the quartet still standing up, was listening intently. With a half-smoked spliff in his mouth, his mind was a sponge that absorbed the lyrics of the militant roots music being played.

The songs reflected the struggle for black freedom and the persecution of the black race throughout world history. The lyrics also had a rebellious slant against the Western world's way of doing things – or, as Floyd and many other blacks called it, Babylon. As he meditated on the words he enjoyed the cussing of the people who represented power. He listened more fervently, and especially liked one song that was about the Rastafarian religion and the connections this faith had with the Good Book.

"Brenton," he called suddenly. "I wanna ask you somet'ing."

Brenton ironed his right temple to indicate that he wasn't in the mood for any philosophical reasoning. "Can't you see I'm crashing?" he grumbled. "Rest your lip, man, and listen to the music – you love to chat too much."

Floyd fish-eyed the girls, who were half-asleep and listening to the cooing of their distant beds. He wanted to press home his point and ignored his spar's plea.

"No man, seriously, do you believe in God?"

"No, I don't believe in God! Does that answer your bloody question? Am I speaking loud and clear? I don't believe in no God! Can I rest up now in peace?"

The weary-looking Sharon began to take an interest in the conversation. She watched Floyd keenly, waiting for him to question Brenton, and he kindly obliged.

"Give me a good reason why you don't believe in God."

Brenton inhaled deeply, trying to control something that was shooting through his throat. He felt compelled to answer. "'Cos I don't, I just don't."

By now, Carol too had become fascinated by the strange exchange taking place. Floyd had a patrician look about him.

"Give me a reason, man – a proper reason."

"What's your problem, bwai? Haven't I given you a fucking answer? Shit, I don't believe this. It's like being in a beast cell when you're in this blasted mood."

Floyd thought he'd better lay off for the next few moments so he used a plastic smile to gaze at Sharon.

"Look, right," Brenton stated hotly. "If there is a God He hasn't done fuck all for me. My life has been pure tribulation, and there are millions like me, you know? All wondering why the fuck their lives are so fucked up."

Carol leaned forward, attracted by the contours of Brenton's emotive face, and smiled at him approvingly when he resumed his theological malediction.

"What kind of God would let this happen? Nah, it's a dog eat dog world out there, and I'm ready to sink my canines into any Doberman or Yorkshire blasted Terrier who gives me strife. I don't want to worry about any God to pray to. I've got nuff problems already."

Floyd nodded while Sharon, intrigued by the monologue, told

him: "You're very bitter, innit. Life must have been hard for you. It's none of my business, but I reckon you have a kinda chip on your shoulder. What I'm saying is, you're not the only one to have it hard, you know? We've all got it hard. Every yout' thinks his burden is the heaviest."

Brenton was listening, although he didn't meet her eyes, so Sharon continued: "Especially us blacks. You just have to get on with it. Everyone here has probably got their own problems, but we shouldn't let them get us down. You catch me on FM?"

Brenton nodded thoughtfully, cradling his chin, then he enquired: "What do you mean, I'm bitter? And besides, what's a chip on my shoulder got to do with believing in God?"

Sharon smiled. "You know full well what I mean."

After listening to Sharon's birdsong, Floyd pointed to her and remarked: "She makes more sense than any of them fool-fool social wankers that I've come across. You listen to her good."

Sharon and Brenton laughed, while Carol was escalating down into the basement marked semi-snooze, snuggled up against the bed's headrest. Floyd proceeded to build another spliff, using the last of Brenton's Rizla papers.

"Yeah, man," Brenton encouraged him. "Just wrap up another zoot and don't ask me no more God questions. Oh, and you'd better give Sharon a few pulls before she gets a chip on *her* shoulder."

After the last toke was pulled everyone somehow made themselves comfortable on Floyd's single bed, using each other's bodies as pillows. The cannabis and lager had wrought their full effect and the quartet fell into a deep sleep as the suitcase boomed out the Gong's *Easy Skanking*.

CHAPTER FOUR

Revelation

Christmas Day morning, 1979

Brenton sat on the park bench he had adopted wondering whether he should have accepted Mr Lewis's invitation to spend the day with him and his girlfriend. Although the offer of a turkey dinner had awoken the taste buds, Brenton thought he would only be in the way, so had felt compelled to decline the invitation. He recoiled at the thought of the fried corned beef and boiled rice that Floyd had so keenly volunteered to cook; he was at the hostel now, waiting with bone-alerting relish for Sharon's promised visit. Consequently, even at home, Brenton felt he would be in the way, particularly as Floyd was planning a physical dessert for his girl.

He speculated on what his mother would be doing at the moment. Was she stuffing her bird? Or maybe she was winter-cleaning her house for the critical eyes of her in-laws. She might, just might, be thinking of how her lost son was spending the Christmas period, but Brenton doubted it.

The park was serene; even the spirits of the lifeless trees seemed to have departed to attend an oak blues, while the musty, cellar smell of the leaf-laden pond massaged the air with velvety fingers. Brenton looked around for any sign of other people and his eyes tailed a middle-aged man wearing a grey overcoat and cloth cap walking his Labrador dog. He considered that maybe the man was an ear-boxed husband who was trying to avoid his wife and excited, noisy kids on Christmas morning, then told himself that he would never get married; all that cussing and moaning! In fact, Brenton felt he was fated to be a loner. He deemed it was only guys like Floyd who had to have a woman. Then again, guys like Floyd craved nuff women. Nothing seemed to satisfy the hunger of his bone! Brenton had lost count of the number of fit girls who phoned his hostel-mate.

That made him wonder what sort of father he himself would make. Probably a bad one, he acknowledged. Anyway, he had enough tribulations already without a baby adding to them.

The notion of having a girlfriend intimidated him. Floyd had said that Carol loved him off...but Brenton made no moves – he didn't want anybody to get too close to him. Too right, women are too damn nosy, Brenton thought – always wanting to know your business and introduce you to their boring fathers. Still, Carol was attractive, but maybe she was a bit too tall for him.

Lost in thought, Brenton moved slowly out of the park and for a moment speculated on how Terry Flynn would be celebrating his Yuletide – probably by going to a party and drapesing some bwai for his corn.

Skywards, the greying heavens mirrored Brenton's mood. When he got back to the hostel, the smell of fried corned beef struck him like a sock full of sand. He headed straight for the kitchen where, with his shirtsleeves rolled up and a fork in his hand, Floyd was stirring something in a charred, bent frying pan.

"Where've you been, guy? You get up early, innit. I was feeling kind of peckish, so I thought I'd start dinner early."

Floyd was in an upbeat mood. Brenton parked himself on the small kitchen table. Weary but inquisitive, he glanced at Floyd's busy hands and asked: "You've got family around Brixton, innit. How comes you're not spending Christmas with them?"

The question took Floyd by surprise. Turning off the two gas rings, which were heating the boiled rice and corned beef, he opened the fridge door and helped himself to a can of strong lager. After passing one to his mate, he answered, "Don't get on with my parents." He paused, took a serious gulp, then revealed: "My paps booted me out when I was only fifteen – bastard. Said he didn't want no t'ief living under his roof."

Brenton held his drink in front of his face, reading the label on the can as Floyd continued: "My mudder wanted me to stay, but she didn't say anyt'ing. She's too scared of the bastard, you understand? I don't even know why she stays with the selfish sap. He treats her like dirt."

Brenton was giving Floyd his full attention, so he plonked his can on the table quietly so as not to disturb his monologue. "Anyway," he went on, "all this happened two years ago. I've got two older sisters I see now and again, but I'll never go back home. Not while my paps is still there – I hate the coconut. He never stood up for me, and the friggin' idiot will always believe whatsoever the pigs tell him – never me."

Brenton studied his hostel-mate, thinking that he, too, had his problems. Floyd got to his feet and proceeded to share out the dinner as Brenton swigged down his lager. Deliberately changing the subject, Brenton enquired: "What time is Sharon coming round?"

"As soon as she can sneak out her yard without her licky-licky mudder noticing."

Brenton raised his eyebrows in surprise. "What? Sharon's mother is a 'colic? You wouldn't think so, would you? Sharon seems so sort of...wise."

Floyd licked free a tiny morsel of corned beef that had glued itself to a cuticle then remarked: "Even people who seem decent have fucked-up families."

"You like Sharon a lot, innit? Or do you just want to bone her?"

Floyd parked a mountainous plate under Brenton's nose then smiled as he sat down, preparing to taste his own cooking. "Yeah, I do like her," he replied, "she's got sense, man. She goes to Brixton College, innit, but I must admit, I'd love to bone it. She's fit man. Her body's gone clear – you wanna see her in tight jeans – her backside just fits in neatly and t'ing. Yeah, man, that will be a wicked grind."

Brenton grinned, picking at his food. "Yeah, she is nice. Ain't you gonna take her to a club or something?"

Floyd laughed, wondering whether Brenton was asking a serious question. "With my dole corn? Be serious, man. I can't even afford to get my slacks dry-cleaned."

"Then learn to wash 'em by hand and iron them, innit," Brenton scolded.

The pair finished off their meagre Christmas dinner, easing it down with a generous helping of some brutal brew, and then Brenton washed up the plates while his hostel-mate smoked a cigarette. "Lewis let me have his portable TV last night," Floyd enthused, "so we might as well watch the James Bond film or something. The aerial's shit, but I think I can get it to show a half-decent picture if you stand on the coffee table and hold it over your head."

"That's sweet. I thought I'd be bored out of my mind all day."

"So what's your story, then?"

"Ain't much of a story to tell. I ain't got no family, I'm on my friggin' tod; my bitch of a mother left me at social services when I was a baby."

"What about your paps?"

"Don't know of him. Sometimes I think my mother don't know of him either."

Brenton's last statement brought about a brooding silence and he compared his dinner of corned beef and rice to the corn-meal porridge that the Gong sang about in *No Woman No Cry*, but he couldn't see how everything was gonna be all right.

"You know," stated Floyd, stealing the pose of Martin Luther King, "my uncle used to say that when you're on the bottom rung of the ladder the people above you can't push you down any further – so the only way is up."

Brenton fingered his earlobe. "I saw some words on the cell

wall. It went: 'we, the oppressed, far outnumber our oppressor. If we unite and rise up as one, then no shitstem could ever control us'."

"Sounds like a man like Peter Tosh was in your cell before you – serious vibes that," guessed Floyd.

"But what does it mean?"

"Probably that the guy who wrote it was crucially pissed off by the beast and wants to get his own back."

Brenton laughed. "Let's watch telly."

The duo trooped up the stairs and even though they only saw Mr Bond on the dodgy little black and white TV, both felt that Christmas Day hadn't turned out that badly after all.

CHAPTER FIVE

No buts

New Year's Day, 1980

Brenton and Floyd had exhausted all their finances. Neither of them would receive any G's from social security for a few days yet, so they spent the greater part of the morning weeding the ashtrays. They were searching for snout butts, so they could squeeze out the remaining tobacco and pastry a few joints.

Wearing the look of someone who has just missed his last bus home, Floyd complained, "This is no way to live, man – smoking bloody butts. I have to find a way of making corn, 'cos I'm sick and tired of getting my digits dirty messing with friggin' butts. I hope Sharon comes around later on. I'll tell her to buy me some cancer sticks."

After torching his joint, Brenton became aware of his own ash and tobacco-stained fingers so he bewailed, "Shit, I've got ash all over my paws, just for a bloody smoke. We should break into Lewis's room. He's always got snouts on his desk."

Floyd could do nothing but laugh at their plight and joke, "This is crazy, man. We'll be looking for butts in the High Street next."

"Speak for yourself."

The brethren chuckled as Floyd stretched out his hand to place a cassette tape in the laboured suitcase. Mr Lewis had advised them persistently on how to budget their social security G's, and they had always set out to make their money last, but somehow they always seemed to run out of readies just a few days before their next payment. Lewis said they had only themselves to blame, since the government didn't intend its benefits to be used to fatten the wallets of tobacconists, licensees and herb dealers.

Brenton stared at his pal, with his neatly combed hair, heavy-looking gold chain and new trainers. Such a contrast to his own appearance. He asked, "Where did you get the new trainers from, man?"

Looking down at his footwear proudly, Floyd answered: "Sharon bought me them for Christmas. She treats me good, innit? She's always saying I should look smart and t'ing."

Brenton felt a little envious as he compared them with his own battered trainers. Looking at his friend again, he enquired, fingering his chin: "What council home did you go to?"

"St Saviours. You know, the one just off Brixton Hill? It was all right there – not too strict, and the staff were easy. Like you could actually talk to them without them telling you how to become a responsible citizen."

Much to Floyd's annoyance, Brenton spilled a few strands of tobacco on the floor, but he chose not to comment when he saw him bend down and pick up the precious brown shreds. Instead he continued, "But they had some stupid rules, like I had to be in by ten o'clock. That was kind of embarrassing when I used to have some fit piece of beef visit. But in the end they just gave up trying to make me come home by that time 'cos sometimes I wouldn't come back till morning."

Brenton cocked his ears. He had heard of St Saviours and that its rules were less rigid than elsewhere. Floyd asked: "What home was you at?"

"Pinewood Hills," Brenton mumbled, tramping out the tobacco stain on the floor.

"That's that big place, innit? Yeah, I've heard of Pinewood Hills. It's going south, innit, on the way to Brighton."

Brenton turned down the volume of the suitcase. He appeared very solemn, as if he was about to recall the tale of a lost battle. He sat down on the bed with his hands clasped together – he wanted to scratch behind his ear, but he became self-conscious. Captivated, Floyd listened intently as his pal explained: "Yeah, that's right. It's a massive place – it must have about eighty big mansion-type houses that they named after trees and plants."

Floyd rubbed his hands together over the ashtray to get rid of surplus tobacco debris. Brenton went on, "Pinewood's got loads of grounds and fields, and it's so big you could get lost in there. We'd play games like Tim-tam-tommy in the bushes. I grew up in the place and it's kind of strange. Pinewood's like a little town without shops, know what I mean? It's got everything – a laundry, swimming pool, community centre. It's even got its own fucking primary school. But the good thing about it is the big fields and bushes and t'ing."

Engaged in the fable of Pinewood Hills, Floyd inclined towards his spar as Brenton continued: "But there's one serious t'ing though. Some of the staff are evil, believe me – serious t'ing."

Brenton's dial turned into a study of seriousness as he uttered draughtily: "Some kids got beaten up and felt up by those bastards in charge. One kid I got to know was sent away to a mental home 'cos they reckoned his temper was too bad. We used to say some housefather was bumming him. You know, that sort of thing. There are some people who work at Pinewood Hills who should be in jail. I've seen it, man. I nearly killed one of the bastards once, 'cos he tried to touch me up. Nah, man, it's a serious t'ing."

Floyd was appalled and wanted to change the subject. "One of your parents is white, innit?" he said, lighting a fresh spliff.

The question caught Brenton unprepared, like a sprinter who failed to hear the starter's gun. He felt ashamed as he answered, staring at the carpet, "Yeah, it's true. My dad is a fucking white man, and my mother is Jamaican. That's all I know about them, apart from the fact that they don't give a shit about me. I have to live with it, though. It's people like Terry Flynn who vex me, calling me names like 'mongrel' and 'zebra', you know? Stupid names like that."

"Seen." Floyd understood fully, headbutting the air.

"After that roll we had in the blues dance," Brenton resumed, "I saw him on a 109 bus going up Brixton Hill. He spied me trodding, and started shouting 'half-breed'."

Floyd was just about to encase a butt-filled joint, but he paused when Brenton recommenced. "But it's sort of funny, though. White people treat me like I'm totally black – they don't see the white in me. But blacks and even you have noticed that some of my features are white. I was wondering when you was gonna ask me this question, but I suppose I'd rather be fully black anyway."

Floyd gave him the look of an understanding social worker. "I can imagine it's kind of hard sometimes."

"Yeah, but I want to see my mother. I don't know why – curiosity, I suppose. You must think I'm stupid, innit?"

Floyd's disapproval showed in his expression, as if some bowler-hatted white man had told him to look for a job. "What for, man?" he rebuked. "I check it that she ain't made no steps to see you? Nah, forget it, man. Just live your life. Don't waste no time on your mudder. She hasn't done anything for you, so why bother?"

Brenton knew that part of what his spar said was realistic, but he still wanted to justify his need to seek out his mother. Flicking his ash into an ashtray, he explained: "I want to know what she's like, or even what she looks like, you know? It's sort of a gut feeling. Besides, I might have brothers and sisters who I'll get to meet. Lewis says he'll try and trace her. The day before, he told me he had a good lead from an old doctor. Lewis has been reading my files, trying to pick up clues on where my mother is."

Floyd shook his head, like a magistrate hearing the defence of a down and out rastaman, and started to fiddle with a cassette tape. Brenton reclined on the bed, switched his gaze towards the television, and proceeded to twiddle an earlobe. Floyd commented: "You're wrong, man. It might just be a serious waste of time. You don't owe your mudder nutten. Just accept the fact she's not interested in you and probably never will be. If she was, she would've made some sort of move by now."

Brenton's countenance had sketched itself into a scowl and his body clicked into animation when Floyd pressed home his point. "Some people are fucked up and I suppose our parents have fucked up. Otherwise we wouldn't be here in a shit hostel, smoking bloody butts, but that's life."

Brenton wasted no time in airing his displeasure. "Shut up, man! Just shut up! You're the one who's fucked up 'cos you think you know it all. And if I want to find my mother, I don't have to ask you, right? You or nobody else will tell me what's best for me."

Slapped by his friend's volcanic tone, Floyd decided it would be wise to change the subject. So gesturing at the suitcase, he remarked, "I'm bored with that D. Brown tape. It's time for Gregory Isaacs."

Floyd proceeded to change the tape while Brenton remained silent, feeling the palms of embarrassment warming his cheeks. He hauled himself up from the bed and left the room, wondering why he had lost control of himself during the vocal volley. He realised the he was projecting the anger he felt towards Terry Flynn on Floyd. After all, his spar was only giving his opinion – an opinion he hoped would be in Brenton's best interest. Perhaps people were right about him, when they said he was nutten but a stepping volcano. Coching on these thoughts, sprawling on his bed, Brenton stared at James Dean. "Floyd must think I'm mad-up, innit, James?"

Mr Dean made no reply.

CHAPTER SIX
Bad Card

4 January, 1980

Brenton idled on his bed, mulling over what he should spend his dole money on – maybe the new Barrington Levy album? Nah, he thought, ain't got shit to play it on. Glancing down, he examined the injuries of his beat-up trainers and came to a decision.

Expecting his Giro to be delivered any moment, he rose and went to the bathroom to make war with his BO. A short while later, eating his cereal in the kitchen, he saw Mr Lewis heavy-footing along the hallway, carrying a scruffy briefcase. "Morning, Brenton. I wanted to see you yesterday, but you were out."

Brenton's eyes stared into his cereal bowl. "Morning."

"I was down in Area Three Office yesterday to read your files," Mr Lewis informed him. "The doctor whose name appears in your files – well, I've arranged to see him today. He has a surgery in Tulse Hill. Apparently, when you were a baby, you were registered with him. I've got a feeling he knows your mum."

Brenton cocked his ears. "So you reckon that this doctor might know where my mother is?"

"Well, it's a slim chance. You were registered with him fifteen, sixteen years ago. It doesn't say in your files whether your mother was registered with the same doctor, but he might know something, so it's worth a try." Mr Lewis was being very careful not to up-anchor Brenton's hopes.

The social worker turned and was about to enter his room

when the letter box clattered. He stooped down to pick up the mail, went back into the kitchen, and gave Brenton his brown envelope. "Don't forget to pay me your board, and do try to make the money last."

Brenton nodded automatically then hunted among the coats on the banister, searching for his anorak. Forgetting to wash up his cereal plate, he left the hostel, walking more quickly than usual, impatient to reach the small local Post Office-cum-shop.

As always, he was welcomed by an arthritic queue. Why the hell does my G have to come the same day as the blasted old people ram up the Post Office, he thought.

Eleven cashed pensions later, Brenton arrived at the summit of the queue and was confronted by a double-chinned Asian lady. Dressed in Indian attire, she fidgeted uncomfortably on a wailing wooden stool, feeling safe behind the wired glass and metal bars. She peered through her guard and ran her eyes over Brenton's hardlife countenance. "Identification, please?"

Brenton passed his crumpled medical card and already signed Giro underneath the counter. The stool-testing clerk examined the cheque as if it was a faked Picasso, then slowly counted out the sum of £42.25, before pushing the cash and medical card back to the impatient Brenton. Turning and walking out of the Post Office, he whispered to himself, "Now for a pair of decent new trainers!"

He headed towards Camberwell Green, where he saw one of his Brixtonian pals running for a bus. "Yo."

"Wha'ppen, Brenton? I'm going to Peckham to check this fit piece of beef. Sight you later."

Wearing a red, gold and green woollen hat, which seemed to be baiting gravity as it flapped in the wind, Brenton's spar bull-frogged on the bus, bumping into an elderly black woman, who proceeded to cuss the agile youth.

A snout later, the number 45 bus entered the scene, and took him to his required destination off Brixton High Street.

Breezing into one of the many shoe shops that were located there, Brenton browsed around, studying the trainer shoes and fingering their texture. A young white male sales assistant, whose sceptical eyes kept on following Brenton's movements, irritated him. Aware of the fact that he was being watched, he strutted towards the suspicious assistant. "Look, man, if I wanted to t'ief anything, I would of done – right? So why don't you stop clocking me, 'cos I'm paying with real money."

The shopworker backed away and asked another potential customer if they needed his aid. Meanwhile, Brenton made up his mind on what footwear he wanted and searched for the nervous assistant whom he had just humiliated. "Yo, service! I want these."

Holding up the trainer shoes, Brenton watched with a hyena-like grin as the shoe salesman hurriedly rushed over to attend to him, obviously finding his bad-bwai mood intimidating. He handed over the cash to purchase his new footwear, then strutted out of the shop. "Have a good day, won't you," he said smoothly, "and remember – the customer always comes first."

The sales assistant hoped one day he would win a transfer to somewhere like Carshalton.

It was half an hour until noon on a grey day with a vexed breeze. Despite this, Brixton Market was full of eager bargain-hunters and middle-aged mothers inspecting the varied fruits.

Brenton meandered along the vegetable and fruit-filled streets and decided to trod home. On Coldharbour Lane he observed the lively atmosphere of the packed Soferno-B record shack, filled with black youths listening out for the latest releases as the bass-line boxed the shop windows.

What he didn't notice was two black guys standing on the other side of the road, opposite the record shop. They had just come out of the barbershop there, although neither of them appeared to be trimmed. They were brethren of Terry Flynn; Flynn himself was inside, receiving a briefing of the ghetto news.

Brenton walked past the bustling unemployment exchange,

unaware that the youths had summoned Terry Flynn and were shadowing him. Carrying his trainers in a plastic bag, Brenton turned left off Coldharbour Lane, looking up at the white-painted tower blocks on Barrington Road.

The sight of a council carpenter repairing a broken-into front door; a silver-headed black man, draining a brew, watching the day go by dressed in his pyjamas; and a fretful-looking postman, adding undue haste to his last delivery round of the day, were familiar events on the tower block balconies.

Still unaware of his pursuers, Brenton trod past a brutalised children's play area. A broken swing skanked in the chilly breeze as a Cortina mark 2 revved noisily at a stubborn set of traffic-lights.

Terry Flynn and his spars continued to stalk their prey as Brenton strolled behind the back of another tower block. Here the avenging trio saw their chance. Brandishing a flick-knife, Terry Flynn and his cohorts hurtled towards their unsuspecting target.

"Get the half-breed bastard!" yelled a crazed Flynn, drunk on the rum of violence.

Brenton turned around sharply to find three guys converging on him with serious intent. With no time to run, he dropped his carrier bag and dodged the first blow by ducking. But a fist from nowhere struck his jaw and rocked him. Punches rained in on the helpless youth as he swung out his fists in desperation. Suddenly, he suffered an excruciating pain in his neck, and everything became misty as heat galloped through his skull, numbing his senses.

Fretting at the sight of thick blood, Flynn stared at his gore-splattered hand. "Don't fuck with me, right? You ain't no bad man!" Then the three attackers scattered out of the area, leaving their crimsoned victim lying on the asphalt, suffering from shock and stab wounds.

Brenton hadn't spotted the elderly white woman who witnessed the assault from her ground-floor flat. Aware of the victim's injuries, she shakily dialled for an ambulance, then replacing the phone, she parted the net curtain and observed the hurt teenager worming in pain. She wiped her brow, willing the ambulance to come as soon as possible, wondering whether the poor lad would live or die.

The woman dared not go outside and tend to Brenton, as she thought the assailants might still be at large. The pyjama-clad old man, perched on the ninth-floor balcony, had also observed the whole incident, but he remained impassive on his perch, sucking a skinny roll-up.

Five tokes later, the witnesses watched an ambulanceman giving emergency first aid to Brenton. Other onlookers now formed a small semi-circle, viewing the wounded Brixtonian get stretchered into the ambulance, his eyes now closed. The old lady followed the vehicle with her eyes as it sped off into the distance, all of its sirens screaming. The small group of nosy onlookers soon drifted off into separate directions as a council worker approached the scene, dressed in a donkey jacket and armed with enough black plastic bin bags to make anyone's day turn into night. He surveyed the bloodstained concrete. "Kiss me neck, why do dey waan kill each udder? Man to man are so unjust."

Many hours later, Brenton found himself lying in a hospital ward, suffering from a crucial headache. He focused his senses and realised that he was wearing a protective neck-brace. Trying to look around him, he sustained a sharp pain. Grimacing, he stared at the resident of the bed opposite his; a guy whose features were almost totally sheathed in bandages. Somehow, Brenton felt lucky.

The decor of the ward reminded Brenton of his hostel. Beige-painted walls gave the place a dismal appearance, although flowers in small vases, placed on wooden bedside cabinets, brightened up the room a little. The limping tree-trunk-coloured curtains cried out for a laundering.

He noticed a white male, bedridden with injuries to his limbs, staring at him. This made the still-groggy Brenton very uncomfortable, especially as he was only wearing a plastic hospital gown. He quickly pulled up his bedcovers to mask any embarrassment, not wanting no white man to see his privates.

A colour television set was situated high up in the corner of the room, supported by a metal stand so every patient could see it. A white-faced clock with black numerals and hands told Brenton the time was four-thirty; but he wondered what day it was.

Monotony came quickly to the neck-braced Brenton. His only entertainment was listening to the other patients bleat on about their injuries. He thought to himself, Where are the doctors and nurses? Then he recalled the sight of Terry Flynn rushing snarling towards him – tall and dark-skinned, with his short tufty hair and unshaven chin – and quickly reopened his eyes to exorcise the disturbing image.

As he waited for someone to tend to him, many thoughts sped through Brenton's mind. Like, what had happened to his newly acquired trainers? And did anybody know he was in hospital? Suddenly, he thought – *what* hospital? The label on the white bedsheet read *Kings College*, which was a fifteen-minute journey from home.

At ten past five, a doctor finally appeared in the ward, accompanied by a sister and a nurse. The male doctor was clad in an immaculate white jacket that could have been used in a soap-powder advert. He walked with an upright posture, suggesting he felt pride in his work. But what made him look particularly acute was his large forehead, enhanced by a retreating hairline.

The doctor approached Brenton and greeted him with a smile. "How do you feel, young man?"

"I ache all over and my brain's killing me."

"We had to do a bit of delicate work on your neck. You have, er, let me see now, about twenty or so stitches. You might not think so, but in a way you were lucky. You see, the incision just missed a main artery. Some of the tissues around your neck are, like I said, very delicate and will take time to heal. So we don't want you to be moving your neck as you would normally."

The doctor pointed at the neck-brace. "This will stop you from making any jerky movements. But don't worry, you won't be wearing it for too long; a couple of weeks at the most."

Despite the feeling that a twenty-stone wrestler had a thick thumb stuck in his neck, Brenton tried to see the funny side. "Well, I couldn't wear it for more than two weeks anyway. A guy can't look neat in this thing."

The doctor and the young nurse smiled, while the older sister, dressed in a navy-blue uniform, simply adjusted the papers on her clipboard, looking very passive. The doctor, a man in his mid-thirties, edged closer to the patient. "We found a medical card in your pocket, so Reception phoned your address and spoke to a Mr Lewis. At the time, you were heavily sedated, so Mr Lewis said he would be along later to see how you are."

Dismay found a route to Brenton's face as the doctor concluded, "You will have to stay here for a few days, and in that time it is very important to take your antibiotic tablets. They will help fight off any infection that might develop in your wound."

Brenton puffed a sigh. The doctor and sister, in conversation, moved away to tend to another patient, while the pretty young nurse stayed at Brenton's bedside, preparing to take his blood pressure. She admired his well-honed, muscular arm, and wrapped a thick brown cloth-like material around it. "You play sport? You look like a strong lad."

"Nah, not these days. I did play football and stuff at school."

The smiling nurse took Brenton's blood pressure while the patient enjoyed eyeing her curves.

Minutes later, he was bored again, thinking his patience would be shattered if he had to remain in hospital for a few days. With any luck, Floyd would bounce into the ward, carrying his suitcase for his use. However it was not the cocksure figure of Floyd that appeared eventually in the ward, but the worried frame of Mr Lewis. Following the social worker with his eyes without moving his neck, Brenton was amused that Mr Lewis found trouble in locating him.

"Yo! Over here!"

Lewis turned and saw a grinning Brenton sitting up in his bed, sporting his new neck decor. Mr Lewis's colossal backside sank into Brenton's bed. "They called me earlier, when you were sedated," he fussed. "How are you doing now?"

The patient, feeling at a disadvantage in his plastic hospital gown, replied, "Well, apart from this uncomfortable bed, these stupid pyjamas or whatever they're called, and a little cut in my neck, I'm all right. Seriously though, I've got a bad brain-ache and I'm bored." He watched Mr Lewis unzip the sports bag he was carrying.

"What have you got in there?"

Mr Lewis brought out a pair of pyjamas and a change of clothes. "Aren't I good to you? When you're up and about you'll be needing these."

The social worker then opened the bedside cabinet door, which Brenton hadn't realised was for his use. He was relieved to see the trainers he had bought inside it, but winced as he saw the blood-covered clothes he had been wearing at the time of the assault. "I only bought the trainers this morning. I thought I'd lost 'em."

Mr Lewis delved further into the bag, emerging with a large bottle of Ribena. "The things I do for you," he mocked. "One day I might do something really stupid and adopt you. Anyway, let me be serious for a minute. I would like you to tell me what happened – if you are ready."

Brenton had his eyes on his new trainers as he rubbed his forehead. Mr Lewis spoke in his most diplomatic tones. "I don't want to rush you, but it seems obvious that someone knifed you. Now, I don't know if you recognised who did it, but I would strongly advise you to press charges. You could have died. I don't want you to become another statistic in the *South London Press*."

"Nor do I."

"You know who did this to you, don't you?"

Brenton didn't answer.

"So you're not prepared to tell me all about it – what led up to this."

Brenton remained silent, his eyes resting on the clock.

"The police are there to protect and seek justice for you as well as anyone else," Mr Lewis stressed.

"What are you trying to say?" snapped Brenton. "You want me to go to the beast, innit?"

"Well, yes. For Christ's sake, you could have died! If you tell them what happened, they would have to investigate."

"Don't make me laugh. They don't help blacks – they just lock 'em up."

"They are not all bad. I admit that perhaps some of the younger elements in the police are too gung-ho. But there are some good officers who treat everybody fairly."

Brenton's laughter was curtailed by his injuries. Mr Lewis shook his head. "Anyway, for the moment, just get better, all right?"

"Yeah, well, thanks for coming and bringing me the drink and my clothes, Mr Lewis, but don't expect me to wear those pyjamas. They look like something a battyman would wear, know what I mean? I think I'll keep this overgrown nappy on."

The man smiled broadly at the joke, then looked gravely at his charge. "I know you're making light of what happened, but it must have shaken you up a lot."

Brenton scratched his uncombed hair and thought about it. "Well, of course it's kind of scary," he admitted, "but I'm still here. The funny thing is though, I never saw the knife coming. I just felt a pain, a sharp pain. It happened so fast. I turned around and saw them rushing me. Then I felt the pain."

The social worker listened attentively with a disturbed expression. Why were so many youths fighting and stabbing each other? Then, rising, he prepared to leave. "I was going to see that doctor today – you know, about your mother. But after what happened, I postponed the meeting. Don't worry now – I'll be seeing him in the next couple of days."

The tedious prospect of being holed up in a hospital bed suddenly invaded Brenton's mind. "If you see Floyd, tell him to bring his ghetto blaster so I can listen to my music."

"If you're allowed a tape recorder in here, don't play it too loud, will you? This is not your home, it's a hospital."

"I know that. I can tell the difference, you know."

Holding his empty bag, and sporting a wry smile, the social worker left the ward.

Next morning, Brenton read every article in the day's newspapers, keeping a look-out for the pretty nurse who tended him yesterday, but she didn't seem to be on duty. Thoughts of reprisals entered his head for a short while. "Terry Flynn, you're gonna know which side blood run on a pumpkin belly," he said internally. He didn't know what the phrase meant but had heard Floyd voice it many times when vexed with his spar Biscuit. Maybe he could be the small axe that felled the big tree. Brenton thought it was uncanny how he could use a Gong lyric to suit his circumstances – Flynn could be the dark oak.

The idea of making a statement to the beast disturbed Brenton; he hated the police just as much as he loathed Flynn. Besides, even if the abhorred Flynn was convicted, he guessed he would only get about a year's oats. And if he behaved himself in prison, Brenton's adversary would only eat oats for eight months. There was also the possibility of losing the respect of his Brixtonian peers if he got the law involved.

Brenton surveyed his ward, momentarily glaring at a patient who had kept him awake for most of the night. Apparently, the head-bandaged patient, moaning and groaning, felt the need to attract the night nurse's attention continually. Pouring himself a glass of Ribena, feeling apathetic, he wished the blackcurrant juice would transform itself into a strong lager; at least that would make him sleep easier.

A 45 bus, crawling towards Camberwell via Coldharbour Lane, only had room for standing passengers. A tutting woman, sitting beside Floyd, was slowly dropping into a pit of anger. Her annoyance was caused by Floyd's suitcase, which took up most of the legroom in the small aisle between the seats, but Floyd was dismissive of the problem as he peered aimlessly through the window.

Floyd had suspected that the ill-famed Terry Flynn would hook up with Brenton sooner or later, and wreak his revenge. He wondered now whether he should have told Brenton in much stronger terms, to keep undercover. He felt sympathy for his hostel-mate, but thought maybe Brenton was too much of a 'lionheart' for his own good.

From a pool-club banter, it had ended with someone nearly losing their life. Why was there so much ratchet-sketching and blade-jousting going on? Hardly a day passed without some story of So and So, or Whatsisname getting his face etched with a serious piece of Sheffield steel. Brooding, Floyd felt it was the fault of people like Terry Flynn. They had massive egos and would knife someone in order to keep their bad-bwai rep intact.

The hospital was just a minute's walk from the bus stop and while Floyd made his way there, he recalled what Mr Lewis had told him earlier in the day: "Don't laugh at Brenton's neck-brace." So Floyd allowed himself a little chuckle in the hospital corridor, flushing the humorous scenario out of his system.

One side of his body was anchored down by his suitcase as he entered the ward where his spar was recuperating. He found Brenton reading one of the newspapers most people normally associate with bowler-hatted businessmen. Floyd strutted towards his pal. "Lewis told me you were bored, but this is getting drastic, innit, for you to start reading that. Anyway, how you feeling?"

"That's a fool-fool question. Why does everyone ask how I am? I thought it was obvious I'm not feeling well, know what I mean? What do you want me to say? 'Oh, I'm feeling fine thanks, apart from a little itch on my neck'."

Floyd parked on the bed, unable to take his gaze off the neck-brace. "I see you haven't changed since you've been in here, but you look like you're wearing a whole 'eap of church collars."

"Is that why you come here? Just to take the piss?"

"You're so ungrateful, man. I've carried this heavy suitcase all the way from our yard and all you can do is moan. I've got some wicked tapes in my pocket as well."

Floyd proceeded to pull a few cassette tapes out of his brown suede jacket and presented them to his brethren.

"Thanks man," Brenton sighed. "I seriously needed that. I was going cuckoo with boredom. Now I've got my roots music, I'll get back my sanity. Yeah Floyd man, I owe you a favour. But ain't it usual for a visitor to come to hospital bringing drink and nuff food for the patient? I'm telling you, a starving hog wouldn't eat the crap they dish out here. And you couldn't even buy me a bloody Mars bar."

Floyd grinned and tried to hide his guilt by showing his palms. "I'm broke, man, I'm a pauper. I don't get my big G till tomorrow."

Brenton gave Floyd a magistrate's look. "Your G usually comes a day after I get mine, so you should have got your big G today. You're lying, innit. I bet you spent most of your corn on herb."

"What you saying, man? Besides if I did, I would deal with you, innit."

"Yeah, I suppose you would. But you still could have bought me a bloody Mars bars though."

"I signed on a day late, like I had t'ings to do on my signing-on day. I was fixing a lock on Sharon's front door that day. Her paps, for the first time in months, turned up in the middle of the night. He had more alcohol in him than blood and was shouting and t'ing, and then he mashed up the door 'cos Sharon's mudder wouldn't let him in. Anyway, she called the beast on him. So you know what I'm saying, I got tied up 'cos Sharon was upset and t'ing. I had to give her some tender care, you know the runnings."

"Yeah, yeah Floyd, if you say so."

Floyd stood up and scanned the ward, noticing the beige-painted walls and the metal beds. He thought to himself that if you disposed of all the medical items and replaced them with small toys scattered on the floor, the ward could resemble a council children's home dormitory he once attended.

Floyd decided to have a nose in the bedside cabinet, where he found something to stir his interest. He picked up Brenton's new trainers, examining them like a goldrush digger. "Not bad man, not bad. A pity you can't step down the street in them just yet. How long are you gonna stay in here for?"

"I dunno, a few days."

Floyd, still studying the trainer shoes, was suitably impressed. "Disappointed I didn't buy plimsolls, are you?" sniped Brenton.

Feeling bored, Floyd put the footwear back in the cabinet and prepared to make his exit. He spotted the attractive young nurse who had tended to his hostel-mate just a day ago, busy changing the blankets and sheets of one of those uncomfortable-looking beds. "Well, Brenton, at least you've got the suitcase to keep you company. I'm heading out now, and if I was you, I'd try and chat up that nurse over there; she's quite fit for a white girl."

Floyd indicated with his eyes the nurse he was talking about, and Brenton discreetly glanced across the ward at her; she certainly could arouse many heads to turn. His visitor turned and paced out of the ward, grinning to himself.

CHAPTER SEVEN
Catalyst

25 January, 1980

It was a spliff end of a desolate afternoon. A vexed rain took out its fury on South London as Brenton idled on his bed, listening to the tune of the weather.

He fingered the jelly-like wound in his neck, considering how unsightly it must look, but at least he now owned two polo neck sweaters that Mr Lewis had thoughtfully bought for him. Although the neck-brace had been taken off over a week ago, he couldn't move his head as freely as before the stabbing. Caressing the scar, he glanced up at Mr Dean. "No one stabbed you in the neck. If they did, you would've killed the bastard - right, James? Terry Flynn's gonna suffer for this."

Brenton had been told by the doctor at the hospital to rest as much as possible, so he spent many reflective hours alone in his room, sometimes talking things over with the omnipresent Mr Dean.

Full of boredom, he was examining his new trainers, when someone slapped on the door. What does Floyd want now? he thought. "Only come in if you got any liquor or herb, otherwise remove ya," he called out.

The figure of Mr Lewis popped his head around the door.

"Oh shit, it's you."

"What do you mean by herb? I hope it's not what I think it is," scolded Mr Lewis, who secretly thought his charge's cannabis smoking was no more harmful than a trip down the pub.

He then produced his trademark frown and it seemed he had untold worries, but didn't know how to solve them. "Brenton, would you come down to my room? I have something important to tell you - it concerns your mother."

Brenton sat up, ready to give a reply, only to see Lewis disappear out of his room. Dressed only in jeans and vest, he shadowed the other man down the stairs, wondering what he was about to reveal to him.

He entered Mr Lewis's room and found him clearing many papers and items of correspondence off his desk, appearing very preoccupied, scarcely aware of Brenton sitting down opposite him. "Oh, er, sorry. I didn't expect you to come down straight away. I'll be with you in a minute, Brenton. Just doing a bit of tidying up - my desk's in a right mess."

Brenton telescoped the table for evidence of any snouts and spotted a half-full packet, partly concealed by a brown envelope. "Don't mind if I take one, do you?"

Mr Lewis simply nodded his head and cleared his throat, preparing himself for what he had to say. From a drawer in his desk he pulled out a large file and placed it in front of himself, then he steepled his hands together and looked up at his eager charge.

"Right, my young friend, this is your file and as you can see, it has a lot of material in it. I don't know if you are aware, but it's like a kind of logbook. It starts from when you came into care, and chronicles your life until the week you moved in here."

Acting like a child on the day before his birthday, Brenton nodded in anticipation, to show he understood. "This file contains all the school reports, staff reports, doctors' and social workers' reports and even some psychiatric reports on you. It's quite amazing really. For the life of me, I can't remember ever seeing a file as thick as this."

"Yeah, yeah, get on with it."

"It's even got details of case reviews and meetings concerning you from when you were a baby."

The social worker paused to light up a cigarette as Brenton sat uneasily. "I haven't got all day, you know."

Mr Lewis secretly thought that someone should have told Brenton about the contents of the file years ago. "I have had this stuff for the past week and you would not believe how much trouble I had getting access to it. These files are like national secrets."

Brenton slid downwards, indicating to Lewis to get a move on. Mr Lewis darted a glance at the teenager. "Anyway, before I tell you about your mother's whereabouts, I feel I have to explain the circumstances of when you were born. Is this all right with you? Do you know anything about what happened at the time of your birth?"

"I don't know much, just that my mother is Jamaican and my paps is a white man. I've always reckoned my bitch of a mother gave me up."

Brenton felt the hot vapour of frustration moistening his eyes. Wanting to hear the full novel, he began to tap his feet. The social worker noted this, but he'd planned this talk for the past few days and was determined to do it in his own way - he would not be rushed, no matter how much impatience Brenton displayed.

"Not even a lion rejects her cubs or even a rat rejects, er, whatever they have. I have to know why she done it."

Flicking his ash in the ashtray, Mr Lewis set his gaze on Brenton. "It's not quite as straightforward as that. I wouldn't call it rejection; maybe another word is appropriate."

Taking his arm off the desk and sitting upright, Brenton fought for control of his tongue. "Then what would you call it?"

"Look, it says in your file that around the time you were born, your mother was already married to somebody different from your father."

Mr Lewis thought for a while then decided to give his charge more information.

"It appears your mother was very intelligent, by all accounts.

51

The records say she came over to England in 1961, late in the year. The exact date isn't given, but I suppose it was November or December."

Mr Lewis flipped through the pages of the file to try and find the notes he wanted to concentrate on. "Apparently she came over from Jamaica to study nursing. At her night college, she met your father. I don't know how accurate this is, but that is what it's got down here. Anyway, your mother's husband was in Jamaica at the time."

Brenton leaned slightly further forward and tried to read the text of the file upside down. Then he re-routed his gaze to the social worker.

"Unfortunately for you, I suppose," Mr Lewis said quietly, "your mother's husband came over to England unexpectedly, just before Christmas 1962. It must have been a big shock for him to find his wife pregnant. You can imagine the trouble and problems this caused."

Lewis paused, then went on: "The first contact Lambeth Social Services had with your mother was in February 1963. The desk clerk wrote that on a freezing cold day, your mother came into the Area Three office complaining about domestic violence. She went there after advice from a friend. This also says that your mother was having complications with the pregnancy, so it was decided by her doctor and social services to keep her in hospital until you were born."

"What happened to my paps? What was he doing at the time? I bet he chipped."

Mr Lewis thumbed through the pages again, while Brenton felt the need for another smoke; it was difficult to swab all this information. No one had ever sat down with him before and explained his early life.

The social worker stumbled upon the page he was seeking. "Ah - here we are. When your mother's husband came over from Jamaica, Mr Brown, your father, kept very much a low profile. In fact, Lambeth Council had no contact with Mr Brown until summer 1964. It says here, that after you were born on the twenty-third of March, 1963, your father actually took you from the hospital when you were only a few days old."

"Why?"

Lewis glanced at the pages in front of him to refresh his memory. "A few weeks after you were born, your mother came to see the social worker attached to her case. The social worker had written to her, apparently, saying that she had a choice. She could either keep her marriage intact, or lose her marriage and go it alone with you. The records don't say whether she had any other children, but it's clear that her husband ordered her to give up the child she had just given birth to - you. It gets a bit confusing here and I can't quite make out what went on. But to cut a long story short, she opted to stay with her husband and she entrusted you to your father."

A disbelieving look spread over Brenton's features as he confronted this tale of his infant life. He would never have imagined that he'd been cared for by his white paps. The revelations from the file were distressing him, so he decided to stand up and step towards the front window to mask his turmoil. He heard Lewis continue.

"Your father was probably struggling to look after you and maintain his studies. The files don't say whether someone helped him take care of you. There's no mention of Mr Brown's family or background."

Brenton turned around, paying full attention.

"It's rather strange, because there is plenty of information about your mother. Anyway, the fact is, your father placed you in care with Lambeth Social Services in September 1964. After that, he appeared to have vanished. There has been no contact since."

Mr Lewis closed the file and watched Brenton re-seat himself. Aware of the youth's despair, he counselled, "Look, you have to realise that in those days, there was a big stigma if a black person had a relationship with a white person. Even more so, if one of them was married - it was unheard of. So I imagine both your parents were under some sort of pressure. Even so, I don't excuse him for abandoning you."

Brenton began to feel a hot impatience. "All right, you have told me her background, now where does she live?"

"Er, West Norwood, a few miles up the road."

Too late, the social worker realised he'd told Brenton of his mother's whereabouts before he planned to. "It's ironic that she lives so close. I finally met up with your mother's doctor last week. He acted as a go-between for us. She didn't want to be seen by any social workers or be called on the phone, but she left an address with the doctor which he passed on to me."

Brenton slowly shook his head. "So bloody close." It filtered through his mind that he might well have seen his mother in the flesh without realising it. He recalled the many times he had walked through the streets of West Norwood. "It's a small world."

Now that he'd told Brenton his mother's whereabouts, Mr Lewis hoped his charge would stay longer for some counselling. Opening a drawer in his desk, he pulled out a small slip of paper, but before waiting for the paper to be given to him, Brenton reached out his hand and snatched it from the scandalised Lewis's grasp. Brenton quickly read the address scrawled on the paper.

"Your mother's name is Cynthia Massey," Mr Lewis said, ruffled. "I don't know if she is married, but the doctor told me he hasn't seen Mr Massey for years. Now Brenton, take it slowly, don't rush anything! I don't know if you're expecting a happy ending, so just see how things go."

Brenton soared from his chair, making sure his mother's address was safe in his jeans back pocket. "Don't worry, I ain't got no expectations. Why should I?"

Striding towards the door, he stopped in his tracks and decided not to leave the room just yet. He turned around and addressed the older man once more. "I just want to know what she is like. I don't even know what she bloody looks like! I want to see her reaction when she sees me for the first time since she gave me away at the hospital. I've waited a long time for this."

Mr Lewis clasped his hands together, studying Brenton's determined face as the teenager resumed, "When I was a little brat, I used to sit up in bed and wonder where my mum was. Now I know."

For a couple of seconds, the pair stared at each other, both fully aware of the significance of the occasion. "You sure you can handle this?" Lewis asked. "Do you want me to go with you?"

Brenton slowly shook his head, as though he'd been asked if he needed to be escorted to school by his parents, even though he was fifteen. "I'll be all right, and thanks for what you've done. I might not show it, but I do appreciate it. For a social worker, you're all right. Everyone calls you Mr Lewis, innit? What's your first name?"

"Arnold."

With a grin, Brenton opened the door and disappeared out of the room. Arnold rocked back in his chair, hoping he'd done the right thing, praying that Brenton Brown wouldn't get emotionally damaged for life.

Brenton looked into the mirror on his dressing table, deciding it was time to start a fight with his hair. Trying to remember where he'd last seen his Afro-comb, he crouched down at the foot of the wardrobe and parted the clothes that were hanging there. Seconds later, he discovered it in the bottom corner. It was too dusty to put through his hair, so he marched to the bathroom and ran a hot tap over it. Satisfied it was dust-free; he gazed into the mirror above the washbasin and forced the metal teeth through his tangles. Grimacing and wincing with pain, he was determined to make himself look presentable. He didn't want his mother to think he was a hopeless youth who didn't care about anything.

As he was warring with his hair, doubts cannoned his mind, as well as many questions. What if his mother was still married? What if there were brothers and sisters? What sort of job did she have? Would she have grey hair? Was she fat? She might be one of those mad church people, singing praise the Lord songs all the time.

With the comb meshed in his hair, Brenton, suddenly not so confident of the situation, ambled back into his room. Was it wise to face his mother after so many years? Perhaps Floyd was right when he said he might be wasting his time.

He had indeed waited a very long time for this day, and wanted to confront his mother thinking positive vibrations. Still struggling to comb out his hair, he made up his mind to leave the hostel at half past six. He didn't want to leave too early, because he suspected he might slap her door, only to find there was no one home.

It was twenty-five minutes to seven. Wearing ironed jeans, and a denim jacket borrowed from Floyd, Brenton appeared quite smart as he laced on his new trainers. Before opening the front door, he made sure he had the piece of paper with his mother's address written on it, safely banked into his back pocket.

As he emerged into the street, trodding to the bus stop, he wondered what he should say to his mother. Should he be polite and courteous, saying: "Good evening, Ms Massey, I am your long-lost son. Could I speak with you, please?" Or should he be acid-tongued, like? For instance - "Hi, Mum, long time no see. In fact, a very long time no see, you bitch!"

Hands in his pocket, he braced himself against the spiteful wind. The rain had called off its deluge, but small puddles rippled in the streets.

He stopped off at a small newsagents run by an Indian family, where he shifted from foot to foot impatiently until the young mother with a child in front of him bought a box of matches. Then Brenton paid five pence for a single snout. Seconds later, he reached the bus stop and peered through the rain into the horizon of the main road, seeing no sign of a number 68.

Camberwell High Street was still busy with the butt end of

rush-hour traffic. To pass the time, Brenton read the posters in shop windows advertising items in the winter sales. As he checked the bargains on offer in a shoe shop, a number 68 arrived. An anxious Brenton boarded it, seating himself at the rear of the upper deck. Taking the fag off his ear, he asked a well-dressed African man sitting in front of him for a light.

The bus reached Brenton's destination quicker than he'd wanted it to. He jogged up a road opposite a college, feeling moths and many other things flying about in his stomach, and then he wondered if this adventure was a good idea. His heartbeat felt like a heavy bass-line as he stood still to read his mother's address once more.

He found himself on his mother's road, and was impressed by the large semi-detached houses in it. The cars parked along the road seemed more expensive than the motors he peered into around his home streets. He wondered what sort of job his mother had, to be able to live in a road like this. Maybe she married some rich white guy, he considered.

Walking on slowly, he noted the numbers of the houses, his eyes straining as he saw the figure of 41- it was number 17 he sought. Quickening his pace, Brenton became aware how quiet the street was. As he approached his mother's abode, all he could hear was the sound of the now mild-tempered breeze passing though the leafless trees skirting the road.

He stopped to study the attractive numeral of 17, coloured in gold on a varnished hardwood door, and finally realised the reality of standing outside his mother's house. His heartbeat moved up-tempo as he gradually neared the front door. There was a doorbell to the side of the door, but he decided to use the knocker of the brass letterbox. His hands began to feel clammy - a hot rush of adrenaline showered through his body as he braced himself and slapped the knocker three times. As he waited, he shuffled his feet nervously, scratching behind his ear.

Through the letterbox, he peered into the darkness of a

hallway, then he closed the flap and looked upwards to see if any lights were switched on. Suddenly the small gap at the bottom of the door became illuminated. Something strange stirred in his veins. Composing himself, he stood upright, expecting someone to come.

The front door gaped slowly. It revealed a worried-looking, middle-aged black woman. Her stature was vulnerable and short, and her physique was slim and fragile. Her tannish forehead was etched with deep-set fissures, and her eyes seemed to have lost their sparkle and life. The cheeks searched for an outlet within her taut skin, and a wide negroid nose was set on a milky, caramel face, dotted with small dark freckles.

Mother and son gazed speechlessly at each other for a few seconds. Time had downed tools and gone on strike. Ms Massey knew immediately that she was looking at her son. Finally, she broke the silence, saying in a soft Jamaican accent, "You'd better come inside. Breeze is blowing, rain is falling and it col' outside."

Brenton entered the house, wondering why he had expected his mother to be big and imposing. The first thing that caught his eye was a picture of a European-looking Jesus Christ, back-dropped by a red patterned wallpaper. Brenton felt the urge to call Mr Lewis on a white telephone that was neatly parked on a small mahogany table. As his feet sank into a Burgundy-coloured carpet, he couldn't escape the irony that his mother had images of Christianity on her walls. Silly hypocrites a ga'long der, he thought. After all, not seeing her son for sixteen years was not very Christian-like.

Brenton looked up in awe at the gloss-painted, elaborate wood beading that charmed the ceiling. Maybe she was married to some white lawyer or something, he convinced himself. Following his mother into the front room, he wondered how much money she earned. Ms Massey beckoned her son to sit down on a comfy-looking, button-filled brown sofa. Situated directly opposite him was a teak wall cabinet, filled with ornamental plates and porcelain statues. A colour television set stood proud in a corner, but it was the stereo that really lusted Brenton's eye. It was powerful-looking and attractive, and he would love to play his reggae tapes on this control tower.

Ms Massey apprehensively sat down in an armchair facing her son, not enjoying the anxious silence. Then she immediately hauled herself up again. "I'm jus' about to mek a cup of tea. You mus' feel like somet'ing hot as you jus' come in from de col'. How much sugar you take?"

Brenton found it difficult to come to terms with his mother speaking in a Jamaican accent - it didn't seem real to him. "Two," he answered. Cynthia Massey disappeared out of the room. Brenton took this as a cue to rise up and nose around. He ambled towards the wall cabinet, drawn by a statue of a pathetic woman carrying a heavy basket. The helplessness of the figure seemed to pluck a bass-note within Brenton and a sudden anger swept through him. He was ready now to ask a few questions.

Two minutes later, Cynthia reappeared holding two mugs of tea. Very carefully, she placed them on two small drink mats, resting on a circular glass coffee table in the centre of the room. Brenton followed her every move like a leopard sizing up its dinner.

Ms Massey was aware of her son's glare headlighting upon her as she slowly snuggled back into her chair. Sitting down and crossing her legs, she tried to find welcoming lyrics to say to the boy. She glanced at him, only to find him glowering back at her.

"Why? Tell me why!" he said in a hoarse voice. "Why did you leave me so young?" Ms Massey was unable to answer, or even meet her son's eyes as he quivered his head. "Give me one good reason why you left me when I was a baby! One good fucking reason!"

Bravely, Cynthia reared her head. "T'ings were kinda hard back in those days. Your fa'der promised me he would mind you.

59

Y'understand, look after you. My 'usband, dem time, did not want me to mind you."

Exploding from his chair, Brenton patrolled the room, still fixing his cold gaze on his ashamed-looking mother. "Not good enough! Shit, just not good enough! You could have come back to look for me, or even tried to find out where I was, but no. I was left to rot in that hell of a children's home."

Cynthia sat motionless, peering into her hot drink as Brenton raged. "Not knowing any family! You won't believe the shit I've been through. But you seem to be all right, innit? Nice yard, I must say. It beats the home I had! You just didn't give a shit, did you?"

"Every day I have lived wid your baby wail, every day," the woman whimpered.

"So why didn't you come to look for me! *Why?*"

"I couldn't face it."

"Couldn't face it! Couldn't face it! I HAD NO FUCKING CHOICE. And you're telling me you couldn't face it! YOU MAKE ME SICK!"

Brenton's yelling seemed to have caused some movement upstairs, but he was deaf to this as he let loose again. "While you've been living a cushy life, I have been fighting and struggling just to stay alive, and sometimes, believe me, I didn't think it was worth it."

Then a tall, very beautiful black girl sporting an Afro hairstyle entered the room. Her face was a picture of wonderment as she stared at Brenton. His temper won control over his curiosity as he loaded his mouth with hurtful lyrics. "I like to watch them animal programmes! There was one on the other day about the gorilla. Now, when these adult gorillas feel that their young are threatened, they get very violent! So, in a way, they're better than you, innit? 'Cos at least they try something!"

"Who are you to shout at my mother!" demanded the young woman.

Brenton's head snapped in the direction of Ms Massy's

daughter. What is going on? he thought. Fuck my days, this might be my sister!

After the verbal onslaught, Cynthia was an anxious wreck, fighting against the flood of tears which was welling up inside her.

The young woman stood at the entrance to the room, glaring at Brenton. An eerie silence followed, until Ms Massey decided it was time for an introduction. So, spluttering with emotion, she gestured towards the young lady. "Juliet," she said weakly, "dis is your younger brother, Brenton."

Brother and sister studied each other as if they had just seen an extra-terrestrial from Outer Space pushing a shopping trolley through an underground Tube tunnel. Brenton was the more startled of the two. He began to rub his temple furiously.

Addressing her daughter, Ms Massey explained, "Well, he is your half-brother. Remember I did tell you about him after the divorce."

Ms Massey's son just could not take his eyes off his sister. She's beautiful, he said inwardly. What is going on?

He looked for any resemblance they might share - but there was none. Brenton thought she was too attractive for them to look alike. Slightly darker than her brother, Juliet's posture was upright and elegant. Her hair was immaculately set and the gold earrings she was wearing complemented her dark-coffee complexion. But it was her big, round, happy eyes that made her a blessing to look at - it was obvious that she enjoyed laughing. After searching her brother's expression, Juliet in her turn thought that Brenton probably lost his temper nuff times.

Brenton stopped his menacing march around the room and, lost for words, glanced at his mother to see if she could provide any. Ms Massey struggled out from her chair, looking as if the evening's events had lined her forehead even more. She picked up her half-full mug of tea. "I don't know what to say. I can say sorry for the rest of my days, but it can never be enough."

"You can say that again," barked Brenton.

Cynthia summoned up the courage to look her son straight in the eye. "Brenton, I always had it in mind to look for you, understand. But the longer I put it off, the more difficult it was for me to face reality. The last I saw of you, you was only a few days old. I remember saying to your fa'der that I will see you from time to time. But your fa'der vanished, an' to this day, I don't know where he is. Months turned into years, an' I could not handle the stress of looking for you again. Maybe I was too 'fraid of my 'usband finding out."

With her two offspring gazing at her, Cynthia bowed her head and wearily plodded out of the room. "I'm tired an' not feeling well today, Brenton, but feel free to come again. I know you must hate me, but I want to see you again, y'hear? I have to go upstairs and lie down - I can't take this."

"I had to take it!" shouted Brenton, his eyes chilled.

Cynthia carefully made her way up the stairs, leaving her son and daughter gawping into a bewildered space.

After a few seconds, the pair began to exchange wary glances. Brenton took off Floyd's denim jacket and decided to slouch in the armchair his mother had vacated. Juliet, wearing a cream-coloured silky blouse and a blue skirt, sat down elegantly on the sofa, folding her arms. Brenton rubbed his chin with his index digit. He was the one who finally chopped the silence. "How old are you?"

"Eighteen. I'm nineteen in May."

Juliet was fascinated by this half-brother she had never seen, and was dying to ask him all sorts of questions, but she was angered by his treatment of her mother. Meanwhile, Brenton was trying to come to terms with the fact that he had a brand new sister. He wanted to cuss his mother but felt the need to show his sister he was a decent sort - not a bad bwai.

He clawed the side of his head. "I'm seventeen in March and I must admit, I didn't think I had an older sister. It's sort of weird."

Juliet's eyes were fastened on the scar on her brother's neck. "I was born in Jamaica," she told him. "My father and my grandparents looked after me when I was a baby. Soon after I was born, my mum went to England."

The pair inspected each other across the round glass coffee table, which still had a mug of cold tea placed on it. "How did you get that scar on your neck?" she asked.

Brenton fingered the unsightly mark on his neck with his right hand. "Some guy who couldn't handle me with his fists did it. Well, you know what the record says: 'Fist to fist days are done, the knife take over'."

Juliet was fascinated, but she had noticed the mug of cold tea. "Want a hot cup and something to eat?" she enquired.

"Please."

And Juliet departed from the room, contemplating the brain-jarring fact that she had a bad-bwai brother. Brenton, meanwhile, felt his trip to his mother's house had been worth the trod, although he could never forgive her for the past.

When Juliet reappeared, she was carrying a plateful of thick cheese sandwiches and a mug of fresh tea. She placed the refreshments on the coffee table before settling down on the sofa, making herself comfortable. Brenton picked up his mug. "Thanks."

The girl watched her brother sip his tea. "Do you live far away?" she asked.

"No, Camberwell. I live in a sort of hostel for kids coming out of care or a Home. You know, something like that."

"It's funny, isn't it? I have a brother, you, who lives so close and I might have walked right past you and we wouldn't of known nutten."

Brenton nodded. "Yeah, it's true. So close and yet so blasted far, you know what I mean? I'm glad I sort of found you, but saying that, I didn't even know I had a brother or sister." Pausing for a moment, he glanced around him, then locked his gaze on his sister. "Are there any more? Are you the only brother or sister I've got?"

Juliet's face curved into a delicious smile as she unfolded her arms. Brenton wondered what the joke was - he looked at his sister with slight suspicion. "No, as far as I know anyway. Unfortunately for you, I'm the only sister or brother you've got. I'm what they call an only child, and I hate that 'cos people think I'm spoilt."

Juliet sank into the sofa and stretched out her long legs under the coffee table, feeling totally captivated by her new-found younger brother, and wanting to prolong the conversation for as long as possible.

She studied Brenton in a way that made him feel uncomfortable. He fidgeted in his chair. "What do you do?" he asked. "Work? Go to college?"

"I went to college for a year, but I got bored of it. You know, I wanted to earn some decent money. Anyway, I got a job working for a bank in the City."

"What city?"

Juliet laughed, nearly choking on her sandwich. "It's where all the big banks and money buildings are, just over the river. Kind of opposite London Bridge. Well, that area is called the City. The centre of it is the Bank of England."

"Oh yeah? It's where that Bank underground station is, innit?"

Juliet smiled at her brother's ignorance. "What do you do?"

Brenton jolted his shoulders. "Nothing. I was kicked out of school. I didn't take no shit from the teachers. Sorry about the French, but me and teachers just don't agree."

"You must try to do something," she said reprovingly. "If you can't decide on what to do, go to college. Sometimes it's easier for a person to do well at college, rather than at school."

Brenton shook his head slightly as he fed himself another sandwich. "No, I'm not the type to study books and revise and so on. I'm more practical, see – good with the hands. Woodwork and t'ing."

"Then go to college and do a course about woodwork or something practical," Juliet interrupted. "Colleges don't just do courses for English and Maths, you know."

"Yeah, I suppose you're right. But like you, I would rather have a job and make some money. I'm sick and tired of buying my clothes in cheap shops. I wanna start to buy them up the West End, you know what I mean?"

Juliet was determined to get her point across, thinking that because of his schooling problems, Brenton should prepare himself at college before lining up for the rat race. "Apply for a grant, you should get one," she advised. "If you do, you'll get more money than just dole, and you'll be learning something constructive at the same time."

Brenton was defeated by his sister's persistence on the issue of college. "All right, all right, I will step down to Brixton College and if I feel like it, I will check out Vauxhall College as well. I will ask what courses they're dealing wid. Will that satisfy you?"

Juliet smiled and felt a small sense of achievement. It was as if she'd taken it upon herself to be her brother's guru. Brenton wondered what his mother was doing upstairs. Maybe she was bawling – serve her right!

Juliet saw him staring into space; she found it hard to think of the right thing to say. "Hey, Brenton, I know it's probably hard for you coming here and meeting me and my mother. Shit, hold up. I mean *our* mother, sorry for that."

Brenton grinned, making Juliet think her brother did possess some humour in his make-up. She resumed, "I am not going to defend what she did or what she didn't do, but I can say this – she did care about you, and she told me I had a little brother when I was seven. Many times she has been thinking what you were up to, especially on your birthday. It's in March, innit?"

Brenton nodded silently. "I know she feels guilty," Juliet went on, "and sometimes so did I, knowing I had a brother somewhere out there. But take it easy on her, Mum's not well these days. She suffers from high blood pressure, so any stress is not good for her."

"Hasn't done me much good either."

Looking pensive, Juliet paused and gazed at her younger brother, who didn't appear convinced by what she was telling him.

The reality of it all finally hit Brenton. He wanted to pinch himself, because he could not quite believe that he was having a conversation with his sister in his own mother's house. He had reduced his mother to tears and began to regret not bringing Mr Lewis with him.

Brenton closed his eyes for a split second and then released them, half-expecting to wake up in his hostel bed, staring at Mr Dean. But this was not to be. What would James make of it all? he asked himself. He found Juliet staring at him inquisitively. This was a stare too far for him. "Look, um, thanks for chatting to me, but I better chip now. It's getting a bit late."

Juliet glanced at her gold-coloured watch, noting that the time was past ten o'clock. "How you getting home?"

"Er, by decker, innit."

Impatient now, Brenton propelled himself forward, sitting on the edge of the chair. His sister stood up and went over to the front window, where she parted the net curtains and gazed through the glass. She heard the wind whistling outside, slamming the rain onto the window. "I'll order you a cab. It's freezing out there."

"You don't have to do that. I'll be all right."

As he got up out of his chair, Juliet was showing some mild displeasure in her face, like a bewildered commuter who had thrown a busker a coin, only for the busker to get up and walk away, ignoring the gift. "Hey, I'm calling you a cab, and before you go, you can write down your address and phone number. Mum and myself would like to know where to contact you."

Juliet stepped into the hallway to make a phone-call to a cab office, while her brother stood, hands in his pockets, wondering whether his mother would come down to bid him goodbye.

Following the phone-call, Juliet's head poked around the front-room door. "A few minutes."

Then she trotted upstairs, leaving Brenton staring out at the raging night, still attempting to come to terms with the evening's events. Seconds later, Juliet sauntered back into the room, holding a five-pound note, a page of notepaper and a pen. Smiling, she placed the cash, paper and pen on the coffee table. "Write down your phone number and address on this. The fiver should cover your cab fare."

Brenton eyed the money. "It won't cost that much."

"Don't worry about it."

Brenton reluctantly picked up the bank-note and pushed it deep inside his back pocket. When he'd finished writing down his details on the piece of paper, he gave it to his sister. "You have to understand, I'm not used to people asking me for my address and phone number. The last time somebody did that, I was in a beast station."

This last statement mopped the smile off Juliet's face. She was about to say something, but was interrupted by a shriek from a car horn. Brenton quickly paced through the room towards the front door, his sister close behind. "Look after yourself and I'll call soon."

"Yeah, thanks and t'ing, and I'll sight you later."

Juliet watched her brother step into the waiting cab, wondering how Fate had treated his sixteen years, and how he'd been brought up. As the taxi moved away, she felt an unfamiliar anger towards her mother for being too weak-hearted when abandoning the infant Brenton. Sympathising with her brother's plight, Juliet vowed to try and make it up to him, wanting to compensate him somehow.

In the taxi, Brenton glanced upwards, to see if his mother was there at an upstairs window, bidding him goodbye. But she was nowhere in sight. He dropped his head, staring at the mat.

As soon as Juliet closed the front door, her thoughts turned to her mother. What with her high blood pressure and meeting Brenton for the first time, the evening must have given her heart a stern test. So she scampered upstairs and tapped gently on her mother's door before entering.

Ms Massey's room was attractively decorated with pink and white striped wallpaper. A matching beige double wardrobe and chest of drawers gave it a furniture catalogue appearance, while the deep red carpet was warm and cosy. Gold-framed photographs hung from the wall, many of them snapshots of the young Juliet Massey. Various school certificates and exam passes were also hung about the walls or propped up on the dressing table.

Juliet found her mother sprawled across the double bed, obviously very troubled and upset. She stood in the doorway, waiting for her mother to notice her, but Ms Massey's head was tombed in her quilt. "Mum, Mum."

Slowly, the distraught woman turned around, her face saturated in tears. Juliet felt a deep compassion for her mother, imagining the torment she was feeling. She sat down on the bed beside her. "You should have talked to him more, Mum. I know how you feel, but it looked bad when you went off upstairs like that."

Swabbing her tears with one swipe of her hand, the older woman sat up to face her daughter. It had indeed been a heart-wrenching experience, setting eyes on her son after sixteen years; she hadn't known how to cope with the situation.

"You know, I did want to hold him," she said tearfully, "but him look so vex, so upset, I jus' could not go near him. It mus' be somet'ing for a woman to be 'fraid of her own son."

Juliet gave her mother a forgiving glance as Cynthia went on, "I did want to tell him that he has been in my thinking for a long time now – since him was born – but I don't think him would have believed me. The trut' is, I have failed him. When he did need me, I wasn't there. I couldn't even look him in the eye. Him mus' really hate me y'know, but you can't blame the poor bwai."

Concerned, Juliet lay down on the bed, propping her head on her right hand, looking kindly on her mother, trying to reassure her that the situation might not turn out that bad.

"Hey, listen to me," she said gently. "He looks well, healthy enough, and we now know where he is. It's gonna take a little time to get to know each other. Just be glad that he's found us. Now it's up to the two of us to show Brenton we care."

Tears began to reappear on Cynthia's cheeks. "When I saw him at the door, I knew it was him. I could have died from shame. But the worse t'ing was, I jus' treated him like any udder visitor to the house. I did not be'ave like a mudder should. I jus' stood there like a frightened john crow, staring at him."

Both of them wondered what Boy Brown would do now he had lifted the lid of his hidden past. Mother and daughter simply sat in silence, only interrupted by Cynthia's quiet sobbing.

Brenton arrived home, paying the cab driver two pounds fifty for the fare. He checked the front-room window of downstairs to see if Mr Lewis was working, but no light was visible. So he pushed his key inside the door, feeling a sense of belonging, like a lost lamb who has found his shepherd.

A mug of chocolate and bed seemed a good idea as Brenton was feeling as if someone had just wrung his brain. He ambled into the kitchen, only to find there were no clean mugs in the cupboard. He peered into the sink where several unwashed mugs had been abandoned. Thinking Floyd must have had spars visiting earlier, he cursed him and didn't bother to make his late-night hot drink. He trooped wearily off to bed, hearing giggling sounds as he passed Floyd's bedroom door. Biscuit laughs like a blasted horse, he thought.

He collapsed fully-clothed on his bed, only stopping to kick off his new trainers. Looking up at Mr Dean, Brenton admired the rebellious pose.

"Got someone else to chat to now, James," he murmured.

"You wouldn't believe how pretty she is. She works in a bank but she should be a model. As for the bitch of a mother I've got, she looks in need of a doctor."

He stretched out a foot to kick the bedroom door shut and with his mind debating on his new-found family, he fell deeply asleep.

CHAPTER EIGHT

Concrete Jungle

26 January, 1980

At nine o'clock in the morning, someone entered Brenton's room and flicked on the light switch. Brenton was still half-asleep. "What is this?" he grumbled. "Jailhouse? Do I have to slop out now? Whatever happened to privacy?"

Mr Lewis, noting that his charge slept in his clothes, produced his university-taught 'confide-in-me' smile. "Stand by your bed, laddie. At the double!"

Brenton seemed to have weights on his eyelids that day. He raised them slowly, focused, and found a grinning Mr Lewis in his sights. Parking himself on the end of the bed, the social worker asked eagerly: "Well, what happened?"

Thinking that Arnold Lewis was a bit too keen to find out his business, Brenton took his time in answering. "Er, I saw my mother. It was weird and didn't seem real. She didn't say a lot and I kinda had a go at her. She reckons she's sorry for what happened in the past. I'll tell you one thing though, she's got a nice bloody yard!"

Brenton paused his tale as he struggled to sit up. Lewis waited patiently, adjusting his glasses that always formed a red blotch on the bridge of his nose. "I've got an older sister, Juliet," Brenton resumed. "We chatted for a while and she was kinda all right. I think she's eighteen. Anyway, I gave her my phone number and she said she'll bell me soon."

"Is that it? How did your mother greet you? Did she welcome you? Was she pleased?"

"Yeah, that was about it. I had a little go at her but nothing serious."

Mr Lewis stared at Brenton, expecting him to disclose a bit more, but the teenager just sat there, wondering if last night's meeting ever took place, and whether his mother was thinking about him. Eventually Mr Lewis interrupted the silence. "It must have been a shock to the system for your mother to see you after so long. I'm not saying she's the best mother in the world, but give her a bit of time. Give yourself a bit of time too to get used to the idea."

Brenton half-glimpsed James Dean, almost expecting him to say something about the matter. Mr Lewis got to his feet. "I'm glad for you Brenton, you deserve a break. I hope this is the start of something good for you, and maybe now you will begin to value yourself."

At that, the social worker departed the room. With any luck, now Brenton had found his family, he might just start to think about a career. The social worker's hopes were not penny-in-well thinking, for even now Brenton was preparing himself to take a look at the local institutions of further education.

Half an hour later, Mr Lewis emerged from his room to find Brenton stepping down the stairs, ready to leave the hostel.

"Where are you off to? It's not like you to be up and about so early."

"Down to Vauxhall College," Brenton replied casually, taking perverse pleasure at the social worker's surprise.

Mr Lewis produced a self-satisfied smile, but before he could add some encouragement, Brenton disappeared through the front door.

With his hands set in his trouser pockets, he breezed towards the bus stop, feeling a new sense of purpose. Once aboard a number 36, he began to recall the lyrics of his sister Juliet the night before, and wondered if he could get a course and a grant just like that.

After a change of buses at Vauxhall BR station, he finally reached the modern-looking college on the Wandsworth Road. The college had a large paved area at the front and side of the building. Brenton decided to nose around the perimeter of it before entering the main entrance. He then set course for the reception area, walking past two smartly dressed white guys whose eyes betrayed their suspicion. A middle-aged woman, perched on a stool, was busily typing a letter, which provoked reminders for Brenton of Borough police station.

He approached the counter and waited patiently for her to notice him. "'Scuse me, I wonder if you could help me out? I wanna go on a carpentry course."

The receptionist swivelled round and arose from her stool. "I'm afraid that our carpentry and joinery courses don't start until September. These courses lead to a City and Guilds examination. Are you an apprentice for a building firm or local council?"

"No."

"Most of the building-trade students are sent on the college courses by their employers. Usually they are day release, and the fees are met by their employers as well."

Not quite understanding what the lady said, Brenton studied the many leaflets on display. "Oh, right. Uh, what about a grant?"

Bending down slightly, the woman collected a couple of leaflets off the table. "This is a form for students requiring a grant, and the other one tells you about the range of craft courses we do here. But do try and join a building firm who will offer an apprenticeship."

Brenton grabbed the information and thanked the receptionist, then paced towards the exit door. He scanned his surroundings and whispered to himself, "Fuck my days - me at *college?*"

Once outside the building, he chose to walk through the gaps in the high-rise tower blocks, taking the shortest route to Stockwell. He wondered how he would feel living at the top of one of these concrete-boxed homes of squalor. Perhaps at night he would peer out the window after smoking a mellow spliff, and invite the high yellow moon out to play.

When Brenton reached Brixton, he sauntered along Atlantic Road, where he came across a small assembly of people watching someone skanking in the street. Brenton took a closer look and found the object of attention was a white dreadlocked man. Dressed up in crude attire, he skanked with no rhythm at all to the thumping bass of a market record stall. Why do all these man who have gone cuckoo, come to Brixton and skank in the street? Brenton questioned himself.

Just as he was about to move on, he heard his name being called. "Brown! Brown!"

He spun round to see the grinning dial of his spar Biscuit, who was wearing a leather cap with the peak nearly covering his eyes. "Say wha'ppen Brown, long time no see. Where's that joker-smoking Floyd?" asked Biscuit, while performing an extravagant strut that would have put a peacock to shame.

"He's probably in his bed."

"What are you gonna do about Flynn?"

Brenton's eyebrows angled. "I will deal with him in my own time. So what are you selling now?"

Biscuit neighed, a horrible-sounding laugh that was more nose than mouth. "Well, everyt'ing. You know me. Floyd was interested in a crucial camera I showed him last night, but he hasn't checked me today so I don't know what he's dealing wid. More time, if you're interested, it's a bad camera - A-1 class, I'm telling you. I saw the Queen the other day in a magazine and she was posing with a camera just like the one I'm selling. Nah man, it's a serious camera. I've also got a chops and some crocodile boot to sell, but that's seriously out of your budget range."

The brethrens started to walk towards Coldharbour Lane. "I ain't got the corn to buy a friggin camera. What am I gonna take pictures of - the yards on Coldharbour Lane?"

"All right then, maybe it's not within your budget. I can

understand that, nuff man in a hard-time style and living on ghetto menu of dry bread and polo mint. But you have to listen to your music, seen? I've also got this wicked Brixton suitcase, brand spanking, crisp biscuit and officially new. Japanese and t'ing. I weren't gonna sell it 'cos it sounds so sweet, nuff bass-line. But you and Floyd are my spars so I'll be open to a serious negotiation. It's got a whole 'eap of gadgets, and you wanna see the size of the instruction book. It's t'ick, man. You can only get this suitcase up the West End in dem royal appointment shops, and Brenton, as you're a brethren, I sell the goods to you for sixty notes, nutten less and nutten more. And if you offer me somet'ing less, me an' you ain't no brethren. And believe me, man, nuff man will get red eye when you carry the tape recorder in the park and just let off the bass-line. I was gonna ask man an' man for eighty sheets. But as you're a brethren, I give you twenty pound squeeze."

Brenton couldn't help but smile at the hard sell. "Biscuit, man, what the fuck is wrong with you? I can just about scrape up the corn to buy myself a patty. Me and Floyd had to do some serious butt building at Christmas. You're chatting to the wrong man. I mean, you crack me up. Why don't you ask them soundman if they will buy the t'ing? They start taping dances now, innit?"

The duo ambled into a West Indian bread shop and came out with two meat-filled patties, wrapped in serviettes. As they walked and talked, Biscuit's eyes were magneted to a fit gal sporting tight jeans. His mind tremored on wondering how she managed to squeeze her solid, vibrating batty inside the denims. "Hey, Brenton, check the legback on that steak over der so."

Brenton was more interested in the hot patty.

The sight of the well-honed steak spouted out any thoughts in Biscuit's mind to make a sell. He changed the subject.

"So where you raving this weekend, Brenton?"

"I dunno. There's a big dance up Norwood Hall where Shaka is playing, I know nuff man will go to that. But like I said, my budget is low, so I might just coch at my yard with a big head of herb and feel merry. So where are you raving, Biscuit?"

"We're gonna check out Cubies, up Dalston Junction. Nuff steaks go der, and any man in there is guaranteed a crub if he ain't too ugly an' if he gets his head trim. Finnley did check some piece of beef up dem sides two weeks ago. He reckons he's boning it regular now. Yeah man, it's about time I was dealing with them fit steaks from north side, you know what I mean?"

Brenton nodded, thinking Biscuit's idea of heaven was an inch away from a fit gal's rocking batty.

The brethrens stood on Coldharbour Lane, both clocking a beastman questioning a dread. "Look, Biscuit, I sight you later and I'll tell Floyd about the camera, but I don't know where he will get the corn from. I have to dally now, so laters."

"Yeah, more time Brenton, man."

The couple proceeded on their separate ways. Brenton trundled towards home, while Biscuit strutted to the high-decibelled record shop - maybe he could hatch a deal in there. Brenton pondered on whether he should check out Brixton College, but he felt too lazy and quickened his pace home.

As Brenton turned his front-door key he was confronted by a wall of cussing in the shape of Floyd and Sharon in the hallway. "She's just a friend, man. I did know her from school, she used to go out with my spar."

Brenton dodged around the quarrelling couple as Sharon insisted, "You too lie. Friends don't climb over each other at a party all night."

"I only danced with her for two records," Floyd argued.

Brenton opted to park halfway up the stairs to ear the amusing argument. Meanwhile, Sharon was pointing her fore-digit right in Floyd's face, nearly jabbing him in the eye. "What do you mean, two dances? My friend told me you danced with the blue-foot all friggin night."

Glancing up at Brenton and desperately seeking back-up in his tiff, Floyd pleaded, "Hey Brown, tell Sharon Sylvia is just an old school friend and I'm not dealing wid her."

The warring couple looked on Brenton at the same time. Brenton loathed being caught in the middle of one of Floyd's gal tiffs, but he felt obliged to support his hostel-mate. "No, well, I haven't seen Sylvia round here anyway."

Brenton was lying through his teeth and Sharon appeared far from convinced, fixing hot accusing eyes on her man. "There's still no excuse for you to rub her down like you're trying to start a fire with her dress and your briefs. Carol did sight you, Floyd, she didder. She told me that you and that leggobeast were so tight, you had a print of her knickers on your Farah's."

"You know how Carol exaggerates."

"Well, if me hear that you're palavering with any gal again, I will sack you so quick, you won't have time to think of some trickster explanation."

"She did rush me, innit. I didn't want to shame her in front of her spars if I said no to a dance."

"Lie you a tell."

"Sticksman honour. She did rush me."

Sharon kissed her teeth.

Finding it hard to keep a straight face, Brenton stood up and made his way up to his room, assured that Floyd would chirp his way out of his 'caught black-handed' situation.

Later on in the evening, at six-thirty, Juliet arrived home from a trying day at work. The crowded trains and buses made her feel agitated - especially as she found herself in the smokers' carriage, standing all the way home.

In the morning, she had felt the need to repel the advances of a white male work colleague. This guy wondered what it would be like to sleep with a black girl. Juliet told him that if he was all the male sex could offer, she would gladly turn gay.

Juliet remembered that she'd promised to bell her new-found

brother, but she needed to rest up and grab a bite to eat first. She walked along the hallway. "Mum! Mum!"

Trudging into the kitchen, she hoped to find steaming pots of welcoming food, but all she saw was a spotless kitchen, with all the pots and pans hanging in their places from wooden pegs on the wall. Giving a sigh of frustration, she sighted a note on the kitchen table: *Sorry, no time to cook, had to go out.*

She didn't fancy the notion of braving the weather again to buy a takeaway meal, so she switched the electric kettle on and satisfied her hunger with a mug of tea and a two-storey cheese sandwich. With mug and plate in her hands, she went back through the hallway where she noticed another scribbled message, by the phone this time: *Phone Garnet when you reach home.*

Juliet smiled to herself as she placed her mug and plateful of sandwiches on the bottom stair, then dialled Garnet's number. "Hello, could I speak to Garnet, please?"

She heard the phone being dumped down as a young voice shouted, "Garnet, phone for you!"

Silence for a few seconds, then the clattering sound of somebody picking up the phone.

"Hello, Juliet, that you?"

"Yeah, I got a message to call you. How's life treating you?"

"Life would treat me a lot better if you would rave with me."

Juliet chuckled. Garnet could always bring a smile to her day.

"Hey, Juliet, how about coming to a party with me on Saturday night? If you say no I will stalk you wherever you go."

Juliet skinned her teeth again. "Garnet, I would love to come, but I promised my mum I would go to East Street Market with her early Sunday morning. So if I go out Saturday night, I'll be too tired, innit?"

Disappointment traceable in his voice, Garnet accepted the excuse. "Well, er, maybe next time then."

"Yeah, all right. Look, um, I'm busy getting myself something to eat. Call me another time, yeah?"

"Yeah, I'll bell you tomorrow. Later."

Juliet put the phone down, feeling a touch guilty. Although she was fond of Garnet, she perceived he wanted to dominate her most of the time.

Her thoughts drifted towards her brother, so after a gulp of tea and a generous chomp of sandwich, she dug out a slip of notepaper underneath the phone book. Feeding herself another mouthful, she studied the telephone for a few seconds, apprehensive of what her brother's response might be. Eventually, bracing herself for the worst, she dialled his number.

"Hello, could I speak to Brenton Brown, please?"

It was Mr Lewis who picked up the phone, and he was surprised that a female caller didn't ask for Floyd. "Yes, he's in. Who should I say is calling?"

"His sister Juliet."

Mr Lewis, who was sitting behind the desk in his room, became animated all of a sudden. "Yes, he has told me about you and your mum. I think he's very excited about it, and I hope it all works out. I'll just go and get him."

The noise of the phone being placed down on the table was so loud that Juliet thought the social worker had dropped the receiver.

Mr Lewis dashed into the hallway. "Brenton!"

At the top of the stairs, a trod-weary Brenton appeared. The social worker newsflashed him. "Your sister is on the phone for you."

The revelation seemed to act as a stimulant to Brenton and he bounded down the stairs and into Mr Lewis's room. The counsellor tactfully lumbered through to the kitchen to prepare himself a cup of tea. Brenton eagerly picked up the phone. "Hello?"

"Hello, little brother. So how's your day been?"

"Not too bad. Went down to Vauxhall College and got some advice about courses. They gave me some forms and leaflets, but I was told it would be easier if I found a firm to work for, 'cos the workplace would then pay my college fees, you know what I mean? Anyway, the course I want starts in September, so I'm gonna apply to Lambeth Council for an apprentice job."

"That's all right then, innit? It's a start and least you are showing an interest. I just hope you can get some sort of job doing what you want."

"Is my mother there?"

"No, I think she went back to work. She's a Sister at Guy's Hospital. Hey, Brenton, all she talked about last night was you. She feels very guilty and a sort of shame about you. I know it was probably wrong for her to go upstairs when she did, but when you left, I found her crying. So be easy with her, won't you? I mean, after all, she is my mum too and she has treated me all right."

Despite what his sister said, Brenton still felt a venomous grievance towards his mother. "Look, I owe my mother nutten and she owes me everything. She's the one who left me when I was a baby, remember?"

Juliet pondered and understood his anger. After a slight pause, she considered it might be tactful to change the topic. "Hey, Brenton, what are you doing Saturday evening?"

"Well, apart from smoking single snouts and losing at domino to my brethren Floyd, I ain't doing nish."

Juliet chuckled. "Would you mind if I took you out somewhere, buy you a drink and maybe something to eat?"

Surprised by his sister's offer, Brenton became tongue-tied. "Where?" he managed.

"I'm sure I'll find somewhere. I'll even buy you a pack of cancer sticks to make sure you turn up."

Brenton smiled - there was no way he was going to turn down an offer like that. "So do I come up to your yard or what? Where shall we meet?"

Juliet paused for a moment, thoughtfully rubbing her chin with her thumb and fore-digit. "Be at my place about nine, then we'll go out from there, all right? Oh, by the way, I will get Mum to bell you before that."

"Yeah, that'll be all right. I'll see you then, bye."

Before Brenton could put down the phone, his sister added, "Why are you so eager to cut me off? Anyway, it doesn't matter; I'm feeling peckish and have to get something to eat. So I will see you Saturday, then. Bye."

Juliet placed down the phone, heartened by the way her relationship with her brother was developing. Meanwhile, on the other end of the line, Brenton wasn't quite sure what to make of it all. He scanned around the room and whispered to himself: "The only girl to offer to take me out and she's my *sister*. This ain't happening."

CHAPTER NINE
Freak Out

The following Saturday evening, Floyd's room at the hostel was a suitcase of noise. Everyone rocked their heads in unison to the incessant bass-and-drum-powered rhythms of the Revolutionaries, the baddest session band in Jamaica.

Floyd was entertaining three of his friends - one skinny male, and two Brixtonian females. He cleared the dressing table so a domino game could be played.

Gazing at his palm of dominoes, Floyd poached a glance at his opponent to see if he had a confident look about him. His challenger was nicknamed 'Finnley' - no one had ever bothered to ask him what his real name was. Finnley was christened with many monikers at school, but the one he hated most was 'Dreadlock'. It was a well-known yarn, that after a games lesson, the scrawny Finnley would take a shower and would have to skank about to get wet. Another joke that did the rounds was Finnley's apparent similarity to a black biro refill. He possessed an almost angelic face, topped off with a neat Afro hairstyle. Although he fended off many jokes about his scrawny build, Finnley possessed a charming ability to laugh at himself.

The girls lounging on the bed were exchanging idle chatter, only interrupted by fits of giggles when they discussed past experiences. The louder one was Angela. She was wearing a headscarf, wrapped partly over her forehead. Brown-skinned, she had an athletic build, which her lithe legs displayed, pressing out her seamed jeans. Her main feature was her unnaturally large-nostrilled nose. Angela had achieved fame in her school by being known as 'Shotgun', as represented in the double-barrelled variety. Other people commented cruelly that her nostrils were as big as two holes in a cow - a massive double-speaker box.

By contrast, Angela's friend Verna was very eye-catching. Long, relaxed hair graced her shoulders and the whites around her eyes seemed as perfect as an untouched pool of silky milk. Half a shade lighter than Angela's skin-tone, she too, was sporting seamed jeans. What Verna didn't notice was Finnley's roving headlights, scanning and undressing her body.

Floyd was engrossed in his domino game and, excited by the thought he could notch a game up, slammed down a domino on the dressing table with unnecessary force. "Easy nuh man, you waan mash up the table?"

"Your double six is dead, man," Floyd snorted. "It's as dead as that wort'less sound you used to be in."

Angela chuckled. "Finnley, what sound you used to be in?"

"Silver Chalice."

The two females burst into spasms of laughter with Finnley and Floyd looking on mystified. In between giggles, Angela explained, "We went to a Silver Chalice dance last year and their set sort of blew up. There was this big bang and nuff smoke was coming from the amp. My God, that was funny. Everyone was killing themselves skinning their teet'."

The girls launched into uncontrollable mirth once more, this time joined by Floyd, who nearly tumbled off his chair. Finnley consoled himself by opening one of the cans of Special Brew that were huddled around his feet. He offered Verna one of these, but she declined, thinking Finnley had an ulterior motive. "So you can't offer me one?" snapped Angela.

"Ease up. I was going to, give me a blasted chance."

Finnley reached out to give Angela the beer, then proceeded to fish out his Rizlas from his back trouser pocket, wondering how he

83

could deflect the conversation from his ill-fated sound. "Biscuit's dread. He was trying to sell me some big-up suitcase yesterday. He's so fool, he knows I'm on government corn."

Floyd, holding his domino sticks, gave an impatient scowl. "It's your play. Is it all right if you make it this week?"

Finnley kissed his teeth and continued to build his spliff. "Biscuit should keep his runnings quiet - too much undercover squealers about."

Then, unaware that Floyd was entertaining guests, Brenton breezed into the room, dressed only in unzipped blue slacks and an Afro-comb dangling from his confused hair. He surveyed the inhabitants of the room and felt a sharp slap of embarrassment. "Wha'ppen, Finnley? Long time no see. You all right, Angela? Verna. How's t'ings?"

"T'ings are all right, you know. Can't complain. We were just chatting about the great, great sounds of Silver Chalice."

Everyone smiled at the wit, apart from Finnley, who finished decorating his big-head spliff. Arsoning a match and about to light his joint, Finnley checked the crusty torso of Brenton. "Where's your shirt, man? Don't you know it's winter? And do up your flies. We don't want to see no ugly sights today, boss."

Everyone chuckled, but Angela seemed more interested in Brenton's physique than the latest joke, licking her lips at the sight of the jutting pectorals. Brenton didn't realise he was being so closely appreciated. He plonked himself on the edge of the bed, and gestured at the enticing liquor on the floor. "Typical black people, smoking herbs, drinking brew and playing domino. Anyway, give me a Rizla so I can build up. Finnley, I beg you a brew, man."

Finnley passed on the liquor, as Floyd dipped into his back trouser pocket, pulling out a scrawled ball of betting slip paper containing the exotic herb. Brenton grabbed the marijuana and Rizla with relish.

"Thanks and praises, man. Hey, did you hear about Paul

McCartney? He was in Japan or one of those ching-chong countries and he get fling in jail for smoking herb. Yeah, seriously, I heard it on the news yesterday."

Floyd shook his head slowly. "They're all smoking the herb, innit. It wouldn't surprise me if all them group like the Police and Madness smoke the herb. Then again, Madness look like they're on something more crucial than the sensii. They probably snort the Charlie and yam dem dirty toadstools."

"See how them man stay though," Angela concurred. "They only cuss the Gong for smoking the herb, but they don't say nutten about them white pop group who take the heroin and that kind of t'ing."

Becoming misty-eyed, Finnley joked, "I wanna know what dem punky rocker group are on. They must be on something serious, the way they jump about and do that mad-up head-slapping skank."

Everyone laughed as Finnley hoovered mightily on his spliff. Brenton turned his dial on Floyd. "I wanna ask you a favour. I need to borrow that Cecil Gee top you've got, 'cos I'm going out tonight."

Floyd reluctantly put the domino sticks back in their case. "Yeah, it's in the wardrobe."

Brenton nodded his thanks and started to construct himself a spliff. Meanwhile, Finnley persuaded Verna to take a couple of puffs of his joint. "How do you smoke that stuff?" she coughed.

"You have to get used to it," replied Finnley with a sly grin, wondering whether the herb would act as an aphrodisiac.

"Well, I ain't getting used to that."

Pissed off with Finnley ignoring her, Angela kidnapped Finnley's spliff and started to inhale the weed. "I was going to give you some," Finnley admonished. "Where's your patience? You're too grabalicious!"

"Yeah, of course you were. Probably next week." Eyeing Brenton once more, she exhaled her smoke in his direction.

85

"Where you going tonight, Brenton? Taking a gal out? I've never seen you with a comb in your head. I'm surprised they actually make a comb that can go through your head-top."

Everyone laughed, but Finnley wasn't sure whether he was laughing at the jibe or because of the effects of the lager and herbs cocktail.

Two spliffs and three lagers later, Finnley felt his inhibitions abruptly march away from him.

"Verna, Verna. My God, you are fit! I don't care, it has to be said, you're seriously fit. You've got a wicked body and I want to count the hair molecules on your scrumptious thighs."

Floyd, astonished, glared at his spar, while Verna, Angela and Brenton collapsed on the bed in a seizure of giggles. "Finnley, stop friggin about, man. Let's play a next game of domino."

"Stuff your dominoes, man. I wanna chat to that masterpiece of fitness called Verna. They say that once you make a woman skin her teet', you've got a serious chance of boning the steak. So Floyd, stick your dominoes up your arse and you will definitely murder the double six. Awwuah! Verna, what are you saying? You t'ink me and you can wine, dine and grind? You don't have to fret 'bout getting big belly, 'cos I always carry a caterpillar's raincoat in my wallet - not like Floyd who will ride his filly six furlongs bareback. Can't you come to my yard now? Believe me, when I'm finished wid you, you'll wanna marry me."

Then the gangly Finnley tried to get up from his chair to where Verna was laughing hysterically, but he tripped over the edge of the bed and landed flat on his right cheek. Now, even the subdued Floyd joined in the laughter. Angela and Verna helped Finnley get up and park on the bed. Floyd shook his head as he clocked his spar tree-bending on the bed. "Finnley, you can't take your liquor and herbs, man. Look at you, you're like them white man who come out of the pub on a Friday night."

Finnley found himself beside Verna, and couldn't help but admire her legs with a stupid grin. "God, please forgive all my sins and t'ing, and for what I am about to receive I'll be seriously grateful."

Howls of laughter filled the small bedroom. Then Finnley called, "Floyd. Hey Floyd!"

"What?"

"Floyd!"

Now with anger in his voice, Floyd said, "Yes - what?" Finnley was on the verge of bursting out laughing as he muttered softly, "Sod off."

Everyone crumpled yet again in mirth, and Brenton almost forgot he had a date. So somewhat groggily, he pulled himself up. "Look, I'll see you lot later, or should I say I might see you but you won't see me, especially the way you're carrying on."

After collecting Floyd's brown cardigan top from the wardrobe, nobody seemed all that bothered whether Brenton departed or not, apart from Angela. "Yeah, I'll see you later. Take care."

Before he left, Brenton turned and surveyed the room. He could see Verna trying to edge away from the lecherous-looking Finnley, Floyd attempting to arson the remains of a joint, while Angela was leaning drowsily against the wall, her eyes wondering where her own bed was.

One and a half hours later, Brenton trod at a brisk pace down his mother's street - the closer he got, the slower he walked. He still felt a little nervous about seeing his family, but sporting his friend's cardigan gave him confidence. Why does my sister wanna take me out? he wondered.

After a slight pause, when he momentarily gazed at his mother's front door, he knocked on it once.

Wearing a headscarf, Ms Massey opened the front door. Her son, like before, simply stood there, motionless for a couple of seconds. He analysed his mother's stark features, concentrating on her tragic eyes. It was as if someone had ripped out the happiness from within her spent body. She could do with a spliff, Brenton thought. The worry lines on her forehead seemed to be as deep as the etchings on a gravestone. He thought his mother must have been through trying times, but he was not going to sympathise with her yet. "Come in, Brenton. Don't stand up in the cold. Come inside."

Brenton stepped into the house, trying to avoid catching his mother's eye. This time, he was led to the kitchen where Cynthia switched on the electric kettle. "You want a cup of tea?"

Walking around the kitchen, observing the wallpaper, Brenton nodded.

"You like it wid cow's milk or condensed milk?"

"Ordinary milk, please."

Brenton glanced up at the ceiling, while his mother followed her son's path with her eyes. "Juliet will soon come, she jus' getting ready. I'm so glad that the two of you are getting on all right."

Brenton acted as if he wasn't listening. Cynthia continued, "Brenton, I'm sorry for the udder night, y'hear? I was very upset and I did not want to say goodbye to you 'cos I t'ought you would cuss me and distress me. Y'understand?"

"That's all right."

An uneasy silence followed. Neither mother nor son quite knew what to say to each other, and both of them mentally willed Juliet to come down the stairs.

A click from the kettle and steam protruding out of its nozzle prompted the next exchange. Pouring the boiled water into a plain white mug housing a tea bag, Cynthia admitted, "I know I 'ave been no mother to you at all. But I hope you believe me when I say you 'ave been always 'pon my mind."

She paused as she watched her son take a chair at the kitchen table. "Always."

Brenton guessed that his mother was looking for some sort of forgiveness, but he wasn't in a merciful mood. "Are you religious? Do you go to church?"

Puzzled by the question, Ms Massey hesitated slightly before answering. "Well, er, yes, I suppose I am religious. I attend church now and again."

Picking up his cup of tea, Brenton gave his mother such a fierce look that she expected him to explode with a volley of stabbing words. "I wouldn't call you a very good Christian, leaving your son when he was just a baby. Not a good Christian practice, is it? Not even a good animal practice."

Brenton was interrupted by the sound of dainty feet coming down the stairs - a sound that brought relief for the anxious Ms Massey.

Juliet entered the kitchen, looking stunning in a blue polo-necked sweater with a thick belt around her waist. A matching light-blue pleated skirt made her look as if she belonged in the centre pages of a fashion magazine. "I hope you two are getting to know each other."

Switching her gaze towards her brother, she added, "Sorry I'm a bit late, but that's how us girls are, never ready on time. Anyway, I've called a cab, and it'll be here in a few minutes. I'm just going upstairs to put my shoes on - soon come."

Juliet disappeared again, leaving her mother and brother sitting at the kitchen table. Brenton scrutinised the brown tiled floor, while his mother felt uncomfortable once more. She hoped her son wouldn't say anything else to make her feel guiltier than she already did. She decided to make herself a sandwich while Brenton maintained an intimidating silence.

Juliet reappeared, wearing black shoes to please her smart black blazer. This was a cue for Brenton to rise up and place his half-full mug of tea in the empty sink. He tried not to notice the sheer beauty of his sister. "You ready now?"

Juliet wondered why Brenton was so keen to leave the house as she watched her mother bravely smiling at her son, buttering slices of bread. Then Juliet enquired, gazing at her brother, "Did you hear the cab horn? I didn't."

"Er, no. I forgot we were going by cab."

Juliet high-heeled along the hallway to see if she could sight a waiting cab from the front-room window, but before she reached there, a car horn barked its arrival.

"Brenton, the cab."

Brenton hurried out of the house, passing his sister on the way as Juliet watched her mother, walking slowly behind her. "Bye, Mum," she said gently.

"Enjoy yourselves."

Cynthia watched the taxi drive away from the front window, then pulled the net curtain back in place, pondering on how she could convince her son to see her in a more favourable light. At the moment, sensing a North Pole bitterness confronting her in the shape of Brenton, all was hopeless. It was as if the skeleton had jumped out of its cupboard and was now pulling faces at her. She couldn't help but think her son's hostility towards her was the price of falling in love with a white man.

Meanwhile, inside the cab, Brenton was feeling more at ease with himself. "So where are you taking me?" he asked his sister. "Not to the fish and chip shop, I hope. I have enough of that during the week."

Juliet smiled radiantly. "West End - get dropped off at Piccadilly Circus and find something to eat. Then we can walk down The Strand and check out the Lyceum."

"The Lyceum, that's a soul place, innit?" Thoughts of black guys with parted hairstyles and wearing baggy trousers, granddad shirts and winkle-pickers made him smirk.

Even in the siege of winter, Piccadilly Circus was a mass of people, some seeming to be very much in a hurry, and others who aimlessly wandered about, dazzled by the bright lights.

Brenton and Juliet climbed out of their cab and headed towards a McDonald's restaurant. Brenton scanned around him, sensing the vitality of the place, looking here and there. He was a little awe-struck as this was his virgin night in the West End - but he didn't want Juliet to know this. He knew Floyd came here often, mostly to check out the Cecil Gee menswear shop, but he'd always thought it was a place for tourists and white people.

Juliet, with Brenton following, entered McDonald's. The

workers behind the counter were trying frantically to keep up with the ravenous demand.

"So little brother, what do you want?"

"Just some fries and a cheeseburger, please."

Juliet joined one of the patience-testing queues, while her brother stood and observed the lively streets outside.

One young man, who had obviously had too much to drink, was being brutally sick opposite the restaurant, while his spar, who was in the same condition, stood by laughing his head off. Further up the road, a young woman sank to her knees, cursing. By her gestures, Brenton guessed someone had just taxed her handbag.

Approaching the restaurant was a young suited Englishman who, very politely and patiently, was trying to direct a group of foreigners who were hopelessly lost, even though some of them were clutching their Guide to London leaflets in their hands.

A tap on the shoulder reminded Brenton he was out with his sister. He gratefully accepted the fries and the cheeseburger, and as there were no seats available, the couple stood by the entrance to consume their food. Wolfing down nearly half of his cheeseburger in one bite, Brenton mumbled, "So this soul place. No reggae is played there, is it?"

"No, just soul. People go there to freak out, you know, get loose. Some just dance until they drop."

Sensing that the sting of embarrassment was waiting for him, Brenton quipped, "Well, I'd better tell you now, I can't dance to save my life. I'm to dancing what a diddy man is to basketball."

Juliet almost choked on her fries. Pleased, Brenton joked again: "I'll be an embarrassment to you. I'm about as co-ordinated as a one-legged cyclist with a serious puncture." He'd heard that one from Floyd.

Juliet had to put her fries down on a table as she laughed heartily. Her brother smiled, at last feeling he could just be himself in his sister's company.

The pair walked along The Strand, nearing the Lyceum disco

night-spot with Brenton feeling like a fish accidentally calling in on a camel commune.

As they entered the club, Juliet was in her element. She revelled in the flashing lights, dancing bodies and the sheer vigour of the place.

Weaving his way through the sweating ravers with his sister excitedly following him, Brenton sought out the safe haven of the bar, fingering the loose shekels in his pocket. "Do you wanna drink?"

"Something soft. I'll have a Coke."

Onstage the DJ seemed intent on playing non-stop dance music until everybody before him collapsed from exhaustion. Around the fringe of the stage, the throng seemed determined to find out how a rice grain feels in a steaming pot. Despite pleas from the DJ, telling the rousing hordes to move back, they paid no heed.

Brenton noted the cosmopolitan crowd - blacks, whites, Asians and others. They all appeared to be enjoying themselves - apart from one bewildered guy who just reached the bar. Brenton addressed the bartender. "One lager and a Coke, please, squire."

"Yes, sir."

While he waited for his drinks, Brenton turned around to try and catch a glimpse of his sister in the swaying crowd. He sighted her among the mêlée of dancers, looking superbly co-ordinated in her dance routines. After he'd collected the plastic tumblers, he carefully threaded his way back to Juliet, carrying the drinks slightly above his head, so no wayward soul-head could topple them.

"You don't waste any time, do you? I hope you don't expect me to join you," Brenton said, gazing around at the jiving bodies.

"No, I don't. You'll probably mash up my foot or something. I just love to freak out, know what I mean?"

For the rest of the evening, Juliet danced, rested a little, then danced again, while her brother smoked, drank and walked around a lot. The DJ did entertain him though, by staging a female wet T-shirt competition. The winner was the girl who displayed the most visible breasts, greeted by cheers from the male revellers. But generally, Brenton was bored. He went through his snouts quicker than he planned. But one thing was evident to him though - the friendly atmosphere. He'd been used to the sometimes menacing atmosphere of reggae raves, especially blues dances, where one false step could lead to a stitched cheek.

On the way home, Juliet hailed a black taxi to take them south of the river. She plonked her head on her brother's shoulder, making him feel jittery.

"Thanks for coming with me," she said sleepily. "Most guys I know hate soul clubs and they wouldn't step near the Lyceum. But I like to go there and just shake a leg, you know what I'm saying?"

Brenton nodded as Juliet resumed, "I'm sorry I left you on your tod for a bit, but I didn't want to force you to dance."

"That's all right, I ain't the type to freak out anyway. I suppose the club is all right if you are a soul-head, and it's all friendly and t'ing, but I must admit I prefer my reggae. If my brethren Biscuit was there, he would have had an asthma attack. Him and soul don't get on."

The time was twenty past two. As the black taxi motored over Vauxhall Bridge, Brenton could see the illuminated lights of Chelsea Bridge in the distance. He didn't say much on the way home, for his unease was turning into a ringing alarm inside his skull; the more he looked at his sister, the more he was attracted to her. Why am I feeling like this? he asked himself.

Within a few minutes, the taxi pulled up outside Juliet's home. She climbed out, then gave a mesmeric gaze into her brother's eyes. "There's something about you I don't quite understand."

Before Brenton could ask his sister what she meant, Juliet kissed the tips of her digits and gently touched her brother's forehead. Dazed, Brenton watched Juliet turn her key into the front door as the taxi did a U-turn. His brain was so spin-dried; he had to pause before being able to direct the taxi driver to his hostel.

Half an hour later, still taken aback at the night's events, Brenton lay down on his bed, gazing first at the ceiling, then at his poster. "Why the fuck did she breeze a kiss, James?" He thought maybe it was her way of showing she was concerned about his life. Perhaps Juliet wanted Brenton to feel the closeness of a family.

Questions went unanswered in his head as he grew tired, and images from his childhood began to march through his mind. These images were getting clearer and clearer, and it was like travelling back in time . . . One memory was very strong now.

The child Brenton Brown was seven years of age. He was lying on one of seven metal-framed beds in a large dormitory; the other six were unoccupied. The white-painted walls reached high and felt refrigerated, cocooning the bedroom in an odour of sadness. A few Matchbox toy cars were haphazardly scattered on the uncarpeted floor - giving the only evidence of the room being a boys' dormitory. The sun, winking in through the large wooden sash windows, informed the young lad that it was still daytime. Then he heard a voice which instilled fear in him.

"Brenton? Come down these stairs immediately!"

It was the voice of Miss Hill, otherwise known among the kids in the Home as 'The Belt'. She was a short, squat white woman with long straggling brown hair. Aged in her mid-forties, she smiled rarely and had a feverish hatred for anyone under the age of eleven.

The young Brenton Brown was summoned downstairs, dressed only in his striped pyjamas. He knew what his fate was. Although the door was slightly ajar, he knocked on 'The Belt's' study door with trembling knuckles.

"The door's open, come in," she boomed.

The Belt was seated at her bureau, pen in hand and wearing spectacles that gave her the classic English schoolteacher appearance. "Close that door and come towards me."

Brenton slowly shuffled towards the lash-happy Belt. He knew that any sign of disobedience would mean more punishment.

"Mrs Willis tells me you called her an insulting name. You know I will not tolerate any kids in my charge calling staff names. Well - what have you got to say for yourself?" asked The Belt, knowing any explanation wasn't worth hearing.

The young Brenton gazed down at the carpet beneath him as he stuttered a quiet reply. "She, she called me a nigger."

"I see. Not only do you call my staff names, but you are a liar as well!"

Tears began to fall down the cheeks of the young Brenton. The Belt ignored this distressful sight and shot out of her seat to look for her serious strip of leather.

Hanging from a screw in the wall near the window was a thick brown leather belt. Grabbing it, Miss Hill headlighted Brenton with sadistic glee. "Bend down and touch your toes, you little bastard. I will teach you not to lie and call my staff names if it is the last thing I do."

Brenton endured six hard slaps of the leather. He was determined not to make a sound, although the tears were flowing freely.

Nine years later the teenaged Brenton Brown awoke in a cold sweat. It wasn't just a bad dream - these events had actually happened. He often had these recurring dreams of reconstructed episodes from his childhood. He felt it was strange, that he always seemed to snap out of the nightmare at the greatest moment of pain.

Adults are sometimes so unjust to children, he thought, and you don't know who to trust.

He still could not sleep with a peaceful mind.

CHAPTER TEN

Trouble In Store

Early February, 1980

It was a Saturday evening cold enough for the down and outs to don balaclavas and mountain-man socks. Brenton was inside his hostel room, ironing out never-ending creases in his jeans and wondering why his sister hadn't belled him since their trip to the Lyceum a week ago. As it happened, Juliet had phoned him mid-week, but Brenton was out palavering on the street with his spars at the time, and didn't receive the message she left for him. His mother had also called several times, but Brenton had already instructed Floyd to tell her he was out. He wanted her to sip a small spoonful of rejection, and see how she liked the taste.

He glanced at Mr Dean. "I don't know why I'm ironing these for. I ain't going nowhere."

Then as if by fate, Floyd came bounding into the room without slapping the door.

"So wha'ppen, you can't knock on the door?"

Floyd flashed his sweet-bwai smile. "Yeah, it's true, you might have been playing with yourself again."

Three seconds of cackles later, Floyd examined Brenton's strenuous efforts to erase the creases in his blue jeans. "Stepping out?"

"Nowhere, man, I'm doing this 'cos I ain't got nutten better to do."

"You should do what I do, man. Before I go to my bed, I put a pair of jeans under my mattress, and when I get up in the morning, the jeans are as good as ironed. Sweet as sugar inna Milo."

Brenton quivered his head from side to side, finding it hard to believe what he'd just heard. Going to throw himself on the bed, Floyd almost tripped over the limb of the ironing board. Noting his pal's heavy-heart mood, he said sympathetically: "Thinking how you're gonna deal with your mudder?"

"Yeah. I dunno whether to go up her yard and strangle her or kiss her."

Floyd sat down. "It must be weird for you. I mean, I know my mudder inside out, and I know if I go visit her, she'll be checking my teet', ask if I'm eating proper and wondering if I was in bad-bwai company. But you kinda got a mudder overnight. That would jangle up my head."

Brenton scratched behind his ear. "Thanks a lot. So you think I'm going cuckoo."

"Nah, you ain't ripe for no fool-fool house yet."

"Yet!"

"I didn't mean it like that. Just take it every day as it comes. Try and be cool with her, see what she has to offer. I know seh you want to cuss her and you did. But in time, you might feel a way about it, and then it'll be too late."

Brenton rubbed his chin, thinking that Floyd was not a bad counsellor when he stopped thinking about gal pum-pum. An uncomfortable silence followed as Floyd braced himself to put his next question. "So how you gonna deal wid Terry Flynn?"

Brenton's eyes drilled into the poster of James Dean. "His time will come - when he ain't expecting it. He thinks he did-der in heaven, but hell is chasing after him."

Silence again. The quietness this time made Floyd visualise flashing blades. He wanted to lighten the mood, so with an impish shimmer in his eyes, he proposed, "I'm going late-night Kung Fu pictures tonight. Wanna come?"

Brenton parked the hot iron in its rack and picked up what amounted to thirty pence of loose change off the dressing table. "What - with this? This is all I've got in my budget."

"Don't worry about it. I'm leaving in half an hour, we're going to the one down Croydon."

"Why Croydon?"

"You'll find out."

It was nearing eleven o'clock when the 109 bus parked a few skank steps from the cinema. Floyd and Brenton disembarked and immediately noticed the throng of predominantly black males gathering outside McDonald's. Floyd, who was carrying a holdall in his hand, asked his spar, "Wanna burger?"

Brenton nodded while clocking the young black faces around him. It was apparent that most of them had just arrived from a big reggae sound-system clash in the area. As Floyd and Brenton entered the restaurant, they were surprised to see so many rootsheads in an outer-city place like Croydon.

Brenton recognised someone he knew from schooldays; his old friend Andrew. Andrew had dedicated his life to sound systems, hence his attendance at a sound clash this far out of town. Only seventeen, but tall and heavily bearded, Andrew caught sight of him. "Brown! Hey – Brown!"

Andrew knifed his way through the black jam, looking genuinely pleased to see his boarding-school spar. Brenton noted the changes in the guy he used to play truant with, noticing the beard first. But there was no getting away from Andrew's hat, which made him look like a black Hovis boy.

"Brenton Brown, long time I man don't see you. What are you doing now?"

"Not much, just bumming about on the dole. I might go to college in September though."

Andrew noticed the scar on Brenton's neck, partly concealed by the anorak he was wearing. Declining to comment about the ratchet sketch, Andrew chose to wax lyrical about the evening's sound clash.

"Just followed Deepbass to a dance, man, and it was ram jam, nuff people there. We booted Observer's batty and made them look like Tony Blackburn was selecting the tune for dem. They haven't got any good tune and they would have had better luck playing a punky rocker dub plate. All the crowd told dem to sign off their sound. Yeah man, we kill a sound tonight."

Just as Brenton was about to question Andrew's version of the night's events, Floyd returned with a bagful of cheeseburgers, fries and milkshakes. In his other hand he clutched about twenty straws and an uncountable number of napkins. Brenton looked on amazed. "Why so much straws and napkins, man? Are you buying food for everyone who's going late night?"

Floyd crouched down and put the surplus straws and napkins in his holdall. "You never know when you might need them. Look how many times we've run out of batty paper in our yard."

Andrew looked on bewildered, as Brenton introduced him. "This is Andrew, old school brethren. He's been telling me how his sound, Deepbass City, clapped Observer's batty all over the damn place."

Floyd smiled while munching his fries. "Is it, is it? In the queue I was chatting to Danny Dread, a sound man of Observer. He tell me say that your sound is pure distortion and hiss noises and t'ing. He reckons that a horse boning a hedgehog sounds better than you lot."

"Lie him a tell," Andrew countered.

Floyd and Brenton were experienced enough not to believe everything a sound man said.

Arching his back so he could get a clear view along the High Street, Floyd beckoned to Brenton. "Come man, the queue's starting to build up."

So the two spars made their way out of the restaurant, hastily eating their takeaway food. Andrew bade them farewell by raising his arm in the air, clenching his fist and shouting, "Later!"

While seating themselves inside the cinema, Brenton found himself hearing the call of his bed. He probably would have fallen asleep if it hadn't been for the constant roar of the audience whenever someone on screen executed a stylish and fatal kick.

The stuffy air was invaded by the distinctive smell of marijuana, which didn't seem to bother anybody. Some guys even had the front to bring suitcases to listen to in the auditorium. A few others took the late-night movie show as an opportunity to strut through the aisles and sell cannabis, wrapped up in betting-shop paper. The management seemed to switch off their headlights to all these bad-bwai customs.

At around three o'clock in the morning, the two Kung Fu films ended and most of the cinemagoers were streaming towards their motors or cab ranks. It was a polar bear night. Brenton wanted to seek the temporary warmth of a mini-cab office, but Floyd, clutching his holdall, had different ideas, strutting along the High Street in the opposite direction from anyone else.

Brenton voiced his disapproval. "Why the fuck are we walking this way for? I'm tired, it's friggin freezing and I want my bed."

"'Cos I want a brand new ghetto-blaster. They always display them in the window of Allders in the Whitgift Centre, so I'm going to kuff the window, hol' the goods and chip to a brethren's house who's expecting me. I've worked it all out, man; no problem."

Brenton stopped walking and kissed his teeth while looking up to the dark heavens. He glared at his spar, but Floyd was oblivious. He kept on walking, leaving Brenton a few paces behind. Brenton quickened into a trot and came alongside Floyd. "And what am I supposed to do while you nick a Brixton suitcase?"

"Keep a good clock, look out for the beast and give me a shout."

"And what do I get for that?"

"Well, if I get my t'ings, you can have my old suitcase."

The two spars tottered along the High Street, trying to look as if they had too much to drink, so the beast, if they passed, wouldn't suspect them of any wrongdoing. Entering the Whitgift Centre, Brenton noticed instantly the big Allders department store, which seemed to stretch out for the length of a football pitch. There was nobody about. While Brenton constantly checked behind him,

Floyd impassively strolled along the shopfront of the big store until he reached a section that displayed different types of hi-fi. Spotting a suitcase, he hissed, "Brenton, Brenton! See it der."

Brenton was mightily impressed, but feeling a little apprehensive. He took a look around and behind him, noticing the assortment of shops and boutiques. Only the jewellery shop, about thirty yards away, had a protective metal grille placed in front of it. In the middle of the shopping area was a fancy pub, probably the watering hole of outer-city husbands.

Brenton turned to clock Floyd admiring the many knobs and gadgets on the suitcase. Then Floyd crouched down to unzip his holdall and took out two bricks, placing them in a plastic bag. Brenton suddenly became very animated, checking for any signs of movement in the area. Then: "Go for it!"

Floyd swung the plastic bag containing the bricks, until he whipped up enough momentum to knock out the thick glass. Then he unleashed the bag and consequently, there was an almighty crash. Protecting his face with his arms, he gaped as he saw that the whole section of window had been demolished. Brenton too looked on in amazement. They both took a second to grasp the reality of the situation, then Floyd climbed through the obliterated window section and grabbed his much sought-after merchandise. He squeezed it into the holdall and burned his soles away from the scene of crime, with his accomplice in his slipstream. Behind them, they left the shattered glass and debris, and an alarm bell that chased them through the brass-monkey air.

Floyd decided not to make his getaway via the High Street, choosing instead the back entrance of the shopping centre. Following much frantic checking to see whether the police were in pursuit, the two raiders scampered their way from central Croydon to the back streets near East Croydon train station.

"So how far is it to your brethren's yard?" gasped Brenton.

"Not far. Just around the corner and we're safe, man."

"You must have woken up the whole of Croydon. Did you have

to fling the bricks like them man who fling hammer in the Olympics?"

"I don't give a damn, man. I've got my goods and t'ing."

The duo now felt safe as they strode leisurely through the quiet streets, gradually moving away from the Dallas-type buildings of central Croydon. After a couple more turns into streets of terraced houses, Floyd and Brenton eventually arrived at their rendezvous. Floyd slapped the letter box rather louder than necessary.

"All right man, ease up nuh. Me nuh deaf, y'know. You wan' wake up me forefaders in Africa?"

The door opened to reveal a string-vested black guy of chicken-breast build, wearing pyjama bottoms. His hair was uncombed and he appeared to be in his late teens or early twenties. He clocked the suitcase that Floyd was pulling proudly out of his bag. "Kiss me granny dutty toenail, I did t'ink you were joking, but you actually t'ief the blaster. Don't mess about, do you?"

Floyd followed his spar into the house with Brenton behind him. "Now Bennett, do I ever joke about anyt'ing? You should know how I stay already."

Floyd pointed at the hand-rubbing Brenton. "Oh Bennett, this is Brenton. He helped me out, you know, keep watch and t'ing. And Brenton, this is Bennett, he's living it up 'cos his people dem have gone to Jamaica for a month. He reckons he's having a party next week, but I feel so he's running up his mout'."

Brenton and Bennett exchanged nods while Floyd analysed his new toy. He started to fiddle about with the many gadgets and knobs, unable to wait to find out how heavy the bass-line would be.

The threesome settled themselves in the dimly lit kitchen at the end of the hallway, and Brenton fell into a semi-sleep. Floyd noticed this and remembered how earlier Brenton was bawling for his bed. "Bennett, man, ding me a cab. We're both tired after all that running about and trodding, know what I mean? But still, it's worth it, innit?"

Bennett smiled. "I don't know why I told you about it. I should have kept quiet and got the damn t'ing myself."

Bennett disappeared into the front room to make the phone call, leaving Floyd to whisper to himself, while gazing lovingly at his new plaything. "Wicked, man. Wicked. When Biscuit sees dis he's gonna be so red eye."

CHAPTER ELEVEN
Stir It Up

A knuckling on the room door. Brenton rolled over on his bed to squint at his alarm clock; five past eleven. "Who the blouse an' skirt is going to knock on my door at eleven o'clock on a Sunday morning?"

Suddenly he was anxious. Could it be a pig, investigating the night on which he stood watch as Floyd declared war against a department-store window? Brenton picked the sleep out of his eyes as he heard another impatient knock. Adorned only in briefs and T-shirt, he opened his bedroom door.

And there, standing before him, smiling tentatively was his resplendent sister Juliet. Dressed in a beige-coloured woollen coat, thick black pullover and royal-blue slacks, she appeared as elegant as ever. Brenton shaped quickly under his covers. He felt ill at ease. What's she doing here? he asked himself.

Juliet glided into the room. "So is this what time you get up every day?"

"No, it's Sunday, innit. I always lie in on a Sunday morning."

She parked herself on the bed, scanning the room at the same time, noting the general untidiness, but she had half-expected this. She glanced curiously at the poster on the back of his door. "So you like James Dean then?"

"Yeah, I like his films."

"I called during the week and left a message that I'd be coming around to see you Sunday morning. Then later on, I'd take you back to my place for Sunday dinner. My mum, er, I mean our mum is expecting you. So please say yes."

One glance at his sister's eyes and Brenton knew his answer couldn't be no.

"Yeah, I'll come. I'll go anywhere for a free meal."

Anything will be better than my Sunday dinner of bully beef and brown bread, Brenton thought; no ghetto man menu today!

The reply brought another sunny smile to Juliet's face, prompting her to stand up eagerly. "Great, so you can get out of your bed and we'll take a walk somewhere, then go back to my place."

Juliet departed and waited on the landing outside, expecting Brenton to get ready. Inside the bedroom, Brenton hauled himself from his bed and fished around in his chest of drawers for a clean pair of socks. Then it suddenly dawned on him; who had let his sister inside the yard? Was Lewis downstairs? Must have been Floyd. Climbing into his blue jeans, he heard his sister shout, "I'll be down in the kitchen. Hurry up."

Looking for a decent pullover, he contemplated the prospect of seeing his mother again. He would have preferred to avoid her for the time being, but Juliet had asked so nicely. Perhaps he could play the loving son for her sake.

Two sprays of deodorant later, Brenton sprang down the stairs, where he found his sister inspecting the decor. "Ready! Where're we going?"

Juliet arose from her seat, smiling at her brother, then sauntered straight past him towards the front door. Brenton had an enquiring look on his face as he followed his sister outside. What's with her? he thought.

Brother and sister walked down the street wondering what the day would bring. It was mild for the time of year, but the sun decided not to clock on for work yet.

After a few paces, Juliet had a staid look about her. "Try to be nice to Mum, won't you," she began. "She's trying her best to make up for the past. It's kind of understandable why you're bitter, but all I want is for you two to get on."

Walking along with his hands in his pockets, Brenton scowled slightly, pondering on how he should word his reply.

"You could never begin to know what the feeling's like when you are a kid in a children's home," he told her slowly. "The friends I had went to various relations to spend some time over the Christmas holidays. And me? Well, no relation for me to go to, was there? That time I spent on my own, I used to do a lot of thinking, you know what I'm saying? Yeah, I used to think nuff. I thought about my mother, and shit, I hated her badly; I still hate her."

Juliet's emotions quaked on hearing the last sentence. Her natural instincts urged her to give a supporting hug to her brother, but she thought better of it. Brenton's natural instincts were to trod towards the park.

"I don't think I'll ever forgive my mother, or my paps come to think of it," he told her flatly. "I suppose you can call it deep emotional scars or what you like. Even now I still have nightmares about when I was a kid. Me and my mother, in time, will probably get on and be polite to each other. But don't ask me to forgive. Not while the memories are still so clear."

As he concluded, Brenton was throttling the anger surging within him, like a little devil trying to jump up in his throat and activate his tongue. Juliet was beginning to realise that family reunions are not quite as straightforward as you see on TV. She studied her brother's stormy countenance. "There won't be another Christmas with you being alone," she whispered. "You got us now."

Brenton looked away to avoid his sister's eyes. Juliet found herself being powerfully drawn by her brother's angry, emotive face. So much pain behind those eyes, she thought.

The next few minutes, the siblings were silent to each other as they walked slowly through the streets. Brenton, hands in pockets and hunched shoulders, and in contrast, Juliet, striding tall and elegant. They entered the tranquillity of Ruskin Park, which seemed to relax the tense Brenton.

"I always come here when something is on my mind," he confided. "I think more clearly when I'm here, for some reason. I dunno. I suppose it's weird, innit?"

"Maybe that's what you need in life; a bit of peace. I wouldn't like to guess at what you've suffered, but now you should look ahead. You have a life to live and the bad days are over. Forget the past and think about making sure you have a better future."

Brenton shrugged, momentarily thinking of Terry Flynn. "Maybe you're right, but I could never forget my past."

Juliet stopped in her tracks and gently tugged her brother's arm to turn him around, facing him square on. "Look, give Mummy a chance. At least listen to her. She really wants to make it up with you. Let her make her peace."

Brenton gazed into his sister's eyes, but didn't answer, choosing to turn and carry on walking, leaving her trailing for a couple of seconds.

The pair watched faithful dog owners walking their enthusiastic pets. The grass felt crisp and firm beneath their soles, and the breeze curled around the twigs of the trees, wondering where the leaves were. A child, clad in woollen hat with matching scarf, was joyfully trying to kick a football back to his proud father. The idyllic scene plucked a string within the onlooking Brenton. "Do you know anything about my father?" he asked.

Juliet paused slightly before answering. "Mummy never talks about him to me, but I know one t'ing though. She loved your father, which is more than I can say for my wort'less old man."

Brenton was disconcerted by the answer. Juliet didn't intend for her reply to make him feel better; it was the truth. She continued, "It must have been a serious shame to be pregnant by a white man in those days. If there'd been no family or outside interference, who's to know; they might have made a go of things."

Brenton produced a wry smile at what he thought was a great

irony. Juliet caught sight of the smile and she did likewise. Then she spontaneously gave her brother a warm hug. This act of affection left Brenton feeling like a dog that has been licked by a cat. Why is she doing this? he thought. He couldn't remember the last time he'd been embraced, or even whether he'd been hugged at all. Juliet sensed her brother's disquiet, but she dismissed it. She wanted to know everything about him.

"You ever had a girlfriend?" she asked inquisitively.

Brenton edged slightly away from her and looked down at the path. He shook his head from side to side as if regretting a crime. "What about you?" he countered. "I suppose you can pick your choice. You must be asked out a lot."

Juliet curved an edible smile. "Yeah, I get asked out quite a bit. But most guys I know just want to get inside my knickers, know what I mean? Put it this way, I haven't had a serious boyfriend, but now and again, I go out with certain guys to a party, club or something."

They walked out of the park exchanging trivia about themselves, and learning more about each other.

While Brenton and Juliet were strolling towards Denmark Hill, Ms Massey was busily preparing the Sunday dinner. Looking forward to getting on better terms with her son, she thought the dinner was a good opportunity to begin the process. During the past month or so, Brenton had hijacked her thoughts day and night. Some nights she cried herself to sleep, provoked by a scorching feeling of guilt. Just two nights ago, she'd felt so distressed, she went to seek comfort from her daughter at two o'clock in the morning.

She deeply regretted the fact that she'd not had the strength to keep her young son years ago. But now she had to endure the heart-kuffing experience of trying to make up for the lost years she'd been apart from Brenton.

As she basted the potatoes and placed them back in the oven, she knew she could never make amends for what had passed. No river flows back upstream, she thought. Perhaps she would have to live the rest of her life with this sharpened needle probing at her conscience. She knew within herself that over the years she had spoiled and over-protected her daughter almost obsessively, possibly as a reaction to losing her son, resulting in her giving all her love to Juliet. The cornerstone of her guilt was that only one of her offspring had received the attention and care every child needed; while the other had received no love or affection at all. Cynthia felt helpless in the assumption that it was too late to make up for those sixteen years of neglect.

Half an hour later, dinner was nearly ripe; just the potatoes needed roasting for a few more minutes. The rice and peas were already cooked, and the chicken pieces were boiled enough to torment a starving vulture. She decided to take a time-out before preparing the salad. Her thoughts went to Brenton's father, the only man she had ever loved. The Gong's *I'm Still Waiting* played in her mind. In some ways, she could see a little of Brenton's father in her son. His forthright nature, for instance.

She acknowledged the bad mistake she made nearly eighteen years ago with her failure to tell Gary, Brenton's father, that she was already married and the mother of a little girl back home in Jamaica. As she brooded more on the early days, she realised that she'd only agreed to marry Juliet's father because she was pregnant at the time and the victim of family pressure; especially from her Pentecostal father. But she at least insisted on following her chosen career, and had headed off to England to train as a nurse, leaving her family behind.

Fondly she reminisced about Gary, who had been the complete opposite of her husband. While Gary was attentive, loving and respectful, Mr Massey was spiteful, mean and a drunk, who used to beat her from time to time. The only good thing about Dwight was his Cassius Clay looks and untold stamina in bed. But he could never handle the responsibility of being a dutiful father.

She was unsure how Gary would have reacted if she'd told him she was married when they first met. She admired him so much, and felt she could stall on revealing her married status. But when she received the emotion-kicking news of finding she was pregnant with Brenton, the truth came out sooner than she'd planned.

Worse than that was Dwight Massey's surprise arrival in London when she was six months' pregnant. Sitting in her kitchen, she shuddered, vividly reliving those days of turmoil leading up to the birth of Brenton. And she remembered the wicked ultimatum she was given by her husband: to choose between her two children. She said to herself at the time, that she could never leave Juliet permanently with her husband's side of the family; she wouldn't have trusted them to feed a nanny goat. Heartbroken to think he was losing her, Gary promised Cynthia that he and his family would look after their child and give Brenton a decent start in life.

Little did she realise, however, that Gary's family were fiercely against him rearing a mixed-race child, and were not prepared to help in any way. So ultimately, feeling desperate and at his wits end, Gary had placed Brenton in care, feeling unable to give his son the proper upbringing he deserved.

Even the people Gary had thought of as friends let him down when he most needed them, refusing to look after the infant Brenton while he completed his studies.

Cynthia had kept a treasured old black and white photograph of Gary, dressed in his cricket whites. But her husband had found it, and ripped it apart one drunken evening. Juliet, her mother thought, didn't know of the burning ember she carried within her heart for Gary. But how could she tell her daughter that she'd never loved her father? And confess that she loved another? Over the years, Juliet had been smart enough to work out the truths and rights of the matter for herself. Not that it mattered to Juliet anyway, because as long as she could remember, she had loathed her father.

Giving a resigned sigh, Ms Massey struggled up from her chair and proceeded to prepare the salad. Just as she began to slice the cucumber, in through the front door walked her daughter, followed by her son.

Juliet appeared in festive mood, while her brother looked as if he didn't want to stay long. "Dinner ready yet, Mum?"

Ms Massey seemed to ignore her daughter, and watched her son slowly walking towards her. "I am glad you are here, Brenton," she said quietly. "It means a lot to me. Dinner soon ready, about ano'der 'alf an 'our."

Without a glimmer of emotion on his face, Brenton slowly nodded, and greeted his mother with his eyes, rather than saying any hellos. She's really trying to be nice, he thought. Well, tough shit.

Juliet wondered what she could do to relieve the obvious tension. "You ever had a Jamaican dinner before?" she asked her brother. "Well, if you haven't, I'll bet you gonna love it. Mum's a wicked cook."

Ms Massey glanced at her son to see what his reply would be, but all he did was slowly shake his head. After a moment's slight hesitation, when Brenton nearly stuttered for the first time in years, he asked, "Er, what are we having exactly?"

"Rice and peas, dat is brown rice, but not de usual English green peas. West Indians use de red kidney beans, but we call dem peas." Ms Massey lifted the lid off the steaming pot. "See, it's about ready."

Brenton peered into the fiery vessel and saw odd strips of onion covering the mass of cooked rice and peas. "As for the chicken, firstly I brown it in the frying pan. After that I jus' boil it over a medium heat wid a liccle pepper an' onion. I don't like to roast the chicken 'cos that make it too dry."

Brenton taking a strange interest in her mother's cookery lesson visibly heartened Juliet, who was quietly observing on a kitchen chair. A toothy smile appeared on her pretty face, noticed by her mother. "What sweet you?"

Juliet laughed. She arose from her chair and headed out of the kitchen. "S'cuse me, Mum. Brenton, follow me, little brother. I want to show you something."

Brenton pursued his sister upstairs, glad to get away from his mother's presence, but felt unnerved as Juliet ushered him into her room. What's she brought me up here for? he wondered.

"Do you have any photos of yourself when you was a young child?" she asked him.

"Nah, except for those photos taken when you're at school. I got a couple of those left; they're somewhere about in my room."

Brenton looked around him. The first piece of furniture to grab his eye was the wardrobe, which was big enough to house four hide-and-seekers. Coloured in light beige, it boasted double doors and stood beside a chest of drawers with a mirror the size of a Monopoly board. The bedroom was very spacious and tidily kept and everything seemed to be coloured in beige or brown. Above the bed were two shelves, filled with books of a romantic nature. Opposite the wardrobe stood a hi-fi stereo system with records and cassette tapes neatly placed beside it. "Never knew you read so much. Is all that stuff Mills and Boon?"

"Sit down on the bed if you want, and no, they're not all slushy romantic novels. I do have a few books about slavery and black history, but I must admit, now and again I enjoy reading a love story."

"What kind of music have you got there?"

Juliet parked herself next to her brother. "Oh, a bit of Rose Royce, Commodores, Heatwave, Stevie Wonder - you know, that kind of t'ing."

"I don't suppose you got any Gong, Gregory Isaacs or Barrington Levy, do you?"

"No, I haven't got them on record, but I have some of their tunes on tape though. Some friends lend me tapes and I copy them."

For a few moments, Brenton seemed to be in a galaxy of his own. This bedroom sure beats the dormitory I slept in at

Pinewood Hills, he thought. Juliet noticed his gaze of envy. "What's the matter?"

"I know I shouldn't, but shit, look at this. Bwai, am I jealous! Nice bedroom, nice yard, you got a job and t'ing, know what I mean? And what have I got? I'll tell you what I've got - one pair of decent trainers and my brethren's old suitcase. Yeah, I envy you nuff."

Juliet gazed into her brother's eyes, suddenly feeling guilty about possessing her material luxuries. She considered showing Brenton her photo album, but changed her mind. "You always just say what you feel, innit? Most guys I know hide what they feel, know what I mean?"

She leaned towards her brother and kissed him quickly on the forehead. Brenton's mind was jolted by his sister's action, and what happened to his emotions, he didn't know.

"That's to show that I care about you," she said seriously, "and don't worry that you only got an old suitcase, 'cos this yard is as much yours as it is mine. Oh, and by the way, I have to act on what I feel."

The siblings gazed at each other silently; both realising their attraction was mutual. What is she on about? Brenton's mind whispered. Juliet suddenly felt the body language was getting too intimate. "Come, let's go downstairs," she said briskly. "It's kind of rude of us to talk amongst ourselves and not include our mum."

Ms Massey was inspecting the tenderness of the boiled chicken when she heard the footsteps of her offspring enter the dining room. Brenton admired the smoked-glass dinner table, which was surrounded by four matching, chrome-legged chairs. Cutlery was carefully placed on plastic mats, and at the centre of the table stood a large bowl of salad. Brenton studied the room, with his eyes roving from side to side, rather than moving his head. He noticed a large wall cabinet, housing various glasses, tumblers, plates and cups of china. The blue patterned walls were bare, except for a wooden cased clock, which tick-tocked opposite the cabinet. Time will tell, he thought.

Juliet sat in an armchair in the corner of the room, watching her brother and sensing his unease as he remained standing near the door. "Sit down, man. Feel at home."

Instead of taking the other armchair near his sister, Brenton opted to sit at the dinner table. "Are you trying to avoid me?" she teased.

"No, it was the nearest chair."

Brenton still felt conscious of the kiss on his forehead - to him it burned like the branding of a sheep. He suspected Juliet was playing cat and mouse with his emotions and even though they shared the same blood, it was hard to ignore the physical beauty of his sister.

Moments later, Ms Massey entered the room, carrying two plates of inviting food, happy to see her son seated ready at the table. "Well Brenton, I 'ope you're 'ungry. Help yourself to the salad."

Juliet took a seat at the table opposite her brother, making Brenton feel somewhat uncomfortable. So he leaned forward to consume his dinner with his eyes never diverting from the plate.

A roast potato later, Ms Massey re-entered with her own plate of dinner, taking her chair and edging it nearer to her son rather than her daughter, feeling confident enough to spark a conversation.

"Brenton, how do the social worker treat you at dis hostel where you are staying?"

"Not so bad, you know. I think Mr Lewis understands me. He does lecture me a bit though, but apart from that, he's all right." But sometimes he don't half go on a bit, his mind added.

Juliet wanted to contribute to the conversation, but sensed it was best for mother and son to take the opportunity to talk to one another. So tactfully, she kept quiet. Meanwhile, her mother proposed to her son: "If you 'ave any problems where you're staying you can always stay 'ere. We have a spare room and bed, so you can stay overnight whenever you want to. Y'understand?"

"Yeah, er, I'll have it in mind. Er, thanks."

Juliet observed her mother produce a satisfied smile, which she hadn't seen for ages. Maybe this was the start of a proper mother and son relationship. She sneaked a look at her brother, who was apparently enjoying his first Jamaican meal like a lion cub tasting the delights of his first wildebeest.

Brenton glanced briefly at his sister, only for her to catch him doing so, at which he looked quickly away. Why is she doing this? he fretted. Then Juliet flicked a look at her mother, hoping that Cynthia hadn't noticed her eyeing her brother. Brenton was desperately trying to conceal any attraction he might be feeling for his sister, but Juliet was only too ready to attract his attention. Ms Massey was the only one of the trio to appear relaxed. "Do you 'ave a girlfriend?" she asked now. "If you do, she will be welcome to visit here as well."

Juliet stared hard at her brother, anxiously awaiting his reply.

"No, I don't. Never had a girlfriend, never needed one."

"You should not say dat. You are a good-looking young man, an' you mus' tickle nuff girl fancy."

Brenton suffered the backhand of embarrassment while his mother smiled. Fortunately, neither one of them noticed Juliet blush also. Unwilling to change the subject, Juliet commented, "I'm sure that in your time, some girl must have fancied you or made some sort of play for you."

Brenton fiddled with his fork, pondering on how to reply to Juliet's interrogation. "Well, er, sort of. But you have to understand, someone of my background finds it kinda difficult to trust any new friends or girlfriends."

"Why?" Cynthia asked.

Unfortunately, this simple poser angered Brenton. He recalled in his mind all the 'why' questions he was asked by the pigs. So after slamming his fork on the plate, he shot up from his chair. "You haven't got a clue about being brought up in a Home. You just don't get it, do you? I still have fucking nightmares about it and you can never imagine what it's like to be on your friggin' tod without anybody. I am not your normal kid or teenager."

Brenton fixed the bayonet on his tongue and aimed it at his mother. "It's all right, you saying I've got a place to stay and whatever, but you don't even know what you're letting into your nice yard. I better tell you from now, you've got one fucked-up son!"

Any confidence Cynthia might have been developing evaporated like a steaming kettle losing its vapour in a monsoon. She remained in her chair, still and ashen-faced, while Juliet, shocked, stared into space, thinking of the reality of her brother's life as a child. Matters were not to be so easy and straightforward as she had hoped.

For a few seconds, an intimidating silence draped over the room as Brenton paced around the dinner table like a wolf circling a chicken yard. Only when his own chair halted him did his thermometer abate. He thrust his hands on the back support of the chair, looked at his mother and with a marked decrease of volume in his voice, said to her, "Er, sorry. I didn't mean to shout. Mr Lewis is always telling me I must control my temper. I have to get used to this, and I ain't coping too good - never had a family before."

This apology warmed Cynthia's heart. It meant more to her than anything her son said to her beforehand. "You don't need to apologise. It should be me who's apologising. Come, sit down an' finish your dinner, it will soon get cold. Finish your dinner, son."

Brenton dropped into his chair and proceeded to finish his meal - it sure tasted good. Although she wouldn't let herself become over-confident again, Ms Massey felt she had just crossed a raging river, but perhaps there were a few more trials to come. She accepted that she could not alter the past and look for forgiveness for it. But she hoped to make a contribution to her son's future, and the first seed of this offering was sown today.

Feeling a little more composed than she'd been a moment ago

Juliet appreciated that there was a lot to learn about her quick-to-anger brother, not least his thin skin. But what an expressive face . . . He would make a wicked dramatic actor.

Ms Massey noticed that her daughter was unusually subdued. "Why you so quiet, Juliet? Usually, I can't get in two words when we sit down for dinner."

Juliet watched her brother swig down a glass of blackcurrant juice. "Just thinking."

Following dinner, Juliet was busy washing up the plates and cutlery. Brenton was in his sister's bedroom, fiddling about with her tuner, trying to get a good reception to one of the pirate reggae stations. Cynthia was talking on the phone to a close friend, explaining how she was getting on with her son. After she had put down the receiver, she climbed the stairs.

"Brenton!" He opened the bedroom door. "'Ave you a minute?" she asked. "I would like to talk to you in me bedroom."

They walked inside Ms Massey's room. The first thing Brenton noticed was the myriad of framed photographs of his sister, smiling down from his mother's walls. He felt a little apprehensive, wondering what his mother wanted to discuss.

"You can sit down on the bed." Nervously clasping her hands, the middle-aged woman set her eyes upon her son. If they shared any resemblance at all, then it must be their tormented eyes. "It's about your fader."

A long pause followed as Brenton's mother gathered herself to say something important.

"One t'ing I 'ave to tell you is dat I loved your fader dearly. In fact, I probably loved him too much. But you see, the problem was, well . . . you probably know by now, but I was already married an' Juliet was born just a few months before I reached Englan'. Your fader was honest, hardworking an' was not too 'fraid to speak his mind, y'understand?"

Brenton nodded. How could she screw a white man? he thought disgustedly.

Cynthia continued: "Back in dose days, people did not accept mixed couples going out together, let alone 'aving a chile. It's not too bad today, but your fader did not give a damn of what people did t'ink. Him tek me everywhere, an' was proud to call me his woman."

Cynthia paused again, as she wondered how Brenton would accept her version of events. Her son was looking strangely docile. "It will tek more than one Sunday evening to tell you everyt'ing. But basically, when Juliet's fader reached Englan', he said to me I mus' choose. I t'ink you know what my choice was. Dem time Juliet was being minded by my 'usband's parents, an' me and dem could never agree on everyt'ing. We had a whole heap of argument about the way dem was treating my daughter. Anyway, back to you now. Your fader tek you from the hospital when you was only t'ree days old. It broke my 'eart, I tell you."

Brenton found the window with his eyes and stared out of it and scratched his right ear. Where's the man with the violin? his mind mocked.

Ms Massey said, almost to herself, "When I look back now, it should 'ave never been a choice. I should 'ave insisted to keep you. I'm not looking for forgiveness, 'cos me know I done wrong. But you 'ave to believe dat I 'ave t'ought of you every day since. Right about now, I'm 'fraid to look upon you, I feel so shame."

Brenton listened intently, looking as though his breath could chill a bonfire night. Although he would not forgive her, he thought his mother appeared genuinely sorry. He glanced at his fretful parent, and still feeling relatively calm, asked: "Is it all right if I smoke?"

"What? Oh yes, of course. I'll get you an ashtray."

Brenton arsoned his snout, analysing the pictures of his sister which up-staged anything else in the room. "Do you have a picture of me when I was a baby?"

"Er, no. Your fader has all de photos. I'm sure wherever he is, he still keep dem safe."

At this Brenton suddenly stood up and abruptly departed the room, leaving Cynthia feeling extremely sorry for herself.

A few sorrows later, Brenton reappeared in his mother's bedroom, informing her that he would be on his way now. He politely thanked her for the dinner, and said he would visit again.

Drying the dishes hurriedly, Juliet heard Brenton stepping down the stairs. "Brenton, you going now?"

"Yeah, I'm tired and I wanna go home."

Flinging down the tea towel, Juliet skipped along the hallway. "Hold up, I'll walk with you."

She disappeared upstairs to don her hat and wedge on her shoes, leaving her brother abiding at the front door impatiently slapping his soles. Ten foot-taps later, Juliet bounded down the stairs, fastening the buttons to her coat. Her brother opened the front door and they ventured out into the street, greeted by a gust of wind. They walked a number of paces before Brenton, who was dangerously troubled, stopped trodding. He clocked his sister. "How do you feel about me, Juliet?"

"What do you mean?"

The short fuse within Brenton torched itself. "You know what I bloody mean! All those kisses, you looking me up and down. Don't pretend you don't know what I'm on about."

Juliet quickly glanced around her, to see if anyone in the street had heard or seen her brother shouting at her. Then she looked at him, feeling her tongue handcuffing itself. So much emotion in his face, she thought.

Brenton urged, "Well, I'm waiting! You must think this is a bloody game!"

Juliet gazed into her brother's eyes, knowing she must be honest with him. She didn't want to create a scene and she hated arguments. She closed her eyes for a long second. "All right, all right. Look, I don't know why, but I'm strongly attracted to you."

Brenton scratched his head in disbelief, then rubbed his temple.

Sure that he would refrain from shouting this time, Juliet added, "I can't help what I feel."

Brenton was dazed. "Oh shit, bloody hell. Well fuck my living days, this ain't happening."

Juliet managed a smile. "You can't talk," she joked. "You've been eyeing me up as well. Now, you answer *me* one thing honestly. So you think I'm sort of, er, you know what I'm saying. Er, do you like me?"

Now it was Brenton's turn to be in the dock. He studiously avoided his sister's eyes, scarcely able to believe the way the conversation was developing. But he felt he had to answer the question honestly. "Er, I dunno. Er, well, I mean yes. But that's not the bloody point . . . you're my sister, for God's sake."

Bad bwai Brown rides to town on a stallion, he thought, only to find his foe's daughter presenting him with a bouquet of flowers - what a confusion!

Then he ambled away, leaving Juliet standing in inky isolation, wondering whether to laugh or cry. She pondered on whether she'd already torpedoed her relationship with her new-found brother, or whether she'd started something special. She looked within herself: what was she thinking? This was lunacy and totally cuckoo! Maybe it was fate, too?

She watched Brenton striding off into the distance, hoping he would turn around and bid her goodbye. But he simply crossed into the next road, refusing to look behind him.

CHAPTER TWELVE
Cornerstone

Mid-March, 1980

The days were closing in on Brenton's seventeenth birthday and during the last couple of weeks, he had found himself some casual work on a building site. A spar of Floyd's set him up for the job, which was a cash-in-hand affair. He was not contributing to the taxman's hoard; neither was he paying National Insurance. A brown sheet a day was paid, and unknowingly to Mr Lewis, he still signed on for his G. Otherwise, the social worker was relieved to know that Brenton had at last found some work.

His duties were mostly labouring, but at least he was learning some useful skills from the craftsmen with whom he worked. At first he always seemed to be stirring cement or making cups of tea, but now and again, a carpenter, or maybe a bricklayer would show him some tricks of their trade.

When Brenton received his first two weeks' wages, he splashed out on a new pair of shoes, a pullover, and two pairs of jeans. But what really pleased Mr Lewis was Brenton buying himself a hammer and a measuring tape. Things were going well for him. Even Floyd was sheepishly slapping on his door asking to borrow money.

One thing bothered Brenton, however. Though he received telephone calls from his mother, he hadn't heard from Juliet. He really warmed to her, but couldn't take it upon himself to pick up the phone and call her. Still, this was the first time his pockets had jingled with cash since he'd lied about his age so he could do a newspaper round as a kid.

It was the fag end of a tiring week and the new employee plummeted on his bed as soon as he reached home from work. In the adjacent room, Floyd, hearing the cry of his stomach, also heard Brenton stumble up the stairs. So, not even bothering to knock, he barged straight into his spar's room.

"The answer's no, whatever you want," Brenton said with his eyes still shut. "It's NO."

Floyd shook his head. "Nah, I don't want your corn. I was gonna do you a favour, man. I was gonna ask if you wanted anything up the spud shop, whether it's fish and chips or patty and chips or what. And all you can do is moan. I don't think I'll even bother now."

Wearily, Brenton got up. "Hold up, man. Get me cod and chips. Oh, and get two brew, one for yourself."

Floyd grinned. "You're a brethren, man, a brethren. I was just about to buy myself a bag of chips with the shekels I've got." Floyd dipped into his trouser pocket and came out with what amounted to seventeen pence. "To get a sausage in batter I need a next thirty pence."

Brenton counted the small change his spar was holding out. "Where're you going with them sixpences? You can't use them again. They're gone out, innit? I think it was a few weeks ago. You can't buy nutten with them."

"Well, kiss me granny armpit, I never knew that. Can you sponsor me fifty pence?"

"Yeah, yeah. Just hurry up, man, I'm starving." Brenton took out a crumpled five-pound note from his cement-stained donkey jacket. "Give me back the change," he warned. "Even the coppers."

Floyd glanced at Brenton's new pair of shoes alongside the bed and felt a whip of red eye. "I could never work on a building site, man. They work you till your digits turn grey, and if I done that, I wouldn't have the strength to crub any steak at the weekend. Nah, I would rather be in an office with my name on the door. Own secretary and t'ing and I would tell her to park her backside on my desk and take down some lyrics."

"Floyd, don't wanna hear about your dreams, man . . . hurry up with that fish."

Floyd grinned like a two-timing fox, while pushing the note deep into his front jeans pocket before departing. Brenton lay gingerly on his bed once more, trying to get comfortable to ease the pangs in his shoulder muscles. With his eyes closed, his mind drifted back again to his childhood.

It was winter, the year 1970, just prior to Christmas.

The children's home had two large coal fires at either end of the mansion-type house. One fire was in the spacious lounge, where the large black-and-white television acted as a baby-sitter for the smaller children. This room was where most of the kids would spend their time if they behaved themselves, or performed their chores to satisfaction. The other coal fire heated the dining room, where two sizeable wooden tables dominated the space. The staff of the children's home would usually discuss matters arising throughout the day in there, over a coffee or mug of tea and a spilling ashtray.

The young Brenton had just consumed his dinner, and was playing quietly with a small model car in the long hallway, when he heard the fear-inducing voice of his housemother Miss Hill - 'The Belt'.

"Brenton, go and fill up the coal bucket."

The seven-year-old loathed this chore, but knew he had to do it. So slowly, he walked into the cloakroom to don his hat, scarf and tatty anorak. He wished he owned a pair of gloves, but that would be a luxury. Beside the back door stood a large coal bucket, once yellow in colour but now virtually covered in coal dust. Next to the coal bucket stood the children's shoe rack, looking like a wire-mesh set of lockers without any doors.

He found his black but muddied wellington boots and pulled them on, hoping the sleet had ceased outside. Then he ventured out into the cold, clutching the coal bucket, which was almost half the size of himself.

There were steps leading down to a paved pathway, and on the other side of this was an outhouse, which contained bike parts, home-made trolleys, forgotten toys and a morbid-looking, headless scarecrow, stuffed with straw and dressed in a torn mac and army trousers. Brenton had found the abandoned bird-frightener in a ditch, near a farm, and decided to give it a home. Many times he had stolen conversations with this scarecrow while he carefully upholstered its limbs, and thought about how he would make its head. He propped it up in a dusty corner and always greeted it with a 'how you doing today?' whenever he entered the outhouse.

Brenton found the pathway very slippery, caused by children sliding on the partially melted snow. So aware of this hazard, he carefully side-stepped his way to the coalbunker, which adjoined the outhouse. Once he'd reached the bunker, he had to feel his way inside, as the light bulb hadn't worked since bonfire night. Unfortunately for Brenton, no coal had been delivered for quite a few weeks. This meant he had to rummage with his bare hands amongst the dust, in the hope of finding a solid piece of coal. There was a shovel he could have used, but the handle was broken and would prove awkward to hold. He dreamed of a pair of gloves, and at this moment, would rather have something to warm his fingers than the Action Man he saw in a television commercial. But he came swiftly back to reality, digging and foraging with his small, tender hands in the search of black gold.

Patiently, with determination, he managed to fill the bucket half-full. Satisfied, he clutched the handle and very carefully trod the pathway back to the home. He dragged the bucket up the outside steps and finally made it to the back door, where he halted and rested for a couple of minutes, feeling his arm and shoulder muscles aching. Then he opened the door, wiping his soles on the vast doormat, and took another breather as he wrenched off his wellington boots. Then he donned his slippers before completing the last leg of his chore.

The coal was required for the dining room, so now the weary child slowly eased his way along the hallway, taking care to keep the coal bucket steady. Alas, he stumbled, causing the bucket to wobble. One piece of coal escaped and danced along the hallway, leaving terrible black marks on the carpet. Brenton could only watch in horror, thinking he wouldn't see another Christmas.

The rounded figure of The Belt stormed into the hallway to see a spread-eagled young Brenton and the coal blemishes, which made the carpet look like the body of a Dalmatian dog.

"You clumsy idiot, just look at that carpet! It has only just been hoovered."

With The Belt rushing towards him with outstretched hand and serious-looking intent, Brenton cowered, covering his face with his arms, adopting the foetal position, expecting the familiar beating.

"Brenton, Brenton! Wake up, man, I've got your goods."

Floyd was looking down on his spar, wondering why he was sweating. "Are you sick?"

Mopping his face with his hands, Brenton's eyes focused on the two white paper bags Floyd was holding.

"Where's the brew, man?"

Grinning, Floyd emptied his jacket pockets to reveal the strong after-dinner liquor.

The two friends quickly consumed their meal.

They were draining their beer when Floyd asked, "I see your sister is A-class, man - wicked-looking and t'ing. So I was wondering if you could have a word, know what I mean? You know, say something good about me so I can deal wid it positively - set me up with the girl. I'm sort of asking you back the favour for when I controlled you the job."

Brenton nearly choked on his beer. "Set you up? Set you up with my sister? You must be friggin joking. Ain't you got enough gal already? The only t'ing I would set you up with is a Muppet. Shit, I don't believe you sometimes, you crack me up."

Floyd, feeling sheepish, glanced at his spar and tried to regain his composure. "All right, just stay cool, keep your Rizla intact, no need to burst a blood vessel and stress out your heartbeat. I only asked. I just wondered, you know."

Brenton shook his head in disbelief, wondering if any gal in South London was safe from his spar's 'keep his bone content' antics. But talking about his sister made Brenton feel it was high time he confronted her. Then he realised he didn't have any cancer sticks to hoover after his meal.

"Shit, I forgot to tell you to buy some snouts. Why didn't you remind me?"

With a grin, Floyd fished in his pockets once more to reveal a packet of cigarettes.

"You bastard, you weren't going to tell me you had them, were you? Don't mess about, man - oh, and give me my change, you ginall."

"I was gonna tell you. I bought them with your corn and I ain't no t'ief. Here's your change, and you can't take a joke, man."

Brenton accepted the change. "Look, I'm sorry, man. I've had a bad day, know what I mean? I've mixed more cement than sound-men have mixed dub-plate."

The duo lit their fags and relaxed to digest their meal.

Two hours later, after Brenton had enjoyed a warm bath, he felt determined to confront his sister that very night, wanting to know if she was still talking to him.

Casually, but smartly dressed, Brenton marched out of his home with a sense of purpose. As he arrived at his mother's house, his heartbeat vibrated through to his throat. He strained his eyes to see if there were any lights on, but no, it was just a streetlight that shone yellow on his mother's bedroom window. Perhaps nobody was at home? Feeling pessimistic, he thumbed the doorbell, and after a few seconds saw a rectangle of light appear around the door.

Looking immaculate in a white frilly blouse and cherry-coloured pleated skirt, Juliet studied her brother with no visible emotion on her face. "You'd better come in," she said coolly, "unless you wanna stand there in the cold."

Brenton silently shadowed his sister into the kitchen, where she switched on the kettle. "So how come you never called me?" she demanded. "You spoke to Mum a few times, but you never asked to speak to me. Why?"

Brenton composed himself before answering. "I thought you didn't want to talk to me - you know, 'cos of what happened. I felt bad about it."

"You mean you feel guilty?"

"Well, yeah, no no. I mean kind of."

This uncertainty caused Juliet to smile; she had never seen her brother so humble in the short time she had known him.

"Where's our mother?" he asked.

"Oh, she's seeing some old friend of hers."

Juliet took out two mugs from the cupboard, made the tea and gave a hot cup to her fretful-looking brother. "What do you feel about me?"

Brenton sipped his tea to give himself more time to work out an answer. "Well, listen, Juliet. To be honest, I haven't a clue what having a sister is supposed to feel like. I mean, I haven't had much practice. But you are sort of caring, and I have to admit I think you're kind of all right. I suppose you can say that I am attracted to you, but this can't be right 'cos you're my bloody sister. But like you say, people can't help what they feel. Maybe it's best if we don't see each other. But it's kinda scary, you know. I'm getting to the stage where I'm starting to imagine t'ings. You know what I mean?" Why am I saying all this? Am I going cuckoo? Brenton agonised. Could I be loved?

Juliet appreciated her brother's straight talking, but hadn't expected him to be this honest. She was thrilled by Brenton's words, despite the battle of her conscience, but unsure what to do next. She arose again and slowly walked over to Brenton, who was standing at the entrance to the kitchen. When she reached him, she gently turned him around, seeking eye-to-eye contact. Only inches apart, Juliet raised her right hand to touch his semi-Afro hair. "I'm starting to imagine t'ings as well," she murmured.

Then she half-closed her eyes and kissed her brother on the forehead. Brenton stood very still, studying his sister's every facial movement. "This is madness," he choked. "I don't know what the fuck is going on, but I ain't resisting this any more." He laughed nervously, then resumed, "You know, since I was a little brat, I wanted to be close to my family, but this is taking the piss."

Juliet laughed heartily, then placed her arms around the neck of her brother and jig-sawed her hands together. The two of them gazed into each other's eyes, both realising that their mutual attraction would have to remain a secret. Juliet was extra conscious of this, because if her mother found out, she knew it would devastate Cynthia.

They both sat at the kitchen table and talked freely for over an hour, recalling their differing childhoods. Brenton even told of his recurring nightmares, which disturbed his sister, but at least she could now identify the torment in his eyes.

Before he was allowed to leave, Juliet embraced him again, this time kissing him on the cheek. He responded by giving her an awkward hug, unsure of where to put his hands.

Prior to opening the front door, Brenton joked, "I just don't believe it. The first woman to hug me up and kiss me is my sister." He mentally pinched himself. Maybe she wasn't really his sister. Maybe she had a different mother. His mother might have adopted her. These things happen . . .

He went home, leaving his sister thinking she was now taking part in her own love story - like the ones that filled the shelf in her bedroom.

Juliet Massey, what have you done! *What the fuck have you done!* her conscience scolded her. As for Brenton, he felt a strange contentment. He bounded off, whistling the Gong's *Could You Be Loved.*

CHAPTER THIRTEEN

There She Goes

9:30 am, the following Monday morning

The postman walked past the hostel without making any delivery. Floyd impatiently prowled the hallway with a corn-hungry look misting over him. He rapped on Mr Lewis's door, then jutted his head around it before stepping in. He found Mr Lewis's head ostriched in paperwork, amidst a plume of cigarette smoke. "You sure my G never come in the post this morning?" he said anxiously.

Mr Lewis glanced up. "No, um, I suppose you should get down to the DHSS Office and ask them what has happened to it."

Floyd would have gladly kicked a cat if he owned one. Mr Lewis noted his charge's anxiety. "Floyd, it's a long time since I've had a chat with you. Come inside and sit down."

The teenager took the chair facing Mr Lewis and slouched into it. "Can I have a snout, please?"

Lewis dug into his pockets and offered him a cigarette. "Now Floyd, I can't remember the last time you told me you had gone to the job centre. Don't you have any ambition? Don't you want to work? Life isn't fair and things don't arrive on a plate for us. Especially for lads like you."

"You mean for blacks like you."

"You are young now, but there will come a time when you are living away from here. Then you will have to stand on your own two feet and support yourself. You can't go through life aimlessly - you must set yourself some goals. I mean, what do you want to do with your life?"

The social worker waited expectantly, but Floyd looked as though he wanted to step out of the room sharpish. "Is there a problem I can help you with?" Lewis persisted. "Like a family problem? You are allowed to invite your family down here - your sisters perhaps? Your mother is always ringing and asking about you."

Floyd knew there were some truths and rights to what the social worker said, but still thought Lewis was a nosy parker. "I ain't got no problems with my family - apart from my paps, right? And even if I did, it's none of your business," he said truculently. "I don't have to tell you everyt'ing."

Lewis drummed his fingers on his desk.

"I don't wanna do no shit job like Brenton," Floyd explained, "where dem boss use you like slaves. I wanna do something constructive, but when you go for the good jobs, dem white bosses don't want to employ a black yout'. You know what I'm saying, Mr Lewis?"

"Well, er, not all bosses are like that."

"Most of them friggin are."

"You can't just give up. You have to try, you know. Like I said, life isn't fair, but you have to make the most of it. You can't just waste yourself like this."

"Look, I will try and get a decent job, but it ain't easy. And I'm telling you from now, I ain't taking no slavery job like working behind a McDonald's counter."

Mr Lewis nodded his head, thinking his charge never listened to his counselling; even Brenton was attentive sometimes. Floyd rose and departed, wondering what the fuck had happened to his G cheque.

Two regrets later, the social worker watched from the window as Floyd cursed his way down the street. Mr Lewis considered it was very true that employers discriminated against young blacks; nevertheless, he couldn't tell Floyd not to bother to look for work! And why wouldn't he see his family? His mother doted on him.

Later on in the evening, Ms Massey arrived home from work feeling that if she was offered retirement tomorrow, she would grab it. The difficulties of trying to explain to a close friend about the reappearance of her long-lost son nagged at her conscience. Could she have fought harder to keep Brenton, or done more to find him? These questions rouletted through her mind and began to make her feel dizzy. She had recently visited her doctor to obtain more pills for her high blood pressure, but she knew there was no medication for this harrowing guilt.

She shuffled along the hallway and without taking her coat off, entered the kitchen. She wanted to make a cup of tea for herself, but for the time being, plonking herself on a chair seemed a better idea. Once seated, she began to reflect.

Her mortgage was almost paid off - thanks and praises for that, she thought. But her early life in England had been hard graft - tending to the incontinent, taking crippled old people to the toilet, and administering undignified standing baths to them.

Her instincts kept telling her it was too late to form a natural mother and son relationship. The closeness she experienced with Juliet would never materialise with Brenton. Maybe, she thought, it would be best to concentrate on the future and not dwell on the past. Then she remembered it was her son's birthday in a few days' time. How could she forget that? She didn't even need to think about what day Juliet's birthday fell upon; it was 25 May. A little more thought was required to remember her son's birthday. Was it 22 or 23 March? She wasn't completely sure.

An interruption of her thoughts came in the sound of the doorbell. Laboriously getting up from her chair, she slowly walked towards the front door while unbuttoning her green trench coat. She opened the door to reveal a frustrated-looking Garnet, immaculately dressed in blue suede jacket and matching blue corduroys. Tall and athletic, he sported three gold rings on his right hand and the barber's spray was still scenting out from his neat Afro. Cynthia thought he was an ideal partner for Juliet, and wondered if they would one day produce her first grandchild.

"Is Juliet in?"

"No, she don't come from work yet."

An irritated Garnet glanced up and down the street. "I can never get hold of her. She don't return my calls, and I haven't seen her for weeks. Where's she hiding?"

Cynthia ushered Garnet inside. "Well, recently we've 'ad a liccle family business, y'understand? Anyway, she shouldn't be too long. You can wait for her until she reach."

Garnet headed towards the kitchen where he knew he'd be offered something hot to drink. Cynthia followed behind. "I was jus' about to make myself a cup of tea. You want one?"

Garnet nodded. "I jus' come from work myself a short while ago," the woman added.

Cynthia made the tea. In between sipping and polite conversation, Garnet kept stealing impatient glances at the front door. He had to wait half an hour until he heard the sound of a key turning in the lock. When Juliet entered, she clocked Garnet peering around the doorway.

"Oh, hi. Long time no see. Soon come, just going upstairs."

A few minutes later, Juliet appeared downstairs, dressed casually in slippers, jeans and pullover. Her mother and Garnet were still seated in the kitchen exchanging pleasantries. "Evening Mum, Garnet. Wanna come inside the front room?"

Without answering, Garnet left Ms Massey in the kitchen and pursued Juliet into the lounge. "Where you been, man? How comes you don't bell me? My sound played out last week, it was a nice dance and the party was ram and t'ing. But where were you? You let me down, man, everyone was asking for you. All Hilary dem were asking me if I was gonna pick you up. I had to tell them some bogus that you were sick."

Juliet had endured a demanding day at work, and the last thing she wanted right now was an argument. "Listen, Garnet," she said firmly. "You don't own me, right? I don't have to go with you every time your stupid sound plays out. Besides, I'm bored with your sound anyway, and as for Hilary, she don't need me to hold her hand. Every time I go out with her, she's always crubbing with Clyde all night anyway."

Garnet decided to sit down, thinking the pretty girl who was slumped in the chair opposite was also bored with him. "You didn't complain when you used to call me so I could pick you up to take you to all the big dances. Yeah, you and your foolish friends. Is that why you went out with me? 'Cos I had wheels?"

Juliet shook her head. "I never used you. Them times I was into roots music and I did love to go to them big hall dances. But now, I'm into soul, you know what I mean? People's taste changes, innit? When's the last time you called me and offered to take me to the Lyceum or up Bali Hai on a Friday night when they play soul? It's always your boof, bang, bing sound system, which breaks down half the time anyway."

Garnet peered into the carpet, not knowing what to say. I don't wanna wait in vain for your love, he thought, realising he might be losing the girl he had chased since he headlighted her riding the dodgems at the funfair. He remembered the day Juliet came round to his yard, where she saw the speaker boxes, records and the sound-system control tower. He felt so proud, sure in the knowledge that the owner of a sound system was well respected and known by all the sweet bwais and bad bwais alike, especially in the council estates and tenements of the inner cities. In some ways, the big sound men were like the film stars of Hollywood. Kids would look up to them in awe and older youths would get red eye of the notoriety they enjoyed. But all this fame and Garnet still couldn't manners the girl he craved.

So giving up the quarrel, he thought he would just accept that Juliet gave him his P45. There were other girls out there who could satisfy him, ones who hung around the sound set when Garnet was playing out - but none as appetising as her.

"Hey, Juliet. I ain't gonna argue with you. Bad vibes, know what I mean? I have to be chipping now anyway, so take care and stay pretty, seen."

Garnet quickly got up, sought out Ms Massey and bade farewell to her. He returned to the front room where Juliet was still slouched in the chair with her eyelids dropping. "Don't bother see me out, I'll check you a next time seen. Later."

"Yeah, I'll see you around. Don't feel no way, will you? You're all right but I need my space, you know."

Garnet departed, wondering how he was gonna tell his brethrens that he wouldn't be dating the fittest girl in West Norwood any more.

CHAPTER FOURTEEN

Ring The Alarm

Saturday, 22 March, 1980

Brenton Brown's last day of being a juvenile coincided with the sound-system event of the year, the Gold Cup competition - a tournament in which the top kick-arse sounds in London would musically cross swords in Brixton Town Hall.

Brenton and Floyd had to be there to support their favourite sound system - Moa Anbessa. Everyone had been debating about the contest for weeks, and fast-talking hustlers, who in the last few weeks became friendly with the promoters of this dance, laid out odds on who would win.

The two spars departed home at six-thirty in the evening, hoping to arrive at the venue early to beat the expected ramjam at the entrance. Apparently, many other roots rockers had the same idea, because the 35 bus, routed to Acre Lane, Brixton, brimmed to over-capacity.

The two friends claimed their seats on the upper deck, taking a sense of identity in the red, gold and green belts and scarves that everybody seemed to be wearing. "Look like this dance is gonna ram," commented Brenton.

Floyd, confident in a grey trench coat, black Stetson and black polo-neck sweater, attempted to make eye-contact with the girls around him. "It's true, Gold Cup dance is always ram. I just hope 'Bassa' can win it. I've heard the sound men have been studio and cut nuff dub-plates."

One beret-topped guy apparently couldn't wait for the music to start. For in the rear of the upper deck, taking up most of the room on the double seat, he had his fingers on the control of an enormous Brixton suitcase - which was more like a London trunk. He was playing a tape of all the latest reggae releases from Jamaica, massaging the appetite of the roots heads.

A fearful conductor emerged from the stairwell, wearing a cap and his ticket machine strapped to his chest. He stole a glance at the DJ's luggage, then eyed the vociferous passengers before slipping back down the stairs.

The conductor was a picture of relief as the throng of black youngsters vacated the bus at Brixton Town Hall. A mass of people grouped near the entrance of the Hall, blocking the path of pedestrians and watching a big white rental van park awkwardly near a zebra crossing.

Walking alongside Brenton, Floyd clocked the disorganised scene and nudged him. "That's Coxone man just reach. Yeah, I recognise Festus the operator."

Brenton turned his head sharply to look at the proud-visaged Festus, who resembled a general arriving at the scene of battle, confident of victory.

All of a sudden, the shutters at the back of the van were raised to reveal about ten black youngsters, none of whom looked old enough to drain liquor. They bullfrogged out of the van and vigorously started their evening's work. They were the 'boxboys' of the sound system, responsible for the lifting and carrying of all the heavy equipment.

A gravel-like voice of Jamaican accent boomed out, "Mind yuh back, mind yuh back."

As the double doors at the entrance swung open, the boxboys bumped the huge boxes, the size of double wardrobes, into the 'arena'.

Meanwhile, Brenton and Floyd queued up to gain entry, hoping to sight Biscuit, Finnley, Coffin Head or anybody else from their posse. There was another liquor-belly man, dressed in army garb and sporting a hairstyle akin to Jimi Hendrix's, receiving the entry tax while shouting in a Kingstonian twang: "One pound fifty fe come in. One pound fifty fe come in. If yuh nuh 'ave it, fuck off an' remove from de gate. One pound fifty fe come in."

The two brethrens paid their tax and made their way to the arena, with Brenton looking here and there, wary of the presence of Terry Flynn, and Floyd wha'appening and greeting fellow Brixtonians he knew. Three threats from the doorman later, Brenton and Floyd finally met up with Biscuit, who was crocodiling a Mars bar, Finnley and Coffin Head - the latter being the owner of the squarest forehead this side of black London.

This was the sound owners' busiest time. Cables of electric wire resembled a giant man's helping of multy-coloured spaghetti. Each of the four competing sounds claimed a corner, scowling at each other as they connected record decks, pre-amplifiers, echo chambers and the like, while the boxboys were busy stringing up the speaker boxes. The only space near the walls where you couldn't find a speaker box was either at the entrance, or where the sound 'control towers' were placed. This was usually aluminium casing, about head height, housing all the amplifiers and the extras topped off by a record deck.

Floyd and his posse were spellbound, like many others, watching the Moa Anbessa controls get pieced together. While the youngsters stared at their heroes, the hall filled up rapidly as the sound guys applied the finishing touches to their routine.

The crowd savoured the almost ritualistic atmosphere, feeling a sense of belonging as they marvelled at the red, gold and green colours. Rastafarians wore their long locks proudly and black females, adorned in their African-type dresses, added a spice of culture to the event. Pictures of the late Emperor, Haile Selassie of Ethiopia, hung or were Sellotaped to the walls. The aroma of West Indian cuisine drifted through the air, blending with the exotic breath of marijuana. There was a serious trade at the bar, where strong beers and soft drinks were selling at inflated prices.

The dreadlocked operator of the Moa Anbessa sound drew the crowd's attention. He carefully placed a record on the rotating table and spoke into the microphone.

"Test one, test one. One, two, microphone test."

The amplified voice was a cue for the people massing around the lobby to rapidly converge in the hall, where they watched the operator finger-wipe the needle of the record deck, producing a heavy scratching sound that earthquaked from the speakers. Looking very proud and clocking the crowd around him, the Moa Anbessa operator announced through the microphone, "In tune to the A1 champion sound of de world - Moa Anbessa!"

Then he proceeded to play a record, which delighted his followers.

Within half an hour, every sound was ready, so the competition commenced. Soferno B, Jah Shaka, Sir Coxone and Moa Anbessa were about to compete for the prestigious title of 'Champion Sound of London'.

The lights in the hall were switched off, which acted as a stimulant for excited youngsters to start shouting, jumping and skanking whenever their favourite sound played a record. Everyone became infected with the skanking vibe, hotstepping on the stage, in the lobby and even in the queue leading up to the bar.

The hall juddered to the relentless drum and bass rhythms of Johnny Osbourne, The Twinkle Brothers, Gregory Isaacs, Dennis Brown and other top-ranking artistes from Jamaica. A lone rastaman grabbed some roots-heads' attention by holding a bongo drum between his knees and trying to keep in time to the music. Skankers in black tracksuits with red and green trims showed off their new moves and party pieces, with onlookers marvelling at the way they controlled their bodies. Most of the youngsters besieged the control towers, captivated by their heroes and cheering every time they were commanded to.

At around eleven o'clock, the competition came to a climax, and the judges declared Jah Shaka the winner. Jah Shaka's followers hollered and whooped their approval, along with the illegal bookmakers. Floyd and his posse, backed up by others, barked their disappointment as they threaded their way out of the building.

The scene at the bus stops could have been the warm streets of downtown Kingston as Brenton and Floyd bade laters to their spars. Brenton looked forward to the Clint Eastwood film on telly that night, but Floyd felt the night wasn't over yet. "Char man, Bassa got robbed. Dem judge are crooks, man. Bassa played the most wicked music."

"I reckon some of them judge are in the Shaka posse anyway," Brenton agreed, scanning the crowd for any sight of his Nemesis, Terry Flynn.

The two spars observed the hordes of reggae-heads jostling and pushing to get aboard a 37 bus. Floyd had an agitated appearance on his dial. "I don't feel like going home, man."

This was the last thing Brenton wanted to hear. He had arranged to go out early next morning with his sister to a Sunday market in East London; Juliet had promised her brother she would buy something for him to wear for his birthday present. Unaware of this, Floyd mentioned, "I have hardly got no herb left, so I might go and check out Chemist. He lives off Brixton Hill, and then we'll go and see what Sharon is saying. She might have a rave."

Although reluctant to go, Brenton tried hard not to show his aversion, knowing Floyd always wanted company when he was stepping the streets of Brixton. So the spars turned right off Acre Lane and trod up Brixton Hill, passing St Matthew's Church.

With his spirits rising up again, Floyd remarked, "Did you see Druffy? He's dread. He should do something about his hair, man. When he was skanking, all dust and rust was coming from his head-top. His hair's as dry as the African desert. I told him, 'cos the shops are closed, he should go petrol station and buy some oil and slap it on his head quick time."

Brenton laughed out loud. "Yeah, it's true, but he don't care, does he? He should at least wear a bloody hat or something."

"What about Biscuit in his 1950's trousers? Doesn't he know that man nowadays wear trousers that reach down to his shoes? I don't know where he's going with dem three-quarter trousers. Check him to me 'bout he's gonna check some gal later on. He ain't checking nutten with those trousers."

Brenton laughed again then stopped abruptly. He'd seen something to alarm him - a beast van travelling slowly towards them, just passing Brixton College.

"Floyd, look, radication squad."

Floyd glanced up. "Shit, stay cool and step it over on the other side of the road. If we have to chip, then we can burn across the grass and into the flats."

The duo crossed the road, both sensing the dark cloud of danger in the shape of a white van overswilling with pigs. Brenton and Floyd kept the vehicle in their sights as they ambled innocently up the hill. The van performed a U-turn and neared the teenagers. "Stay cool," Floyd advised. "Remember, pigs can't burn as fast as us."

The white van pulled up alongside them and out stepped a double-chinned pig. This action prompted the driver of the van to accelerate until he was abreast of the black youths. The pig trotted up to the teenagers and oinked spitefully, "So where are you two niggers going tonight? Planning a burglary? Or are you waiting for a little old dear to walk by so you can nick her purse?"

"Who are you calling nigger, you big white shit."

Floyd's sharp eyes spotted some movement in the van. As the officer closed in, Brenton and Floyd backed off onto the grass verge. "You're a cheeky wog, aren't you? You won't be so cheeky inside a cell."

"*Run!*"

The two brethren burned as hard as they could as the van emptied out another four hungry pigs. Floyd led the way, heading for the flats. Cars stopped on Brixton Hill as motorists watched the beast being outpaced by the two youngsters. Gaining a lead into the council estate, Floyd and Brenton leaped without thought or hesitation, into a large grey metal rubbish bin. Fearfully they waited submerged in garbage and trying to murder their heavy breathing. The sounds of heavy trotters made Brenton and Floyd keep very still. When the beast arrived in the forecourt they hovered around for a while, with two of them searching the balconies. Brenton and Floyd could hear one of the officers grunt after a period of ten minutes: "The charcoal bandits have fucking disappeared. Come on, let's go. There's many more coons out there in the sea."

The radication squad dispersed from the estate, leaving a nervous Brenton and Floyd up to their necks in black bags full of rubbish. Floyd whispered to his spar, "You think the beast have gone?"

"I don't hear them, but even if they are still around, I can't stay in this shit for too long. I stink. Which one of these blocks does Chemist live in?"

"The one just in front of us."

"So why the fuck didn't we go there straight away?" hissed Brenton, glaring at his spar.

"Too risky. Say the beast caught us at Chemist's yard, he would have got pull as well 'cos he's got a big bag of herb at his yard with all scales and t'ing," explained Floyd, sniffing and catching scent of something that might have died in prehistoric times.

Brenton took a peep over the top of the large bin. "Hey Floyd, come on, man. I can smell shit but I can't smell no pigs."

They climbed out of the bin and stealthily made their way to the block of flats nearby, checking behind them all the time. They eventually reached Chemist's front door and Floyd gently slapped the letterbox. Seconds later, the front door opened to reveal a spliff-smoking Chemist, adorned in many gold chains and heavy gold rings. "Quick, close the door."

Topped off by a leather beret, and with an arching scar on his forehead, Chemist was a large imposing figure. "What the hell is going on? And what the blouse an' skirt is that smell?"

Floyd took off his Stetson and inspected his stained, creased hat. He licked the palm of his hand and attempted to rub out the unsightly blemishes. "Radication just chase us innit."

Chemist glared at Floyd. "And you run here! You want two slap in your head or what?"

"Nah, nah, we had to jump in a friggin rubbish bin downstairs. We did wait for a while until the beast dem chip. Then we reach up here."

Chemist's face turned from one of anger into one of humour. "You jumped into that big rarted bin downstairs? You know all man fling their dead dog and t'ing in der? And some man fling their dick macs in der after they just done use it. You're dread, I would rather get pull than jump in that."

Brenton, dusting himself down, alertfully watched around him, not trusting anyone he didn't know too well. "It wasn't you getting chased by the beast, was it? Anyway, they're too slow, man."

Chemist led the way into the front room. "Don't bother coch down on me furniture, y'know. I don't want my woman complaining that my spars come and renk out her yard, y'hear? And don't touch nutten."

Floyd was not amused. "Just give me a five-pound draw and we'll chip."

Chemist laughed. "Yeah, hold on. My t'ings are in my bedroom."

Before he disappeared, Floyd called out to his herbalist: "Hey, Chemist, I don't want no tea granules or thyme mixed up in my herb, man. And I don't want no Brockwell Park grass which you cut up and soak and give to dem fool-fool white man. Just the other day some man down the line gave me a draw mixed up with dem t'ing der. So treat me proper, man, I'm a good customer."

"Just cool, man. Would I do a t'ing like that?"

Minutes later, Chemist returned with a newspaper-wrapped sprinkling of cannabis. He passed it on to Floyd who opened it, with Brenton inspecting the herb as well. Chemist went into his sales patter. "That's a serious herb, man, and I've given you more than a five-pound draw 'cos you two give me joke. You will be charged after one big-'ead, me ah tell you."

Floyd nodded his approval. Chemist resumed, "Bwai, you jump in a garbage bin to get away from the beast. You two are coming like the Marx Brudders to rarted."

Floyd was satisfied with his purchase. "Yeah, the herb smells all right. Can we use your bathroom to dash 'way our BO and t'ing? I'm just about to go to Sharon's yard."

"Yeah, well, you can't pull no gal tonight renking like that, can you?"

Brenton glanced at Chemist cautiously, wondering why this guy thought his misfortune was so funny.

Chemist skinned his teeth again and parked on a sofa, preparing to pastry a spliff.

Two joint wrappings later, Brenton and Floyd had used the bathroom to freshen up and were ready to leave. "Hey Chemist, I'll catch you later, yeah? And if this herb smoke bad, I'm gonna tell every herbalist in the land, and your rep will be so bad, you'll end up lifting up crusty speaker boxes for your supper."

"Yeah, seen, you rarted joker. Come out of my yard, man, and fling 'way your BO inna different direction. More time, yeah."

Brenton followed his spar out of the flat and the two brethren made their way out of the estate. They quickly crossed Brixton Hill, scanning around them for any sign of the beast.

As they turned into New Park Road, their attention was caught by screams coming from the end of the street. Two black youths burned past a startled Floyd and Brenton, one of them clutching a handbag. A distraught white woman of about twenty years old yelled in vain: "You bastards! You fucking bastards!"

She might as well have been a Labrador barking at the flyaway, cunning crow. Every inhabitant of the street must have heard the shrieking, but no one emerged from their shells to see what was occurring. Meanwhile, Floyd and Brenton stood at the other end of the street staring at each other. "It's all happening tonight, innit? Can you friggin believe it?"

"Come, Sharon's yard is just the next right-hand turning up there. Let's chip before we get blamed for this shit. The stupid bitch shouldn't be out this time of night."

"Shouldn't we . . .?" asked Brenton.

"No! Double no."

For a split second, Brenton stood pillared to the spot, pondering on whether to go to the woman's aid.

Then Floyd announced, the pig van nagging at his thoughts: "You know, one day there will be war in the streets between us and the beast."

Still feeling humiliated by his experience in the bin, Brenton nodded his agreement, longing for that day of war.

They arrived at Sharon's home and Floyd banged on the door, while Brenton nervously glanced up and down the street for any sign of the boys in blue.

Sharon's silhouette became visible to Floyd through the misted glass of the front door. She proceeded to unlock two bolts, a mortice lock, and unfastened a latch. "Do you have to slap so friggin loud? You waan wake up me mudder?"

Sharon, dressed in a matching Burgundy blouse and skirt, didn't realise she was talking loudly herself. Floyd spotted an Afro comb in her hair, and guessed she was preparing to go out raving. "Just let me in, man. Where're you going tonight? Party?"

Floyd entered the dwelling followed by his spar, both of them passing Sharon. "All right, Brenton? Carol's upstairs doing her hair. We're going to a party, wanna come?"

"Nah. I'm tired, man."

"I like the way you ask my spar. Wha'appen about asking me?"

Sharon smiled and lifted her fore-digit to her lips. "Be quiet, me mudder's sleeping."

As they made their way to the kitchen, Brenton assessed what he could see of the house. The wallpaper in the hallway had come to the end of its life. The passage carpet was sole weary - you could almost see your footprints in it, and the bulb lights had no shades around them, but they exposed the many fissures in the white painted ceiling.

As they entered the kitchen, Brenton saw a small, circular table, with four simple wooden chairs around it, which made him think of the police station. No modern appliances were in sight, not even an electric kettle - just the bare essentials. It was not like his mother's home in this respect, but despite this, the place looked as tidy as anywhere else.

They parked around the kitchen table; Floyd gazing at Sharon lustfully, appreciating the way she was provocatively dressed.

"Who you a look 'pon? You lose somet'ing?" she asked cheekily.

Floyd smiled, but his face quickly became serious. "We got chased by the beast and we had to chip to the flats at Brixton Hill. I'm telling you, black man can't trod street at night and feel safe."

Sharon nodded as she began to comb through her hair. "There's nuff drapesing going on around here, and the radication are all over the damn place, stopping everybody on the suss. It's like dem few muggers make every innocent black man a suspect."

"What's suss?" Brenton asked.

"It's like a law that says the beast can stop anyone and search them. The only t'ing is, the radication are taking nuff libs."

"Well, the drapesings are true," Floyd agreed. "We just saw some poor white bitch get drapes around the corner. Two crusty looking yout' did burn past us in a serious hurry."

Sharon shook her head in sympathy and Floyd could not help but notice her white bra, teasing him through her thin blouse. "You ain't wearing that, are you?" he asked.

"Yes, I bloody am. No man's gonna tell me how to dress. And besides, it's gonna be hot in the dance. Don't want me renking of sweat, do you? And come to think of it, what's that smell?"

A slightly embarrassed Floyd glanced at Brenton to seek some relief, but Brenton's eyelids were tugged tight. "You two been searching for butts in a bin again?"

"You could say that," replied Brenton.

"Have you been giving him too much herb?"

Brenton answered before Floyd could. "No, he hasn't - just bought it from Chemist's yard. Don't like the look of that guy. I'm just tired and I want my bed. So Sharon, can you call me a cab, please? I'm stepping home."

"I would if I could, but my mudder put a lock on the phone 'cos the last bill we got, went bionic, y'understand? Anyway, there's a phone box just around the corner, although you'll be lucky to find it in one piece."

On hearing this, Brenton painfully got up from his chair and trudged his way along the dimly lit hallway. Suddenly, the wails of a very young baby startled him. "Whose pickney is that?"

"My sister's."

Brenton opened the front door. Aware of a presence at the top of the stairs, he looked up and clocked Carol standing on the landing, holding a small make-up mirror in her left hand and looking very sophisticated, wearing an expensive, close-fitting dress which displayed all her bone-waking charms. Brenton eyed her tall figure as Carol glided down two steps. "Where you going? You're not coming to the party?" she asked.

"Nah, I'm too tired, innit. I've been up since early morning and I have to be up tomorrow morning as well."

Carol, one hand on her hip, glared at Brenton. "It seems like you're scared to rave with me. I don't bite, you know."

Brenton placed his right hand on the door, giving the impression he was in a hurry. "Nah, seriously Carol. I'm tired badly. Look, we'll all rave together the next time, yeah?"

"I'll have to see it to believe it."

Brenton swivelled and disappeared out of the front door, thinking as he strode towards the phone box that Carol must think he was a battyman or something. Pretty as she was, he didn't want her.

The lecherous Floyd was left in the kitchen with the girl of his desires. Now that his spar had gone out, it gave license for his eyes to truly appreciate the beauty sitting opposite him. Sharon was still styling her hair as he rose up from his chair. He pulled her arm to make her stand up, then kissed her fully on the mouth. Sharon responded by embracing him, then suddenly she jerked herself way. "I'm just gonna check to see if Carol's ready."

"Carol can get ready by herself. I haven't seen you all week."

She went off upstairs, leaving her man feeling unfulfilled. He slumped at the table, pushing his head into his hands and quietly muttered, "Women."

When two taps on the front door indicated Brenton's return, Floyd went to open it. "The cab's on its way, be here in a minute," Brenton announced.

"You let me down, man. I need you to come to this dance to manners Carol, innit. Now she's gonna get in the way 'cos she's on her tod. Why are you going home so early, anyway? What are you doing tomorrow?"

"Family business."

A coffee later, a cab horn hollered outside. Feeling relieved, because sometimes you may order a cab in Brixton, only for the car to go missing, Brenton departed, making sure he closed the front door quietly. Floyd was left behind to ponder how could it take two Brixtonian girls so long to get ready for a night out? And how was he gonna get rid of Carol? He would have to try another time to entice Sharon back to his yard.

CHAPTER FIFTEEN
Lovers Rock

Early the next morning, a rap on his room door awaked Brenton. Hurriedly, he slipped on a pair of jeans and T-shirt and then found his Afro-comb underneath his bed. He opened the door to reveal an impatient-looking Juliet, wrapped in her beige camel coat. "Ain't you ready yet?" she nagged. "It's gone half past eight."

Brenton picked up a hand towel. "Yeah, I'm just gonna dash 'way my BO. By the way, who let you in?"

"The guy in the room next to you; he let me in the last time. I think he just come back from a party, he was all dressed up."

"Did he say anything?"

"Like what?"

"Oh, it don't matter."

"Then why did you ask?"

Juliet went downstairs, surveying the decor. The white-painted walls reminded her of her dentist's surgery, and in the hallway, she caught sight of many leaflets scattered on the small table near the base of the stairs. She picked one of them up and read the headline: How To Prepare Yourself For An Interview. Not bothering to read the pages, she ventured into the kitchen, where a notice above the sink read: Leave The Kitchen As You Find It. Juliet smiled to herself, walked out of the kitchen and sat down at the foot of the staircase, careful not to crease her coat. Out of her black leather handbag, she took a small make-up mirror and checked if her hair was behaving itself. She heard her brother heavy-stepping upstairs and the sound became louder as he bullfrogged down to where she sat.

"Did you rave last night?" she asked. "I called about ten and got no answer."

"Me and Floyd went to Brixton Town Hall, the place was cork."

"Them sound dance, I just can't take the grief in my ears any more. All that boof, bang, bing."

She stood up and joined her yawning brother, ready to leave the hostel together.

Petticoat Lane Market, in London's East End, already had a busy vibe, even though it was a quarter to ten on a Sunday morning. Brenton couldn't keep up with the variety of goods on sale, and found it hard to believe that so many people could rise from their beds so early to shop on a Sunday morning. The traders were selling everything and anything. Pots, pans, cutlery, carpets, wallpaper, hi-fis, clothes and more clothes. Biscuit should step down here and get a job, he thought.

Scything through the crowds, he spotted a van selling hot dogs and hamburgers. He nudged his sister. "I have to go and get myself a dog roll. Feeling peckish, man. Do you want anything?"

Juliet shook her head. "No thanks. I cooked myself a fry-up before I reached your place."

Just as Brenton was threading his way towards the mobile take-away, his mind flashed back to another incident in his troubled past.

In his inner vision, he saw not the hot-dog van, but an ice-cream mobile. There were white kids all around him, excited with the thought of tonguing choc-ices and lollies. Brenton was queuing up, eager to satisfy his taste buds. When his moment arrived, he viced the pennies tightly in his fist, making sure not to drop any. Then from a radiant smile, the vendor's face turned scornful and aggressive, glaring down at the ten-year-old Brenton. "We don't serve the likes of you. Go on, hoppit."

Quickly blinking his eyes and quivering his head, the now adult Brenton joined the queue for his morning starter, staring at the cheerful young man serving the hot snacks. As he was about to be served, Brenton never blinked, thinking history might repeat itself. But there was no repetition as he grabbed his hot dog, half mauling it by the time he returned to his sister's side.

Juliet led the way through the streets, side-stepping onto a pavement with more walking space. Every now and again, she stopped and ran her eyes over any item of clothing that tickled her fancy. Her brother was not so enthusiastic, although a collection of hand-made china figures and wooden statues fascinated him.

The couple left Petticoat Lane, with Juliet telling Brenton how criss he would look in a new suede jacket she had bought him. Brenton was more than pleased with his present, eager to sight Floyd's face when he set eyes on it. Biscuit would probably say he had one like Brenton's that was on offer for fifteen notes.

The siblings made their way back to Brenton's hostel, via Tube and bus. All seemed very quiet inside his home. Floyd was perhaps still sleeping, or gone out to visit Sharon, making sure he consumed a decent cooked meal for the week.

Brenton opened his room door and was followed inside by his sister. She took off her coat and sat on the bed, watching him proudly hang his birthday present in the wardrobe. Juliet studied the bedroom, thinking it would probably fit into her own room at least two and a half times. She looked at Mr Dean, feeling uncomfortable under his ever-watchful eyes.

"You must be the only black guy I know who's got a picture of James Dean in their bedroom. I mean, most black guys have the Gong or someone like Dennis Brown. What's with you and James Dean? Do you fancy him?"

"Well, I certainly don't fancy the bastard. I like his films though. He always acts the kind of rebel. I suppose in a way I see myself in him - you know, not quite fitting in."

Juliet listened intently as Brenton went on: "He always seemed to be fighting everybody, as if the whole world was against him. Well, sometimes I feel like that."

"Got any decent soul tapes here?"

Brenton stood up and sifted through a selection of cassette tapes on the windowsill. "Er, let me see. Er, no. But I've got lovers rock."

He turned around to see his sister smiling and nodding her head. Juliet watched her brother switch on the battered suitcase and insert a tape. "There's some Brown Sugar, fifteen, sixteen, seventeen on this tape, and a bit of Sugar Minott. Yeah man, wicked lovers."

Juliet was now totally relaxed, lying comfortably on the bed. "So I bet you and Floyd go to nuff blues and parties and pull nuff gal, innit?"

Still fiddling with the knobs of the suitcase, trying to extract more bass if he possibly could, Brenton laughed. "That's Floyd's scene. I don't go to a lot of blues, and besides, I've never had the nerve to pull a girl in a dance. I'd rather go to a hall dance or something, where they play dubwise."

Juliet hauled herself up and faced her brother. "You waan dance?"

Nervously, he placed his arms loosely around his sister's waist, then, in the aisle of the confined space between the window and the bed, the couple rocked together to Brown Sugar's *I'm So Proud.*

"Not so fast, Brenton." Juliet's hands found her brother's shoulders, appreciating the rugged-hewn, brown rock of torso as she gently taloned his shoulder blades. Brenton was concentrating on the movement of his feet, not wanting his sister to know that he was a virgin when it came to crubbing with a gal. He jerked his head towards the side of Juliet's head, not wanting to look at her face to face. Juliet responded by holding the startled Brenton closer. Now both of them could feel their thighs brushing and rubbing together. Neither one dared to gaze at the other now, as they both felt their conduct smacked the face of moral decency. I wonder if Terry Flynn's got a woman, Brenton suddenly thought. He looked up at Mr Dean for approval.

The bone-wakened Brenton gently placed his hands at the back of his sister's neck and stroked the delicate area there. Then he fished for her jet-black hair, his fingers imitating scissors, pulling and caressing with his right hand. His left hand was still soothingly covering Juliet's neck, like a protective guard against attack. Juliet closed her eyes dreamily, feeling as if she was being embalmed by a healing hand.

Aroused, she arched her back, inviting her would-be lover to caress the front of her neck. Her hands still pressed against her brother's shoulders, but then she dropped them to his waist. Although perspiring, Brenton still wore his pullover, so without any hesitation, Juliet pulled the sweater off and hauled it on the bed, revealing the unironed T-shirt he was wearing. Juliet giggled out loud while Brenton looked mortified. Then she tugged his shirt out of his jeans and slipped her nail-varnished hands onto Brenton's muscular back, skanking her fingers teasingly up and down his spine.

By now, the couple had stopped crubbing, although the music was still playing, having an almost hypnotic effect on them. They stood still, touching and exploring each other's bodies. Brenton lowered his head and softly kissed his sister's neck. Body language told them what they both wanted, so they fell entwined on the bed.

Without daring to look at each other, they undressed themselves. Juliet, not wanting to be seen naked, dived under the bedcovers while Brenton undressed to his briefs. He slowly edged in next to his sister and enclosed his arms around her. For a few seconds they remained gummed in each other's embrace, until Juliet's hands began to trespass over a well-developed chest. The kissing resumed . . . Juliet trailed her fingers along Brenton's thighs from above the knee to the upper part of his groin. Breathing hard he wondered what he should do with his hands, until she gently

153

guided them to her breasts. Brenton slammed his eyes shut as Juliet took off his briefs. Soon, the couple were making furious love to the sound of Sugar Minott's *Never Too Young*.

Tow hours later, Brenton and Juliet were lying still, tired and naked. She coched her head on her brother's chest as he stared into space, not quite believing what had happened. "Somehow, from the first time I did see you, I had a vibe this would happen," Juliet whispered sleepily. "You know that time we weren't talking? I was asking myself: how could I fancy my own brother?"

"Yeah, I know what you mean. I was asking myself the same t'ing."

The couple remained in bed for the rest of the afternoon and early evening. They were without a thought for food, drink or anything else. They made love, talked a little and made more love.

Brenton stroked his sister's hair as he wondered what the hell was going on with his emotions. He kept on thinking to himself, What a way to blast one's virginity. He didn't want this day to end, for his night had run away for the present. None of the childhood nightmares and dramas seemed to matter any longer. The revenge he had promised himself to visit on Terry Flynn was a distant thought, tucked away in a drawer in the cellar of his mind. He knew what it was like to experience the bottomless pit of sadness and depression. But now, Brenton Brown learned that because he'd been so desolate in the past, he could truly appreciate these moments of bliss.

Juliet didn't understand what drove her into the arms of her sibling, but she felt it was something she had to have and savour. My God, I'm actually doing this, she said inwardly.

Her lover looked across to the window and realised he hadn't even drawn the curtains shut. He grinned to himself and his sister turned her head towards him, smiling radiantly. "What sweet you? You've got the smile of a young boy who has just been told he's won a trip to Disneyland."

"You sweet me, this don't seem real, man. Shit, the beast can lock me up for this, innit?"

Brenton gave his sister a tender kiss on the forehead, then decided to rise up and get dressed. Floyd would be returning to the hostel soon, he thought. Juliet followed suit. It was only now that she experienced the first kuffs of guilt, aware that her particular love story was not to be found in her collection of slushy novels. Mum would have a breakdown, she thought. Brenton, however, had no regrets; he wouldn't give morals the time of day.

A few minutes later, the couple were both dressed. Juliet was busy making sure her ebony-coloured hair looked criss, while Brenton remade his bed. As Juliet finished grooming herself, he warily opened his bedroom door, checking if Floyd was about. Thank God there was no sign of him yet.

Juliet, not entirely happy with her hair, squeezed on her shoes and joined her brother. Together they emerged from the bedroom looking as blameless as if they had spent the day flicking through photo albums.

Brenton escorted his lover back to her home. Once he reached there, his mother made sure he did not leave without a hot dinner nourishing his stomach.

Ms Massey asked her son how they celebrated a child's birthday in the children's home. He answered that he would rather forget his childhood birthdays than remember them. His mother tried to reassure him that future birthdays would be more memorable, and then presented him with a twenty-pound note and a birthday card. Brenton thanked her for the gesture, while Juliet remained unusually quiet, finding it hard to come up with a smile.

After Ms Massey conceded defeat in trying to persuade her son to eat any more rice and peas, Brenton prepared himself to brave the elements. He thanked his mother for the dinner and then wondered where his sister had disappeared to.

"Where's Juliet?"

"Maybe she's resting up in her room. She looks tired."

Brenton climbed the stairs, pondering on why Juliet had been withdrawn and not quite herself once she arrived home. He knuckled her door and walked inside. He found his sister rewinding a cassette tape in her stereo. "Something the matter?" he asked.

Brown Sugar shrilled their delicate tones from the machine and it didn't take Brenton long to recognise his lovers rock tape. "Don't mind me taking your tape, do you?"

Brenton shook his head. "No, no. Course not."

Juliet glanced at the stereo, then back at her brother. "I'm gonna cherish this tape . . . look, I'll call you, yeah? I'm tired badly and need some rest-eye. I dunno if I'm going to work tomorrow. Anyway, I'll call you tomorrow night, yeah?"

Brenton stood up. "I'm tired myself. It's been quite a day, innit? I'll see you soon, yeah."

Still a little baffled, Brenton departed the room, leaving Juliet gazing at her stereo, reflecting on the early part of the day. But she couldn't help feeling sinful, whenever she exchanged glances with her mother in the course of the evening.

Brenton had none of these misgivings. He left the Masseys' abode feeling that not even a gluttonous cat in an aviary was as happy as he.

CHAPTER SIXTEEN

Box Clever

The following Wednesday evening

"**W**anna make ten sheets tonight?" Floyd proposed to Brenton, gate-crashing his bedroom. "All we have to do is go to that building site down the road, where they're building dem new yards, and clap out the plywood, chipboard and two by two. What are you saying, man?"

Brenton rolled over onto his back. "Who's it for?"

"Spinner. He's in my room. He said he'll give me twenty notes when he picks up the goods."

On hearing the name, Brenton stood up and his expression stirred suspiciously. "Spinner? That trickster! I'd rather trust Terry Flynn to give me a decent hair-trim than Spinner. Let me chat to him."

Floyd was relieved to see that his spar was showing some interest in the job; palavering about in the dead of night nicking bits of wood wasn't something he fancied doing on his own.

The immaculately dressed Spinner was parking on Floyd's bed, rolling an impressive-looking spliff. An equally impressive black Stetson crowned his unusually large head. The square glasses he wore gave him a mature appearance, and the glint of gold tooth made his smile broader than a horny pimp's.

Examining his joint to make sure it was pastried to his pleasure, rather like a jeweller poring over an uncut diamond, Spinner arsoned his spliff with a personal engraved lighter.

"Wha'appen, Brown?" he drawled. "Backside, you ah get big. I can't frig about with you now, can I?" He glanced at Floyd. "Check his arm section - solid."

Brenton snarled, "You owe me two pound. I did lif' box for your bruk-down sound last year. I want my two pound, man."

Spinner took a deep inhale of the burning weed, then as a gesture of good faith, offered it to his ex-employee. "Here, man, just touch this and cool yourself."

Floyd looked on suspiciously, wondering how Spinner and Brenton knew each other so well. Meanwhile, the herb-hungry Brenton was making a quick hoover of the spliff, the thought of passing it on to Floyd not occurring to him.

"Give us ten pounds now and ten pounds tomorrow," Brenton demanded, "yeah, and we'll get the goods tonight. But Spinner, you're lazy, man. Why can't you get the wood yourself?"

Spinner cackled, then delved into the pocket of his suede top, emerging with a neat, brown sheet.

Half past one in the morning - a sodden March night. Only a blue light from the Chinese guy's yard – situated at the end of the road - illuminated the drab housing. The Chinaman had been unemployed for seven years, and recently decided to reinvent himself by performing yoga exercises through the night. Floyd often peered through his window on his way home from a rave, wondering if he would take up a mad hobby after seven years of G-cheques.

The humming of the sparse traffic mingled with the pitter-patter of rain as Floyd trudged down the street, feeling the chill despite his two pullovers and bobble hat. "I'm seriously cold, man," he whined to Brenton. "Makes you wonder why our parents come to this damned land. We should've waited for a better night. It's freezing! My bottom lip feels like someone put that hardening glue on it, 'cos it's all stiff-like. My bone has shrunk underneath my seedbags, and my nose feels like it's got a friggin tiny fridge in it, used by dem small insects that scientists can only see tru dem serious microscope . . . we might have to make two or three trips."

"Well, if you step it up, we might get it done. So stop complaining and move your backside."

Workmen had begun building a small housing estate at the end of the road where Floyd and Brenton lived, but as yet, they had only completed the excavations and foundations. On an idle afternoon, Floyd had noted a delivery of plywood and chipboard sheets - ideal materials for any serious sound bwai with ambition. Sensing an opportunity to supplement his Giro, he quickly got the word out to all prospective sound-system builders, and Spinner, being a man who would pay the retail price for clothes, but not for wood, expressed an interest.

The two brethren reached the site, where they were confronted by a wire-meshed fence of about seven-foot high. This presented no serious worries to the raiding pair as they used their agility to leap and somersault over it. Having experience of working on building sites, Brenton had wisely sheathed on his army-like boots. In contrast, Floyd was doing his best to dodge the numerous puddles and muddy areas in a pair of lightweight training shoes.

Floyd sighted a sheet of transparent plastic covering near a hut and slip-slided his way over to it. "Brenton. Yo, Brenton! See it der."

The two plunderers didn't waste any time. Within seconds, they carried two eight foot by four foot sheets of board to rest on the fence. Then they went back for more, piling the wood against the whimpering wire-mesh.

Brenton leaped over to the other side of the fence and as Floyd pushed the swagger up, Brenton guided it over onto his side.

Looking back at the huts, Floyd suggested, "Hey, shall we bust open one of them huts? You never know what's inside. Might find some of dem power tools. Check it out, you could sell dem when you go to work to dem other builder man, innit. Or sell dem to Biscuit. You know so he buys anyt'ing. The udder day he bought a friggin tea-maker," Floyd sniggered. "Who is gonna buy dat off him? Apart from his mudder."

"Look, man, I don't wanna spend more time here than I need to, right? So just dally."

The damp weather forced the marauders to work quickly. They soon had the first two sheets of wood stacked in the hostel's back yard, and from then on, only a couple of troublesome motorists impeded their progress, causing them to place the wood flat on the pavement and hide behind parked cars. As for the limb-stretching Oriental, whose silhouette animated grotesquely behind a curtain, they simply ignored him.

They made three trips in all, and by 2:45 am were back in the warmth and safety of their rooms, rewarding themselves for a job well done by hoovering a generous spliff each. Spinner would call in next morning at seven o'clock to pick up the goods and sign the invoices.

Although very tired, Brenton could not sleep, nor even wanted to - Juliet gate-crashed his mind. Looking forward to next Friday evening, when they had arranged to meet, he had exciting visions of embracing her and scissoring her hair . . . His eyes closed as he tried to recapture the moment when he had kissed Juliet for the first time. He felt a strange loneliness in his bed as he bade laters to Mr Dean and drifted off to sleep, hoping for a sweet dream.

CHAPTER SEVENTEEN
Major Worries

A s Brenton lay curled up in bed, fast asleep and dreaming of all things pleasant, Juliet writhed sleepily in her own bed, under attack from morality questions that trampled her conscience. She hated herself for longing to be at Brenton's side.

Her mind was like a battleground, with one side fighting for rampant desire, and the other for what was right. Passion easily won the day.

Seven o'clock in the morning.

Ms Massey had made a pot of tea. Wrapped in her dressing gown, she slowly climbed the stairs to wake her daughter, tapping on the door twice before entering. Before she could say, "Rise and shine, it's seven o'clock," she saw that Juliet was already sitting in front of the mirror on the dressing table, tending to her hair. "Seh how long since you get up?" Cynthia asked, surprised.

"Oh, about half an hour. Couldn't sleep last night."

Cynthia studied her daughter in the way mothers do. "You must be worrying about somet'ing," she remarked sagely. "Anyway, on your way from work, I want you to buy a few t'ings in Brixton Market. You know, yams an' green banana an' breadfruit."

Juliet decorated her face with make-up. "Yes, Mum."

"You sure everyt'ing is all right, mi love?"

"Yes, Mum, I'm just a bit tired."

On the Tube train travelling to work, Juliet aimlessly stared out the window as the crisis about her brother resurfaced from her mind. "There are more questions than answers," her mother used to sing while cooking the Sunday dinner. If she only knew the truth, Juliet would never hear her cheerful voice again, she thought with a shudder.

Once she arrived at work, she was able to concentrate on her duties, leaving her no time to ponder on her personal problems. She talked on the phone to clients, filled in many forms, made phone calls to find out if potential clients were credit-worthy, and she danced her fingers on a typewriter and video data unit. Beside from her chores she fended off the amorous looks and chat-up lines from a few males who worked in the establishment.

Most of the guys she worked with were harmless, she thought, but one or two made her feel very uncomfortable by undressing her with their eyes. What's wrong with married men? Ain't they ever satisfied? she asked herself.

The women at work always seemed to be gossiping about who was allegedly screwing who within the company, and Juliet found that boring, but she got on well with a white girl who lived in the Elephant and Castle. Her name was Tessa, and Juliet found her working class wit very amusing. An attractive brunette with a man-look-over-his-shoulder figure, Tessa could stop the work on many building sites if she sauntered by - especially as she loved to dress in short tight skirts.

This Monday morning, the two colleagues went to a nearby McDonald's for lunch. Tessa got ready to murder a Big Mac. "Steve's a perve, I'm telling you," she said earnestly. "Every time I talk to the bloke, he gawps at my breasts. Anyone would think he'd never seen a pair of boobs before. I mean, what did he suck on when he was a nipper? He can't keep his bloody eyes off 'em. He gives me the bleedin' creeps. I've got a good mind to tell Baldie my boss. Only thing is, I caught *him* staring at me an' all! Christ, they're all bloody perves at that place. They should be castrated."

Juliet sniggered, although her friend was trying to be serious, and she nearly choked on her fries when Tessa added, "How old is Baldie, anyway? Only twenty-eight, ain't he? And he ain't got no bloody hair. I've been here for nearly three years and Baldie's never had any hair. He looks like one of them far-off planets, the poor bastard. We should call him Pluto."

Still laughing, Juliet tried to defend Baldie. "He's all right, though. He treats me OK, and he is fair and can take a joke. He puts up with a lot, with everybody taking the piss out of his head."

Tessa scoffed her burger, looking towards the counter, where customers were lining up to buy their lunch. "That guy behind the counter, he's a bit of all right, ain't he? Wouldn't mind his eyeing me up. Trouble is, the men you don't want to ogle you, do, and the guys you want to notice you, don't. I mean, why do I attract all the poxy low-lifes? It's not bloody fair."

Juliet could do nothing but giggle. "What happened to that guy, Whatsisname? You introduced him to me after work a few weeks ago. He was all right - not bad-looking for a white guy."

"Bloody cheek! Malcolm is much better looking than the bloke you was hanging about with before Christmas. What's his name? Oh yeah, Garnet - Mr Male Model who wears crocodile shoes and a Lee bleedin' Van Cleef hat. He looks like a cross between John Wayne and Shaft. He was so vain, weren't he, with that silly John Travolta walk and imitation silk shirts. I'm surprised he didn't have a vanity case in his pocket. He's another one I caught staring at my breasts. He was the one who had speaker boxes the size of my nan's four-poster bed, wasn't he?"

Juliet found it difficult to locate her mouth as her friend was making her laugh too much.

"Yeah, Malcolm was OK," Tessa said reminiscently, "but he was an idiot as well though, a bloody moron. I'll tell you something about Malcolm, shall I? He would rather get up on a cold Sunday morning, leave my bed and pay one pound to play football in some stupid park. And what's more, he expected *me* to watch! The guy's sex-drive is all in his feet. I mean, what's wrong with me? I used to think I frightened him off because I can be demanding, if you know what I mean. But football, effing football."

Tessa was good therapy for Juliet. She could always be relied upon to bring a smile to her face. Even so, the lunch-break was only light relief, for Brenton was ever present at the back of her thoughts.

The two work mates high-heeled reluctantly back to the bank, knowing the sexist comments would be a little easier to cope with if they stayed in each other's company.

It was 3:30 in the afternoon and across London on a building site, saucy remarks were shouted at passing women. Hammers tapped away like lead-filled drops of water falling into a sink. Bricklayers chipped their bricks with the same sound effects as popular late-night Kung Fu movies. Foremen and charge-hands were trying unsuccessfully to make themselves heard over the hum of a busy crane. Now and again, a couple of men dressed in shirt and tie and crowned by yellow safety helmets, went by clutching rolls of sketches and drawings, which seemed too large to analyse.

A young man walked gingerly away from the building site, holding his back with his right hand and stooping slightly. A black woollen hat covered his head, specked with cement mix. The size of his crusty frame was enhanced by the black, padded donkey jacket he was wearing, and along the pavement in his wake, he left a trail of gooey cement, dribbling off his army-type boots.

Cursing his luck, Brenton asked himself how he could take his sister out now that he'd hurt his back. He struggled his way to the bus stop, grim faced. A few aches passed before a number 36 heading for Camberwell pulled up. He took a seat on the lower deck, something he did very rarely.

After he disembarked near his home, he Long-John-Silvered to a chemist's shop to buy a relief spray for aches and pains in the muscles. Reaching the hostel, he climbed the stairs to his room, where he delicately took off his donkey jacket and thick woollen pullover. He applied the spray to the damaged area, wondering when he would derive relief, but only sensed a numbing coldness. Carefully, he laid on his bed, hoping for the pain to fuck off and leave him alone. Glancing at Mr Dean, he thought to himself that he might as well be in discomfort somewhere he would be looked after - his mother's home.

He faltered down the stairs, hoping that Mr Lewis would be in, but a couple of unanswered slaps on the man's office door prompted the thought that Lewis was probably attending a social-wanker meeting. Time for plan B - struggle down the road to the phone box, and pray that it hadn't been vandalised.

Following a change of clothes, Brenton hobbled carefully to the red phone box. To his surprise, it was in working order, although there were hammer marks on the metal box where the coins dropped.

Brenton dialled 100 for the operator, explaining to her very politely that had pushed his coin in the slot, but lost the call due to a faulty mechanism. The operator asked him for the number he wanted to dial, and he gave her his mother's. The operator then connected him through. Although he was now earning a wage, the crafty habits he had caught off Floyd were hard to cure.

Fortunately Ms Massey was at home having a day off; she was delighted to hear that her son was going to pay her a visit. Concerned about his bad back, she advised him to call a cab to travel to her home - Brenton had been hoping his mother would make this offer.

Sitting in her kitchen, opposite Cynthia, sipping a hot mug of tea, Brenton appeared thoughtful.

"How did Lewis find you?" he asked her suddenly.

"Apparently, it was quite easy for him. The social services 'ad files on you when you were very young. Before you was born, I 'ad to fill in ah whole 'eap of forms, y'know. Dem ask questions like, who is your doctor? Your address, next of kin. Dat kind of t'ing."

Although he was listening, Brenton looked blank, trying to give the impression that his mother's explanation wasn't important.

"In fact, even though I did move around ah liccle in the early days, I always 'ad the same doctor since I was pregnant wid you, y'understand? So anyway, a while ago I had a call from my doctor an' him tell me that a man from social services of Lambet' wanted to talk to me urgently. I knew it was about you, so at first I tried to ignore it, 'cos I felt too much shame. But after t'inking about it for a week, I called my doctor an' tell him that I would like to make my address available for Mr Lewis of the social services. I could have called Mr Lewis directly, but I didn't want to. I don't like social workers."

Brenton stared out of the window, watching an impatient motorist reverse into a space, which seemed too small. He rubbed his temple as Cynthia continued, "It don't sound good, do it? You mus' be ashamed of me."

Brenton switched his gaze to his mother's regretful-looking countenance. Then he slowly nodded. For the first time since he'd met the woman, he pitied her. But he didn't show any signs of sympathy. Instead he sipped his tea again, wondering when the offer of food would come.

"Wid dat sick back, you better go in the front room and lie 'pon the couch an' res' up. In a short while I will bring you somet'ing to eat."

So Brenton painfully hauled himself from his chair and dragged his throbbing back to the front-room sofa.

Twenty minutes later, Ms Massey entered the room carrying a fried-egg sandwich on a plate. She noticed Brenton had taken off his pullover, exposing his T-shirt, and had made himself comfortable, lying down with eyes slightly ajar on the sofa. But what truly drew her eye was the ugly scar upon her son's neck. "I will cook dinner later," she told him, "but 'ave dis snack for the time being."

Brenton sat up painfully and received the offering as Cynthia felt compelled to comment about the wound. "Brenton, do you mind if I ask you how you got that scar 'pon your neck?"

Brenton alligatored the sandwich before answering. "Some bad man did stab me. I don't want to go into it, but these things happen when you're on your own. I was lucky to live, so the doctor told me. But I survived and I'm here. If there's one thing I am good at, it's surviving." The image of the loathsome Terry Flynn hurtled into his mind. You will pay for this, he promised inwardly.

Ms Massey settled into the armchair opposite her son and gave him a lingering, caring look. Brenton glanced at his mother and finished his sandwich.

"You know, your fader got into fights because he went out wid me," Cynthia confided. "I remember one of his best friends got drunk-up one night, an' started calling him a nigger lover. Gary 'ad a very bad temper, an' I screamed when the two of dem clashed."

His interest caught, Brenton listened avidly.

"We 'ad to be very careful where we did go if we wanted to go out somewhere nice," Cynthia went on. "Sometimes we would jus' walk an' talk inna park, y'know. Gary used to like nature an' was always talking about driving to the country for the weekend. One of me best memories was your fader taking me to Kew Gardens. It was such a beautiful day - all the plants, flowers and t'ing look so nice. Your fader did want to take me to the bes' clubs, but it was too dangerous. Even if we went to a black person party or drink-up, people would pass dem comments."

Brenton thought of his adopted bench in Brockwell Park.

"When I look back," Ms Massey said thoughtfully, "I 'ave to say your fader was a very brave man."

"He wasn't brave enough to look after me though, was he?"

Cynthia watched her son try and get himself comfortable on the sofa once more. A few Gary reminiscences later, she departed.

Time passed and Brenton fell into a heavy slumber. At a quarter to seven in the evening, the front door closing awoke him and in walked Juliet, both hands clutching bags full of shopping. She was surprised to see her brother there, snug on the settee.

"Make yourself at home, won't you?" she joked.

Brenton was really pleased to see her but, as so often of late, his mind suddenly decided to rewind to an incident from the past.

Sitting on his metal-framed bed, the seven-year-old Brenton was confronted by The Belt. In her loud shrieking voice, she laid down the law to the child entrusted to her care.

"You, my boy, are going to school. I don't want to hear any more lies about hurting your back while getting in the coal last night. No excuses, you're going with the others. Or else I'll give you what for."

The speed at which Brenton's mind recalled an event from his childhood was the same that flashed him back to the present. He focused his eyes on his sister, thinking about that day of forbidden passion.

"I was mixing cement and I felt this wicked pain in my back," he explained, "so I'm here, getting some tender loving care. Know what I mean?"

With a somewhat embarrassed look, Juliet grabbed the shopping bags again and made haste to the kitchen.

Brenton stayed at his family home for a couple more hours. His mother did offer to prepare the spare room and bed, but he felt awkward staying the night, especially with Juliet in the adjoining room. So he declined her invitation and caught a cab back to his hostel. During the journey, he thought about his mother and her sad despondent face. It was apparent to him that she was still burdened by a heavy sack of coal, and perhaps always would be. Maybe her suffering of guilt would only become worse, now he had dramatically reappeared on the scene.

Reaching home, Brenton shuffled up the stairs and thought to himself he could do with some entertaining chat with Floyd. But there was no answer coming from the other side of the door and no sound of a suitcase.

Floyd was over at Sharon's home, trying to charm her into introducing her pelvis to his. There were together in Sharon's bedroom, which as far as Floyd could see, was an open invitation to a long-awaited taste of nourishing steak. Maybe it was a bit naive of Sharon to have invited him up there, but Floyd's face was a study of determination.

"Look, your mum's out doing her nightshift, your sister has gone and taken the pickney to see your paps for a few days - the pickney will probably end up sucking a bottle of brew - and I'm in your bedroom. So from here, we're suppose to sort of get all romantic Hollywood and t'ing. But you wanna talk about the social conditions of second-generation blacks in England. I don't friggin believe it!"

Sharon was giggling on her bed, enjoying the tease of her man, knowing what he wanted and deriving pleasure from making him wait. "You guys are all the same, just wanna get inside a woman's knickers. Then you tell all your spars you boned so and so, so your brethrens can look up to you. Well Floyd, I ain't so easy, know what I mean? I want nuff respect. When's the last time you took me out?"

Floyd sat down, joining his girlfriend on the bed. "What are you saying, man? I took you out just the other day. You ain't got nutten to complain about."

As he completed his sentence, Sharon took a swipe with her right fist, aimed at her guy's shoulder. She connected and sent him sprawling to the floor. "You facety shit! It was my friend's party! I took you out - and me and Carol paid the cab fare. I'm talking about you taking me out for dinner or a club or something."

Looking at a loss, as if he was selling a gold chain, but a customer discovered the chain was made out of plastic, Floyd rejoined his girlfriend. "You know I haven't got no corn, man. I'm unemployed. If I had a job and t'ing, I would take you out, yes. Believe me, if I had a wad I would take you to dem club where only man with chauffeur driver go and where the bouncers wear dem bow tie. It seems you want a man for his corn. You're not a shine eye gal, are you? Well, I'm just a loving pauper."

The arm that had just sent him rolling off the bed was now

wrapping around his shoulders. The catty grin swabbed off her face, Sharon appeared becalmed. "Look, t'ings will work out, man. I like you a lot 'cos you make me laugh. But I don't want you to treat me like a leggo-beast, you know what I'm saying? Look what happened to my little sister. I don't want the same t'ing happening to me, you understand?"

Floyd put his arm around his woman's shoulders and kissed her gently on the eyebrows. "Can I stay the night? Please? I'll do anything you say - even wash your baggy and clean out the dirt in your toes and scratch any itch in your headtop."

Sharon deliberated for a while, then she stared her man straight in the eye. "All right, then. But you have to be gone by six in the morning. My mum usually comes back from work about seven, so you better chip before then."

Floyd's dial lit up, like a pensioner who just called house. Sharon resumed, "I want you to promise me somet'ing."

"What's that?"

"Promise you won't get involved in this Brenton, Terry Flynn war."

"Me get involved? Me! I wanna keep my pretty boat, innit."

"Good, 'cos I don't want to see you in no hospital."

"Just cool. I've been telling Brenton it's best to forget the past 'cos otherwise it will only end when one of dem is dead."

"One more t'ing," Sharon said. "Er, you have protection seen?"

From a picture of content, Floyd's features turned to a look of grief. "Er, no. Er, I didn't think. Oh frig my living days."

Sharon abruptly took her arm off her man, stood up and proceeded to cuss loudly. "I don't believe you sometimes! You ask to stay the night and you don't even bring nutten to protect me! You've got a nerve, man - especially as you know about my sister!"

Floyd tried to defend himself and now wished he possessed the courage to walk into the local chemist's shop and buy a packet of dick macs. "Just cool, man. Calm down, don't bust no cheek or jawbone. To be honest, it wouldn't have looked all that good if me and you were chatting and all of a sudden, I pulled out a mac. You would have checked me weird if I'd said, 'Can we go to bed now?' You would've kuffed me harder than you just did."

Considering, 'shall I kill him?' she finally found the funny side of the matter and embraced the relieved-looking Floyd. The couple collapsed on the bed, laughing and kissing, but in between the giggles and kisses, Sharon whispered in her man's ear, "You can stay the night, but er, you can't go all the way, y'understand? Besides, there are other ways of doing t'ings, you know."

Floyd was more than happy to accept this, but wondered how his bone would behave itself throughout the night.

The following morning, Brenton was in his kitchen, devouring a bowlful of cornflakes. He had risen late and had no intention of going to work. His back was still proving troublesome, although not as bad as the day before.

Mr Lewis plodded in from his room. "Aren't you going to work today, Brenton? I hope you have phoned your foreman to tell him you will not be in."

"I hurt my back yesterday morning, mixing cement. The boss man already knows I'll be off for a couple of days."

Mr Lewis ran his eyes over the kitchen, checking to see if the dishcloths he had bought were being employed. There were the usual mugs, plates and saucers left unwashed in the sink, but otherwise, everything was in order, probably because the inhabitants of the hostel couldn't be bothered to cook.

"How is the job going? Learning much, are you?"

Brenton shrugged his shoulders. "Well, it's all right I suppose, but there is little time for training. Everything is rush rush. Things have to be done quickly, and everyone has to work fast to get their bonuses. So there is little time for them carpenter man to show me t'ings every day. For most of the time I'm usually mixing cement, making tea, hod-carrying bricks and making more bloody tea, know what I mean? When I'm not too busy, I just watch them skilled man and see how they do t'ings. But it's all right, the guys there don't treat me too bad."

The social worker appeared rather proud as he listened to his charge talk about his job. He recalled how just a few months ago, he couldn't hold a proper conversation with him. Now he was working and had found his family. Mr Lewis felt Brenton was a self-improved young man, and he himself enjoyed a feeling of achievement - maybe his job was worthwhile after all. His superiors had misgivings about the experiment of a hostel for kids out of care, but Mr Lewis had convinced them it would work.

"How is your relationship with your mother?"

"Is there something about social workers? That when they become one, they can't stop asking questions?"

Mr Lewis flashed a rare smile, causing him to readjust his glasses, realising he must have come over like some sort of interrogator. With that thought, he turned around and slothed back to his room.

Brenton placed his cereal bowl in the sink and stepped up the stairs, wondering what he would do for the rest of the day. As he entered his room, he wished his living quarters could miraculously be put in order. Recently washed, unironed clothes spilled out of a wailing laundry bag, and cassette tapes littered the floor, mixed with an assortment of underwear. Brenton simply ignored the mess and carefully laid down on the bed; if anyone were to ask about the state of his room, he could always give the excuse of his bad back.

As he relaxed and fantasised about what it would be like to crub with the Sister Sledge soul group, Floyd barged his way in.

"Knock, knock, please come in."

A wolfish grin buttered over Floyd's face; he was obviously dying to speak of his manly deeds the night just gone.

"Sorry, but I see you come up, so I thought you wouldn't mind 'cos it's me. Anyway, I got my t'ings last night, you know what I'm saying? Yeah, I finally christened her in every which way possible. I was at Sharon's yard the whole of last night. I only reach home just before seven."

Brenton remained lying on his bed, with his hands supporting his head to make it slightly tilted. He gazed upon Floyd in doubt, scratching behind his right ear. Floyd sensed this.

"Yeah, man. She's a tasty steak, she don't hold back, man. I kind of felt awkward at first 'cos I was in her yard, but she practically seduced me. You know, these gal are all the same. They go on like they don't want it, but really, they're as peckish as us, you know what I mean?"

Brenton knew if Floyd told a tale, it would be grossly over-hyped. "Well, you've wanted to bone Sharon from time. Usually, after you get what you want, you leave them. You going to leave Sharon?"

Wondering why his spar didn't share his elation of his service to womanhood last night, Floyd sat on the bed, feeling boxed by the question. "I dunno, she's all right. She ain't stupid like other gal I know."

"She must be, to go to bed with you."

"Very funny."

"So this is a serious t'ing then?"

"Could be, could be. But I wanna know if she can cook."

"When's the last time you was interested in any gal for her cooking?"

"Well, Sharon's passed the sex test, now she has to pass the cook test for me to t'ink 'bout settling down wid her."

"But can *you* cook though?"

"Yeah, man. Don't I cook corned beef an' rice when we run out of money for take-away?"

Floyd's headlights scanned the room for any signs of a cancer stick, but he couldn't see any. Brenton decided to sit up, and felt a twinge in his lower back as he erected himself. "I'm surprised you don't have back trouble," he quipped, "the amount of boning you do."

This brought a proud grin from Floyd, who revelled in his steak-tasting rep, but felt his hostel-mate was missing out on all the juicy flavours. "Hey, Sharon's friend Carol likes you, why don't you deal wid her? She needs a service. I'll set you up, man. You know she's fit badly. So I reckon if you checked it out, you won't get no blank, you know what I'm saying?"

"She's all right, quite fit and t'ing, but she's too long. I think the gal is taller then me. Nah, I will feel weird going out with a gal who's taller than me."

"What's height got to do with it? She ain't that tall anyway. Think about the seriously shaped legback around your V, man. Biscuit, Finnley, Lizard and Coffin Head are all asking me to set dem up with the gal, but Carol's only interested in you. You must admit, her body's gone clear."

Brenton remained silent as Floyd glanced up to the ceiling and kissed his teeth. Laying back down on his bed, Brenton changed the topic. "I'm tired, man, and my back is paining me."

The would-be matchmaker received the hint and stood up. "Look, if you're interested, I'm going with Sharon and Carol to Bali Hai tonight. TWJ play their soul session on a Friday night there. So we're gonna freak out and do what dem weird soulheads do. I'll be leaving about nine to pick dem up, seen. So be ready by then if you want to go."

After checking to see if Brenton's face was showing any interest in his proposal, Floyd left the room, hoping the next spar he talked to would show more enthusiasm for his steak-tasting last night. Biscuit would get some serious red-eye.

Despite the nagging twinge in his lower back, Brenton found himself drifting off to sleep. Wondering why Floyd had asked him to go raving when he knew about his bad back. He wanted to listen to his selection of music, but couldn't be bothered to get up and turn on his suitcase.

Ten o'clock that night, Brenton had just returned from the fish and chip shop; he noticed that Floyd had already left for his soul rave. Sitting on his bed, he was gulping down the last bit of pie when he heard an impatient knocking on the front door. Thinking it was one of Floyd's spars; Brenton pushed a few hot chips into his mouth and then struggled down the stairs. He opened the front door and was greeted by the beautiful figure of his sister. Surprised to see her, he counted his untold blessings.

"Will you let me in then?" she asked. "You want me to stand outside here and catch my death?"

Brenton ushered his sister inside and appreciatively watched her walk into the hallway and up the stairs. Then he glanced towards the kitchen and Mr Lewis's door, hoping that no one was about - there wasn't. So with lusty adrenaline gorging through his veins, he climbed slowly up the stairs to his room, where he found his sister doing her best to make the place tidy. "I was gonna do that before I went to my bed."

"Yeah, sure. And I'm going to be believe that Blair Peach was not killed by the beast. Can't you keep your place tidy? It's only one room. Won't take for ever, you know."

As she talked, she attempted to find matching socks so she could roll them together. Her brother sat down on his bed, feeling a sting of embarrassment. "I've got a bad back, you know," he muttered. "I can't bend down too far."

Juliet kissed her teeth as she picked up all the cassette tapes off the floor and placed them in a neat pile on the dressing table. "My mum always says that men can't take pain. Us women can tolerate more pain than men can, you know. That's why God made us the ones to get pregnant, 'cos men can't take the pain of giving birth."

Brenton looked upon his sister in disbelief. "Rubbish! How can you say that? No, man, that's fuckries."

Juliet gave her brother a shove, which made him lose his balance and nearly drop to the floor. "Don't say I talk fuckries."

Brenton grimaced with pain, clutching his lower back.

"What did you do that for? I've got a bad back and you're making it worse."

"Ahh, does it hurt? I'll bawl for you. See what I mean about men can't take pain?"

Brenton's expression of pain changed to one of meek enquiry. "Somehow, I get the vibe you've come around here tonight to take the piss out of my back."

Juliet laughed heartily, causing her brother to raise a smile; it felt good to see his sister in such buoyant mood. Meanwhile, Juliet hung her coat in the wardrobe. She then sat on the bed and noticed her brother staring at Mr Dean, wondering why one simple portrait of a young, good-looking man, clad in leather jacket and white T-shirt, could have so much meaning to someone like Brenton. "He only made three films, innit, then he died in a car crash," she said softly. "Sad, innit, so young."

"Yeah . . . Ain't you going out with your friends raving tonight? To a club or something?"

"No, I just thought I would come up and see how you were. Haven't got any objections, have you?"

"No, of course bloody not. I always like to see you, you know the vibe."

Juliet reached out to her handbag and took a cassette from it. "I thought I'd bring my own tape 'cos most of yours are pure jumpers music. You've only got one decent tape. Anyway, this one's got Roberta Flack on it."

Brenton looked mystified. "Who's he?"

Juliet tried hard not to laugh. "Roberta Flack is a she. You haven't heard of her? Where've you been, man?"

"Her name rings a bell," he said unconvincingly.

Juliet laughed and then proceeded to sing the first few lines of *Killing Me Softly*. Her brother recognised the song and wasted no time telling his sister, "Oh shit, I know that. Yeah. But the way you sing it, you make the record sound bad."

Juliet retaliated by picking up one of the pillows and swinging it at him, connecting her brother on the head.

"You're too facety."

"Hey, watch my back, man. That's twice now you've kuffed me. Bwai, it seem like you want me to friend-up a wheelchair."

"You and your bloody back, you're like an old woman . . . Hey, I tell you what, lie down on your stomach and I'll give you a massage."

"A what?"

"A massage. You know, relax the muscles and t'ing."

"You ain't touching my back."

One lingering look at Juliet, who was sporting her most sexy smile and Brenton knew he couldn't resist. So he stretched out along the bed without hesitation, flat on his stomach, then his sister sat astride him, hitching up her skirt, exposing her toned thighs. She gently rubbed his crusty shoulders and cupped her palms around the back of his neck. Then she used her thumbs to penetrate deep into her brother's upper back, using a downward motion that teased him ferociously. Brenton felt Juliet pulsating in rhythm with her hands, and his cravings went into over-drive at the prospect of what was to come.

The massage turned into a caress, as Juliet's digits walked inside her lover's T-shirt and string vest. I'm gonna make him want me so much, she said to herself. His eyes closed, he savoured every moment of this so-called massage, enjoying the warmth of her soft palms exploring his yielding back. Bone-wakened, he turned around, wanting to kiss and embrace his masseuse, but as soon as he did so, Juliet sprang up. "Wait, the tape!"

Brenton soon realised that Juliet had planned the evening's proceedings.

She inserted her Roberta Flack tape in the suitcase, then spun around to face her impatient-looking brother. "Not complaining about your bad back now, are you?"

Her hand reached out to switch off the light, and then she felt her way back onto the bed, where Brenton was vulturing to embrace her. He considered kissing her Hollywood-style, but decided instead to yank off her pullover, exposing her firm, round breasts. Juliet knew he wanted her and Brenton couldn't wait to feel the warm flesh of her body against his naked skin. She hurriedly sought out his heaving chest and sketched around his nipples. His hands tremored as he cupped her breasts, feeling her heartbeat as he proceeded to gently knead them. Juliet moaned, half-closing her eyes, and groped for the zip in his denims. She zipped him half-open and paused. Brenton was trembling like an eighteen-inch bass speaker. This feels so good, he thought breathlessly.

She pulled the zipper down as quick as a guillotine, then they undressed each other in a frenzy, kissing as they did so, longing to see each other fully naked.

Two I-love-you's later, they tangled naked together. During their intense lovemaking, the couple felt comfortable enough to gaze into each other's eyes longingly, without any embarrassment. Brenton had never felt so much joyous emotion. He prisoned his eyes, thinking it must be a dream, only to free them and set his gaze on Juliet's glistening body. He marvelled at her nakedness. He couldn't hold her tightly enough to his body and his partner sensed the power of his arms holding her and the pent-up emotion releasing itself from his perspiring body. She pleasured in his strapping body bearing down upon her, and watched the sweat dripping off his ecstatic face. She orienteered with her hands all over his muscular backside and could feel the cries of her own body, wanting to be stroked all over. Brenton couldn't wait any longer as he relished the sensation of Juliet's moist lips pecking his chest.

As he entered her, their faces ironed against each other. Juliet, wondering if God had designed Brenton just for her pleasure, knotted her lithe legs around his thrusting back, urging him into a frenzied exhilaration. He could feel her polished nails pincering his back as the couple gummed to each other, as if they wanted to make themselves as one.

Twice more they made love during the night before Brenton,

feeling only a slight twinge in his back, fell asleep blissfully happy.

Juliet noticed her brother's strange snoring sound and wondered how many times she would listen to it. She gently snuggled up to him, placing her hand on his shoulder and coching her head on his well-constructed chest. She listened to his heartbeat and lay there, open-eyed, tuning into her brother's breathing pattern. She looked at the scar on his neck, thinking to herself, My hero. Exploring his face, she raised her head and examined the thin hairs above his upper lip, forming an immature moustache. Still not quite a man, she thought.

Then doubts bombarded her mind. After all, she was lying in bed with her half-brother. Mum would go absolutely spare, she thought. Desires of her flesh had once more triumphed in battle, and only something brave could halt the march of lust and its allies before they destroyed everything.

CHAPTER EIGHTEEN

Midnight Ravers

The following Saturday night

O n Capital Radio, the ten o'clock news had just reported the concern community leaders in the inner city felt about relations between the police and young blacks, and particularly the suss law. Floyd had heard the vexed rhetoric of the ghetto press, and smelt the aroma of uprising and revolution in the Brixton air. Placing his thoughts at the back of his mind, he prepared to listen to David Rodigan, who was about to introduce his reggae programme.

It was some sort of ritual on a Saturday night for untold reggae heads to listen to David Rodigan's selection for a couple of hours, then head out to a party or a club, or in Floyd's case on this particular night, a blues dance.

Earlier in the afternoon, Floyd had purchased a small black and white television off Biscuit for twenty notes, negotiating the asking price of thirty notes.

The volume of the television was turned down as Floyd lay flat on his back, hands clasped behind his head, watching the football while listening to reggae at the same time.

Dressed only in his black corduroy trousers and black string vest, he was very conscious of the time. For him, it was trodding too slowly. Impatiently, he willed it forward to ten past twelve. By then, he would be on his way to the blues dance where he looked forward to what he thought would be a serious crubbing session.

The sound system, I Spy, was spinning the lovers rock, and they boasted a sizeable female following.

Hanging from the plain brown wardrobe were Floyd's gal-hunting clothes, which consisted of a pair of blue slacks and a blue-black-flowered imitation silk shirt. He knew it would be steamy in the blues, so he planned on wearing a cardigan instead of a pullover. He had been going to ask Brenton to trod with him to the blues, but he felt his spar was acting strange of late, so he didn't bother. Anyway, Brenton wasn't the best company someone could have at a blues dance. All he did was coch against the wall and inspect the crowd. And as for Biscuit, he and Finnley were on a secret gal-hunting mission up Hackney.

Floyd pondered on why Brenton shaped away from chatting and crubbing with girls, and why his brethren was not interested in Carol, who with the slightest persuasion would wide out her legbacks for him. She was criss: Floyd pictured her long elegant body and wondered why any man would reject her. Biscuit was forever asking to be set up, and perpetually asked Sharon where Carol lived, but didn't like the repeated reply of 'SW9'.

Match of the Day concluded. Floyd punched through the channels to check if there was anything else worth watching - apparently not. So without further ado, he switched the television off while kissing his teeth, and laid back down on his bed feeling impatient. But Ram Jam Rodigan made the waiting easier to bear, playing selections from Black Uhuru, Eeek-A-Mouse and the upcoming superstar of Jamaica, Johnny Osbourne.

Fourteen Rodigan selections and a news update later, he strutted to the bus stop, hoping the last bus hadn't gone earlier than scheduled. His shoes were discomforting him as the rims of his leathers almost crocodiled his ankles. But nothing could dampen his optimism for the night ahead.

It was mild for the time of year and Floyd could get away with wearing only a thin blue cardigan over his shirt. As he turned into the High Street, he noticed a contrast in cultures. While many white guys and girls were apparently making their way home, perhaps from a pub or restaurant, here was Floyd and hundreds of other reggae heads all over London, just heading out to their Saturday night, Sunday morning entertainment.

Floyd watched a middle-aged man on the other side of the road, the worse for drink. Pedestrians kept their distance from the colic, as he attempted to place one unsure foot in front of the other.

A trio of young teenage blacks appeared in the distance, trooping in a hurry, as if they were three expectant fathers-to-be, rushing to the hospital. Dressed in jeans and trainers and all of them sporting black berets, Floyd recognised them as members of the newly founded branch of the Black Panthers, based in Brixton. They seemed to have sprung up after the death of Blair Peach, who was allegedly killed by the police on an anti-Nazi march. They preached in secluded corners of Brixton, telling whoever would listen that black people should use arms to protect themselves from the truncheon-happy pigs. Floyd knew the Black Panthers had a small following, but the influence they spread, mixed with the lyrical content of music winging in from Jamaica, bred a feeling of unease and revolt.

Floyd hawked the trio. "All right?"

"Yes boss," one of the teenagers answered, turning around to cautiously examine Floyd. "Cowley estate, tomorrow," another teenager announced. "Reach if you can. Brothers coming in from America to talk to the ghetto yout's. Too muck fockin Babylon man killing our people - so you must reach, and tell your brethrens - Cowley estate, on the green behind the flats."

After this brief exchange, the threesome stepped on their way, with their bodies almost forming silhouettes as they disappeared into the deepening night.

A number 45 finally arrived, soprano-ing to a halt and surprising for this time of night, full of passengers. Receiving his ticket, Floyd sensed the driver was not at ease working at this hour, probably due to the spate of attacks on bus drivers in the area.

As there wasn't much traffic on the road, Floyd reached his destination ten minutes after boarding the bus. He bounded off it and strutted towards the council estate where the blues was being held.

A Cortina mark 2 sped past him with a black youth's head protruding out the window, sneering at the stepping Floyd. "Trodder!"

Floyd glanced up to see the car accelerate into the distance, thinking to himself he would have his own motor one day.

Minutes later, he entered the council estate where the blues dance was being hosted, locating it by following the faint sounds of reggae music.

This was a typical inner-city estate. Brand new cars could be found alongside old, crippled cars. Rubbish chutes were overflowing, reminding Floyd of a bigger version of his overfilled ashtray at home, and he checked the familiar sight of plywood sheets blocking up the doorways and windows of vacant flats. Black teenagers often tore down the plywood and used it to build themselves speaker boxes.

The children's play area, in the forecourt of the estate, had been well vandalised. Even though pets were banned from most council estates, a pack of stray dogs roamed near the large circular rubbish bins, in search of a meal their owners could not afford.

Now the music could be heard clearly. Floyd trotted up the steps of one of the blocks only to find, as usual, that the lift was out of order. This wasn't as frustrating as it might have seemed, because he thought the damn t'ing would reek of piss-water anyway.

He reached the floor of the blues dance to be greeted by a mass of rave-goers all herding around the front door. The doorman was having an argument with a guy who apparently didn't want to pay his tax to get inside.

"I know the girl who is having the dance, man! I ain't paying no rarse pound! Go call her, man," roared the vexed punter, trying to gain admission.

"Sorry, me can't do that, man. No freeness, no squeeze fe anybody. Pound fe come in," ordered the doorman sternly.

This exchange of lyrics was holding up blues ravers who were prepared to pay their tax - Floyd included. In consequence, there was a lot of pushing and jostling occurring near the front door. Other ravers, who probably couldn't tolerate the heat and stuffiness inside the flat, were peering over the balcony wall, hoovering their snouts and spliffs and watching the ash and dead matches flutter down to the concrete ground below.

The tense row at the front door eventually subsided after a compromise was reached, with the still riled guy, trying to avoid payment to the blues, paying 50p for the privilege.

Passing through, Floyd found himself in an overcrowded hallway, lit by a dim red light. He passed the kitchen, which was being used as a makeshift bar, and as he inched his way onwards, he accidentally trod on the foot of a surly-looking lager-swilling yout'. "Watch where you a go, bwai." Floyd remembered how Brenton's feud with Terry Flynn began. "Sorry, boss."

A table was parked across the kitchen doorway, with strong lagers stacked upon it, waiting to be bought. The barman was an overweight rastaman, sporting a knitted red, gold and green hat, and wearing a jacket that a commando might have fancied. "Pound fe a Special Brew or Red Stripe."

Floyd ignored the hard sell and squeezed into the room where the sound-system boys had strung up. Overhead wires, taped to the top of the doorframe, told Floyd that two rooms were being utilised for this dance.

It took him ten minutes to make his way from the front door to the middle of one of the dark rooms being employed. A torchlight, used by the DJ, was the only illumination. Now he was in the centre of the room, Floyd's next move was to go and seek a decent spot to stand where the well-shaped ladies outnumbered the sweet bwais, so as to increase his chances of riding a serious crub.

Patrice Rushen's Forget Me Nots blared out from the speakers - a soul tune, and the crowd two-stepped as if they were part of one entity as the DJ kept on yelling, "Soul break!"

Floyd took the opportunity to move closer to a few girls he spotted in the corner of the room. After another soul break he patiently sort of side-stepped and hot-stepped into prime position. Clocking around him, he couldn't resist a foxy smile to himself as he waited for the DJ to play some lovers rock.

Taking off his cardigan, Floyd held the garment by pushing his hand in his pocket, with the knitwear draping over his wrist. Trying to acquire a good posture, he shuffled his feet a few times. The bevy of girls that aroused his loins were behind him, but the crub-hungry Floyd preferred to be behind them. Fortunately, he received a lucky break when a crusty youth removed himself from his position against the wall, and obviously feeling the need for fresh air, made clumsy efforts to depart the room. Floyd was quick to slip into the position the intoxicated guy vacated.

Following three anxiously hoovered cancer sticks, Sister Love's *Every Bit of My Heart* boomed out from the speakers. Floyd reached out his spare hand and gently pulled the fit girl's wrist in front of him. She turned around and with a polite look, discreetly shook her head. Not feeling too downhearted, Floyd patiently awaited the next lovers rock record. When he heard the intro to Alpha's *Can't Get Over You*, he stretched out his hand again, extending his arm a little further as he 'pulled' another girl's wrist.

Floyd thought she wasn't as criss as the first one he'd pulled, but she was decent enough. After a lingering stare, she willingly stepped into Floyd's clinch. There was an initial confusion over the style of dance, but it was quickly sorted out as the couple settled down to rhythmical groove. Feeling confident and peckish for a tighter crub, Floyd pulled his prey until his hands could meet around her back. Record after record Floyd requested a crub with his keen partner, and the more they crubbed, the tighter the embrace became. It had now reached the stage where the girl didn't bother to rejoin her friends following the ending of a record. She just settled in her bone-tremoring partner's arms.

Thinking hard for something intelligent to say, Floyd whispered, "So, er, can't you tell me your name?"

"What?"

He tried again, this time speaking louder. "What is your name?"

"Rosene," she answered, craning her neck so her mouth could get as near as possible to Floyd's lobe.

The sound of the music was unrelenting, but the couple were determined to get to know each other as they talked and crubbed for the next hour or so. Rosene must have tickled his fancy, because on two occasions, he even struggled through the massed throng to get to the makeshift bar. He was certainly glad his partner only downed soft drinks, as his budget did not cater for any liquor, especially at the prices they were being sold at here.

At half past four in the morning, the disgruntled sweet bwais and a couple of roughnecks who failed to find a partner, loitered in the hallway or were strung out along the balcony, staring aimlessly down at the forecourt, which was now filled with badly parked cars. The two rooms were still packed though, with sweating couples practically making love, standing up in their clothes.

Floyd decided it was time to take in some badly needed air and chat with his dance partner outside. The pair weaved their way onto the balcony, where the cool night air rapidly refreshed their sweat glands down a degree or two. Rosene appeared even more criss in the light, as he studied her clear face and carefully kept permed hair. Wearing an off the shoulder, silky blue dress, she indeed looked stunning.

Floyd bided his time until they passed any would-be news reporters - he remembered how Carol caught him crubbing with Sylvia. The couple stood at the far end of the balcony, viewing the panorama from their third-floor vantage point.

"So, er, Rosene, could I see you again? You know, um, can we go out sometime?"

Rosene seemed to be revelling in the attention. Flashing him a smile, she looked at her admirer with a sexy, sideways glance, causing Floyd to feel a flock of butterflies in his stomach.

"Maybe we could, but it might be difficult, if you know what I mean. I've sort of got a man, y'know."

An expression of curiosity passed over Floyd's face. "What do you mean, 'sort of'?"

"You might know him - everyone else does."

"Why? What's his name?"

"Terry. His spars call him Terror, Terror Flynn."

Floyd's eyebrows shot up through his forehead. "Frig my living days . . . You go out with Terry Flynn?"

"He takes me out now and again - he's a brethren of my brother's. But it ain't serious, if you know what I mean. He ain't that bad when you get to know him."

Floyd began to pick imaginary dirt from his fingernails. "He ain't that bad when you get to know him! Man and man would say your judgement is crucially lacking. He's a bad man!"

Rosene crossed her arms, trying to keep warm. "Look, I said it wasn't serious. We just go out in a posse sometimes and I sort of pair off with him. He always shows respect with me - never tries to manners me or anything."

Trying to look composed and mature, Floyd slowly nodded, while Rosene thought to herself that her dance partner looked like an ant being pursued by a boiling pool of water.

I don't believe this, Floyd was thinking in a panic. Get myself a nice piece of legback for the night and she deals with a warmonger. "Let's go back inside," he said, disappointment in his voice, trying to hide his fear.

"So what? That's it?" Rosene probed, admiring Floyd's devilish looks.

"Er, we might clash again, yeah. But I just come here tonight to enjoy myself."

Rosene kissed her teeth.

"It will be too much strife for anyt'ing to happen," Floyd explained.

"In other words, you're scared of him."

"No! It's just that it would be too much hassle."

"I hardly see him these days. He's too busy selling herbs down the line."

Floyd's eyebrows arched. "He sells herbs down the line?"

"Yeah - he says he's too busy to deal wid any girl seriously."

Floyd's interest gathered pace. "So, er, where does he coch?"

"Vauxhall, near the station. He always jumps on a Tube to check his spars in Brixton. He never checks me at my yard 'cos my fader caught my brother and him downstairs one morning weighing herbs. So you can bell me?"

Floyd ignored the invitation. "Vauxhall? He ain't even a Brixtonian. Dem flats near the cricket ground?"

"Yeah. I have to go back inside for a pen so I can write down my phone number."

"Yeah, safe."

The pair walked slowly back towards the flat, where the blues was still carrying the swing. They passed by another couple going in the opposite direction. Possibly the start of a romance, or the end of a very brief one.

The thought of dealing with Rosene suddenly appealed to Floyd. It could be his revenge against Flynn for an incident that happened in Brockwell Park one afternoon.

On his way back inside the flat, Floyd recalled in his mind his first encounter with Terry Flynn.

Last summer, Floyd and Biscuit were playing football in Brockwell Park. The sun had blessed this particular day and enticed many of the black youth out of the estates and into the swerving hills of Brockwell Park, where they walked and talked, listening to suitcases, watched dog fights and bought the latest batches of Jamaican collie herb.

After a miskick, the ball escaped and found its way to the feet of a fierce-looking black guy, who was hoovering a spliff like there's no more Sundays, on a park bench. Floyd went to retrieve the ball. "Kick the ball back nuh, man."

Silence. Floyd approached the bench-dweller. "Do you chat triple Mexican or somet'ing? I did ask if you could kick it back."

Terry Flynn exhaled the smoke in Floyd's direction. "Who are you ah talk to bwai." He produced a flick-knife from his back pocket. "Next time say please," he smirked.

Biscuit galloped to be at Floyd's side. "Come Floyd man, I wanna get level - you're winning 2-1. The loser buys the choc-ices."

Floyd stood there, mesmerised by the blade. Flynn folded the knife back into his pocket, cackling. Biscuit retrieved the ball and led Floyd away.

"Don't chat wid him," Biscuit advised. "When he was born, God forgot to give him humour. He's just a warmonger."

"What's his problem? I only asked for the man to kick the ball back."

"Come, man. 2-1 to you."

Floyd had yet to tell of this incident to Brenton, but he remembered the anger he had felt and the pointless intimidation. The seduction of Rosene would be a good vehicle for his requital.

CHAPTER NINETEEN

Terror's Lair

24 hours later

Asweet bwai simmering in frustration sat on the bonnet of his 3.5 Rover, knowing there was no chance of escaping the roadblock. Four terraced houses away, Soferno B were rocking the neighbourhood playing endless dub plates of Sugar Minott and Al Campbell. A little further on, the all-night West Indian food shop boasted a queue of raved-out ravers, hungering for a snack of bun and cheese or fried dumpling before heads butted their pillows. Across the road from the shop, a bejewelled pimp sporting a beaver-skinned Stetson sat regally in his Jag, collecting the night's taking from his bruised and swollen-faced whore.

Sinking their Special Brews, teenaged boys employed by the drug dealers watched up and down the road for any sign of SPG vans. A stray dog, sniffing around dustbins looked unsurprised when his snout was nearly punctured by a thrown-away syringe . . . It was a typical night and early morning in Railton Road, or as locals called it, the 'front line'.

In a run-down residence that nobody was sure who owned, about forty steps from the blues, Terry Flynn held court. Sitting in the only armchair, he was surrounded by a catalogue of Brixtonian villains. Apart from one. This one was a rasta, decked in African-type robes, perched on a red plastic milk crate in the corner of the room, squinting out of his one good eye, while sucking an enormous spliff.

"I shoulda drapes his fockin white arse," Flynn regretted. "What's a fockin white man doing at a blues down here? Fockin white people. Dis is our area. Why do they wanna come here for? Nosing in on our business. I shoulda wet him up an' tek everyt'ing he had."

Everyone nodded apart from the dread. Encouraged by the response, Flynn continued his monologue. "If a black man steps in their area, we get arrested quick time. Can you imagine if we were cruising in downtown Windsor? We'll be stopped before we step out of the rarse car."

"Ah true dat," a dealer concurred, scissoring a fresh batch of faded green Jamaican export.

"Yeah, mon, ah reality dat," a picky head youth agreed.

Flynn took out his Rizlas and cancer sticks. "I fockin 'ate de white man. You see, they would never allow us to 'ave de t'ings they 'ave. They don't wanna see us in nice car an' nice clothes. They don't wanna see us in nice yards an' 'ave serious stereos. They jus' wanna keep us in the ghetto. They all 'ate us, y'know, always 'ave, always will. Dem mek me sick, walking in our area in their stoosh suits, doing some fuckery social study."

The monologue slid into a rant as herbalists came and went, silently purchasing the Mary Jane and Charlie.

"I want what they got, man!" Flynn resumed. "I'm gonna get meself a nice yard wid a big garden so I can grow my own herbs. And it'll have a garage big enough for two cars, me ah tell you. An' I'll join the local fockin golf club, just to piss off de white man dem."

Snorts of laughter. "You can't play golf, Terror," a dealer suggested.

"Then I'll fockin learn, innit. Den I will join a tennis club to rarted, jus' for de pleasure of seeing de white man's face when I gi' 'im de money to join. I'll show 'em us blacks are jus' as good as dem."

"Then if you're for your own people, why do you rob dem?" the rastaman asked, peering through the smoke and noting the gasps from the multitude of sinners inside the room.

Flynn glared at the dread. At this moment a hot hatred swelled in his body and he was itching to use the blade close to his chest. No one usually dared to challenge him here. This is me turf, he thought. An' dis dirty rastaman is trying to show me up! "A wha you ah talk to, dread? Wha dem call you? Nelson dread wid de one eye. Ah wha de fock are you doing here anyway?"

"You never answer me question. Why you rob your own people dem?"

Flynn's veins became visible in his throat. His lips thinned and his cheek tightened. It would be easy to just take his knife and wet the dread. But cut Jah Nelson? Every ghetto yout' respected him. Jah Nelson wasn't a man of violence. Flynn knew that in his environment it was easier for a violent man to ratchet-sketch another violent man. "Dem bwai who me drapes are idiot bwai, dem too rarted an' mek people walk all over dem."

"You t'ink even less of de white bwai, so why you don't drapes any of dem yet?" the dread riposted, speaking in a calm manner that infuriated Flynn.

The hierarchy of Brixtonian villainy smelt the sudden tension, along with the wafts of lamb's bread. They didn't think too much of Jah Nelson's chances, expecting him to be another victim of Terror Flynn's overused ratchet.

"Why should I listen to a man who gives praises to a dead African Emperor who made his own people starve to death?" Flynn suddenly countered, gauging the reaction of the rogue's gallery. "Emperor Haile Selassie I, fockin crook who 'ad whole 'eap ah money inna Swiss bank account an' made his people starve. Don't talk to me, dirty dread. Why don't you run an' go home an' wash your dirty head?"

"An' if I don't, what you gonna do? Wet me up like so many others? You t'ink me like dem fool fool bwai who is always around you, nodding their heads to everyt'ing you say. Telling you you're badder than what you really are."

"Shut your fockin mout', dread, before me cut off your dirty locks an' peel off de skin 'pon your top lip!"

"Remember dis," the Rasta continued, his voice still tranquil, "those who induce fear are only hiding their own fears. Jah know!"

Flynn shot out of his chair and went for the dread. The onlookers backed away, putting their merchandise in their pockets. Flynn took out his blade and held it an inch away from the dread's good eye.

"I should jook out your eye, dread. Then everyone will 'ave to t'ink 'bout another name rather than Nelson!"

Jah Nelson sucked on his spliff mightily. "Then you'd better mek a good job of it. Cah if you leave me standing an' alive, in Jah's name I will tek 'way your life. You better believe it!"

Flynn pushed the dread off his crate, causing him to drop his spliff. Jah Nelson readjusted himself as Flynn returned to his chair. "You ain't worth cleaning my blade for," Flynn mocked. "Joker dread, as if *you* could do me anyt'ing."

Jah Nelson relit his roach. "Well, you're not so impregnable. Everyone knows dat a young bwai mark you for life. You'd better start looking over both shoulders."

Flynn cackled - a horrible sound that spelt out utter contempt. His friends laughed with him, thinking that Brenton Brown would never come after Flynn looking for revenge.

"Me nearly killed dat bwai to rarted," Flynn laughed. "'Im probably still der-ya inna hospital. When the rarted bwai fucked with me, he didn't know who I was. He does now. My name's on his rarse neck!"

"Yes," Jah Nelson agreed, "but 'im walking an' living, an' sure dat he is walking an' living, he might be the one to be your Waterloo. Jah know!"

Right now, Flynn would have liked to sink his blade in Jah Nelson's tongue. He wouldn't look so smug then, he sniggered. What was the dirty dread still doing here anyway? He'd bought his herb. Why didn't he fock off to Twelve Tribes or somet'ing an' smoke his herb there with his dirty-head brethrens?

Thinking he had made his point, Jah Nelson stood up and was aware of all eyes on him. He knew he had brought the confrontation to the brink. And he was sure that if he pressed home his advantage, Flynn would be gagging to use his blade. To cause further embarrassment would be folly, especially in front of this audience.

The dread departed, enduring a crazed stare from Flynn.

"Remove ya," Flynn mocked. "Dirty focking Rasta. REMOVE YA."

The dealers went back to their business as Flynn rolled a spliff. What were his peers thinking? he wondered. Did they really think that Brown bwai would look for revenge? He should ah made sure he didn't walk an' live. He should ah wet him from ear to ear, severing his windpipe. Because now he was scared. What if Brown was looking for him? He recalled the vision of Brown's eyes. Eyes that were not afraid, eyes that spelt an insane determination. The fear had embedded itself under his skin, and kept him awake at night, dreaming of those mad eyes boring into him, telling him Brown was not afraid of him. Flynn would have to seek him out and extinguish his light. Finish him for good, rip out those eyes.

And if he did kill Brown, no one would say anyt'ing. He'd just be feared even more, that's all - a good result. Besides, the beast never investigated black on black violence thoroughly. They don't care if they find another young black body lying in a pool of blood on the front line. It's jus' another statistic. An' it's expected. Dem usually asking questions for a little while, an' when they get no response they shrug their shoulders and close the case. A black life is cheaper than a white life. An' Flynn should know, 'cos he's killed two black yout' already.

Flynn made up his mind as he sucked on his cocaine and herb cocktail. *Brown will have to die.*

CHAPTER TWENTY

One Drop

Three weeks later

Brenton and Floyd strode up Brixton Hill on their way to check Sharon. It was a Saturday night, and Floyd wanted to surprise his girlfriend by turning up unexpectedly at her home.

As the two brethren passed a hi-fi and audio shop, Brenton stopped to peer through the reinforced window. "See that amp over there? That's what I want. Nuff power, I think it's about a 100 watt a channel. Yeah, I bet that could drop a few eighteen-inch speakers."

Floyd spotted a beast van menacingly crawling down the road. "Hey, Brenton – beast. Come away from the shop, man, you know how they stay. They're probably bored, and wanna jail up a blackhead for the night."

The brethrens turned into New Park Road, off Brixton Hill. "You sure it will be all right to call for Sharon and she don't know we're coming? It's gonna be well sad if she ain't in."

"She'll be in; she better be."

Before knocking on Sharon's door, Floyd clocked the time; 11:45 pm. Fearing the cuss-happy voice of Sharon's mother, he gave the door a light slap and waited. It opened to reveal a crissly dressed Carol.

"You know, I had a feeling you would turn up here tonight," she said. "We were just chatting about you two a minute ago." Glancing at Brenton, she patted her hair coquettishly. "Hi

Brenton, why you never come to the party last week?"

Before his spar could answer, Floyd brushed abruptly past her. "Where're you two going?" he said tersely. "I thought you weren't raving tonight."

Carol totally ignored the question, and simply waited for Brenton to answer her. "Well?" she prompted him, crossing her arms.

"I had t'ings to do that day and I had to go work in the morning, so if I went, I would have been all tired and mash up."

Carol glared at the contrite Brenton. Then they both walked inside the dimly lit hallway, noticing Floyd waving his arms about in the kitchen.

"How comes you are raving tonight and you didn't tell me?" Floyd questioned Sharon. "You told me yesterday and last week that you're going to rest up and coch in on Saturday night. So where're you going?"

"I don't have to tell you my movements. When you and Brenton go out, I don't demand for you to tell me where you're going."

Carol parked beside Sharon, offering support to her friend. Floyd turned his back on his girlfriend and kissed his teeth. He peered through the cracked window just above the empty sink, then whipped around to face Carol. "Where're you heading tonight, Carol?"

"Don't rope-in me on the argument. This is between you two."

Floyd kissed his teeth again while Sharon calmly combed out her hair. Brenton sat in the remaining empty chair by the table. "Blouse an' skirt, the course of true love."

Sharon yanked herself from her wooden chair and marched along the hallway and up the stairs. Floyd quickly pursued her, leaving Carol and Brenton staring at each other, wondering if the argument would commence again. "Is Sharon's mum here?"

"No, she's at work. She's on nights this week."

"Where are you going tonight?"

"My brother is playing out, innit. It's sort of a last-minute t'ing, 'cos the sound that was supposed to play couldn't make it. I think their van broke down or something. As it's my brother playing, me and Sharon will get freeness, so we thought why not go."

Brenton smiled. "I think Floyd's getting possessive." Just at that moment, a car horn yelled from outside. "Is that for you?"

"Er, yeah. My brother's friend, he's picking us up."

Brenton flicked his eyes towards the ceiling. "This should be interesting."

An irate Floyd came storming down the stairs and tramped into the kitchen, glaring at Carol. "Who's that outside in the wheels?"

"Why you getting so rail up? It's my brother's friend, Smiley."

Floyd stormed back into the hallway where he met Sharon coming down the stairs. "What's Smiley doing outside and where're you going with him?"

"Look Floyd, calm down, man. Smiley's just taking us to the dance. Mikey's playing out innit; Carol's brother."

Floyd heard the horn yell once more. "I don't trust that Smiley, he's got about sixteen pickney already. All he has to do is pull a girl for a crub and they get pregnant with friggin quads. The man doesn't yam or drink; he just has sex. That's what keeps him alive. He should've had his seedbag punctured at birth."

Ignoring her boyfriend's comments, Sharon looked towards Carol, while Brenton tried to stem his laughter. "You ready then, Carol?"

"Yeah. I'll just get my purse from upstairs."

Sharon studied her ego-haemorrhaging man. "Look, Floyd, I'll be all right. I mean, I was raving without you before we met. You have to give me a little space, man. You can't expect me to only go out with you all the time."

Floyd screwed his face into a ball of resentment as Sharon resumed, "Anyway, I can't leave you and Brenton in the yard on your own. So you're gonna have to dally."

"Oh, that's dread; come all the way here to look for you and all you can do is dash me out on the street and step into a man's wheels who possesses the most crucial sperm in Brixton. His pickney dem will ram-jam all the nurseries in SW9 inna couple ah years. Yeah, thanks a lot."

As Carol emerged at the top of the stairs, Floyd became aware of the sniggering Brenton, still parked at the kitchen table. "Why are you skinning your teet'? Come on, let's chip."

The quartet met the sticky night air, with Floyd scanning the occupants of the coughing motor by the kerb. He found the driver staring back then averting his gaze to the appealing Sharon, just as she was about to enter the car. "Hey Sharon, hold up."

Sharon walked towards her man. "What now?"

Floyd glanced at the driver of the car, then deliberately embraced Sharon and kissed her on the forehead. "Behave yourself."

Sharon joined Carol in the back of the motor, and as the car sped off, Carol looked back at Brenton and waved.

The two spars watched motionless as the motor burned off into the distance. Brenton and Floyd trudged off into the direction of Brixton Hill. "I've got somet'ing to tell you," Floyd said. "Should've told you the other day."

"What?"

"You know that party that Sharon and me went to last week? Well, Sharon reckons she saw Flynn outside the dance selling herbs."

Brenton didn't say anything in response; instead, he stared straight ahead and quickened his pace. Floyd struggled to keep up with his spar. "Don't you wanna get him back? I mean, he's marked you for life."

"Don't worry, Floyd. I'll have my day when he's least expecting it."

"Well, I hope you do, 'cos if he's mashed up then I could move in on his girl."

"You're sick."

"She's wasted on him, innit."

"Sharon's wasted on you."

"Frig you. I treat her wid nuff respect."

"Then how comes since you buck up on Flynn's girl you haven't stopped chatting about her."

"She's fit, man. You wanna clock the breast 'pon her."

"You're as bad as Smiley."

Floyd saw the hypocrisy, and grinned. "If he tries anyt'ing, it's me and him."

"Yeah, well, you should treat her nice, 'cos bwai, if you lose her, you're gonna feel it."

"I ain't gonna lose her, man. Me an' Sharon are well solid."

"You ain't gonna be solid if she catches your backside wid dat Rosene."

"Why you so doom an' gloom, man? I know what I'm doing."

"I'm not all doom an' gloom, I'm jus' sayin' that when you get somet'ing precious, you should do all you can to keep it; I know I would."

"What d'you know?" Floyd probed. "You ain't got no steady gal; not that you're telling me anyway. Maybe you 'ave a liccle undercover floozie you ain't telling me 'bout."

Brenton didn't respond.

Twenty minutes later, the two brethren passed the Ace Cinema, where an endless stream of cars were parked and double parked, most of them belonging to the enthusiasts of the late-night Kung Fu show.

They walked on into Brixton High Street, where a rastaman leaped out of a Hillman, dressed in massive dark flares and green safari jacket. He was crowned by a beige cloth cap, which seemed too small to house his locks. The dread pushed a card into Floyd's hand. "Yuh mus' reach; dance haf fe ram."

Brenton snatched the card off his spar and read the wording out aloud.

"'Late-night blues, the champion sound like Tupper King International will rock you until the morning.'"

Then he stopped and read through the remainder of the flyer.

"It's tonight, at Stockwell Park Estate," he told Floyd. "They're all right, innit, Tupper King?"

"Yeah, they're not bad, but I'm going to my bed. I haven't got the vibe to go out now."

Brenton flung the card over his shoulder, and the friends proceeded to pass Brixton Tube station, where Floyd threw a ten-pence coin at the feet of a tramp.

Unknowingly to the Brixtonians, the occupants of an unmarked beast car were keeping a concentrated eye on any black faces. But the brethrens were oblivious to this as Floyd muttered again, "If Smiley tries anyt'ing with my girl, it's me and him."

CHAPTER TWENTY-ONE

Three Meals A Day

11 May, 1980

It was Sunday morning, about 8:30 am. Floyd, who an hour ago had arrived home from a Crucial Rocker blues, paced quickly along his street, peering into the doorways. Catching sight of what he was after, he scooped up two bottles of milk and burned home.

Moments later, he was enjoying a breakfast of corn flakes when his hostel-mate appeared in the kitchen doorway, dressed only in pyjama bottoms. Brenton looked as tired as a dog who'd chased a teasing bird all day. He prised open his eyes and was astonished to see Floyd fully clothed.

"Where've you been this time of morning?" he asked, opening the fridge and pouring himself a glass of milk. "You don't usually know what a Sunday morning looks like."

"I've been getting supplies, innit." Floyd gestured at the bottle.

"If you wanted some milk, I would've give you corn for it," Brenton yawned.

"It's kinda hard to get out of the habit. The other day I took a loaf of bread; I had some serious toast."

Brenton shook his head and proceeded to prepare himself a bowlful of cereal. Floyd switched on the kettle. "You see the Cup Final yesterday?"

"Yeah, West Ham won, one nil innit. Brooking scored with a jammy header. Still, I'm glad West Ham won though. I hate Arsenal, they're so friggin boring."

Floyd wanted a smoke to go with his hot chocolate. "Got a snout?"

"Yeah, but you have to go upstairs. They're on my dressing table."

Floyd raced upstairs, and came back down before the kettle boiled. He then reseated himself at the kitchen table. "You know, I'm sick and tired of being poor, t'iefing milk in the mornings and rolling up butts when you're not here. It's pissing me off. I think I'll start looking for a job. I reckon I could be a dread salesman."

"Salesman? Don't you have to do nuff training to do that? Besides, I can't imagine you trodding street and slapping on people's door all day. In the winter, you will fart when it gets cold."

"Look who's talking. Ain't you gonna freeze when winter comes? Your seedbag are gonna be like round blocks of ice when the cold smacks your backside."

Brenton could do nothing but laugh as Floyd poured hot water into a mug. "You going Sharon for your dinner today?" Brenton asked, wondering why Floyd never offered to make him a cup.

"Nah. Her mudder looks at me strange when I go round there on a Sunday, as if I burgled her yard. It's like she knows I'm partly there because I'm getting something to yam. She's polite and t'ing, but the way she looks at me, she kinda makes me feel shame that I'm there, know what I mean?" Floyd kissed his teeth. "Anyway, Sharon tells me that her mudder asks her if I got a job and t'ing when I'm not there."

He kissed his teeth again. "I'm staying in today, listen some music and coch. I might check Spinner later on, or maybe Biscuit; he's got some herb and the new Lone Ranger album."

"Why don't you come with me? I'm going to my mum's yard for dinner, innit. She's always telling me I must bring a friend or someone around."

Floyd didn't know what to make of the offer. "Er, why not? Yeah, be a change, innit. Can your mudder cook good? Her rice an' peas safe to eat an t'ing? What time you leaving?"

"About two."

Floyd arose from his chair and strutted his way along the hallway, then glanced behind him. "Yeah, all right."

Brenton shadowed his spar until he turned up the stairs. "I'm going back to my bed," he yawned.

Floyd opened the front door and plonked himself on a dustbin to take the morning air.

A few minutes later, a middle-aged woman appeared, dressed in her Sunday best, walking along the pavement towards Floyd. He guessed she was on her way to church. When the white woman caught sight of him, she immediately veered over to the other side of the road and quickened her stride. As she glanced back to check whether Floyd was following her, he stood up and prepared to voice his own sermon. "Scared, are you?" he bellowed. "I bet you're not as scared as my great-great-supergreat-grandad, who was rowing his way to Jamaica to start work as a slave. Don't worry, I ain't gonna drapes you."

Didn't my forefathers slave for this damn country, Floyd thought. Now you look 'pon us with scorn and spend all the friggin corn.

The woman didn't dare look back as she hurried her way along the street. Floyd kissed his teeth in disgust as he strolled back indoors.

Floyd and Brenton approached Ms Massey's home in the early afternoon. The brethren were deep in conversation as Floyd noted the affluent houses. "So how are you gonna get Flynn?" he asked.

"Finnley reckons that every Saturday night, Flynn makes his way from his supplier in Tulse Hill Estate to the front line, where he sells his herb. I check it that I will have a chance to frig him up on the way there. But not on the line, 'cos there's too much man he knows there. So I have to find a quiet spot, then I will jook him up good."

Floyd looked at his brethren. "I'll be with you."

"You?"

"And Biscuit, he hates him an' all."

"Biscuit? What's he gonna do? Take pictures with that friggin camera he's been trying to sell for ten years?"

Floyd laughed and thought that some of his wit was influencing Brenton.

The pair ambled towards the front door, and as Brenton rapped on it, he turned to his spar. "Thanks."

Juliet opened the front door and smiled as she set eyes on her brother, then she suspiciously observed Floyd's wide-eyed grin. "Hi, come in."

Brenton stepped inside the house, trailed by Floyd, who immediately examined the hallway wallpaper. "You done all right, innit."

"Yeah, nice yard innit."

Juliet resumed preparing the salad as the boys followed her into the kitchen. "Well, what do you do?" she asked Floyd politely.

"A bit of this and that. You know, a bit of hustling. Can't find myself a decent job yet. I was thinking about taking a job as a trainee manager."

Brenton parked at the kitchen table. "Where's Mum?"

Juliet swivelled round abruptly: she had never heard him call their mother 'Mum' before. "She's on the phone upstairs."

Floyd sat beside his mate, enjoying the scent of boiled chicken. "Why don't you go inside the front room?" Juliet suggested. "Dinner will be ready soon and it's more comfortable in there."

Brenton and Floyd marched into the front room. "This is like the Hilton Hotel compared to my mum's yard," Floyd remarked, impressed. "At my mum's yard, we had to wallpaper the walls wid the fool-fool drawings we done at school to make it look good. Our carpet was so damn thin it made tracing paper look t'ick. Hey, Brenton, why don't you coch here?"

Brenton snuggled himself comfortably in one of the suite chairs. "It wouldn't feel right, you know what I mean?"

A shout was heard from upstairs. "Juliet! Juliet!"

The girl trotted upstairs, and seconds later, poked her head around the front-room door. "Brenton, Mum wants you. She's in her bedroom."

Brenton leaped up the stairs, wondering why his mother hadn't been downstairs to greet him when he arrived. He went straight into her bedroom, and found her lying on her double bed, with the extension telephone beside her.

"You all right, son?"

Brenton stared at a photo of his sister. Cynthia noticed this. "She look pretty der, innit?"

"Yeah, she looks all right."

Brenton self-consciously decided not to look at any more pictures of his sister. He found this very hard, so he stared at the floor instead. "You look a bit down," Cynthia said, studying her son's face.

"Nah, I'm just a bit tired."

"I was jus' talking to your aunt in Jamaica. She well want to see you, y'know. Hopefully she can reach next year an' you can meet."

Brenton looked up at his mother. "Is your mum still alive?"

"Yes, she is a strong woman. She's in her eighties now, but really she act like she jus' fifty."

"Does she know about me?"

"Yes. My God, she give me some cussing about you. In her letters she still does. One day I 'ave to tek you to Jamaica an' see all the family."

"So she should cuss."

Silence. Cynthia pushed herself off the bed. "When I was a girl-chile back 'ome, I remember my mother always cussing me about 'ow I should do good at my education. When I reached 'ome from school, she would ask me what I had learned dat day. I remember I used to be tired after the long walk from school. It mus' 'ave been about two mile from the school to my 'ome. And more time, when I reached 'ome, all I wanted to do is jus' find my bed for my afternoon sleep. But my mother insisted

205

that I should tell her what I had learned before I could sleep."

Brenton listened attentively, more in love with his mother's accent than the recollection she told. "So you got any other brothers and sisters?"

"I 'ave two older brothers, but jus' the one younger sister. She come over to Englan' about t'ree year after I come. But she get 'omesick an' she gone back 'ome an' never return."

"What's she doing now?"

"She married now, an' she 'ave t'ree children, your cousins."

"What about your brothers?"

"Well, we don't really keep in touch, y'know. After the t'ing wid your fader, it sort of upset dem. Dem don't like the idea of me going wid a white man, y'understand?"

Cynthia wiped an imaginary tear from her cheek and resumed, "Even my sister did not like it, but she get used to the idea after a while, an' she start cuss me about you, jus' like my mother. But my brothers don't keep in touch. I can't change the past, y'understand?"

Brenton nodded. "If you had kept me, they might have had more respect for you."

Ms Massey approached the bedroom door. "Juliet mus' 'ave dinner ready by now. Come, let's go down an' eat some food."

Brenton bullfrogged down the stairs and into the front room, expecting to see a hungry Floyd in there. But his spar was in the kitchen, laughing and joking with Juliet. "I've been saying to Juliet that maybe she should come out with us on one of our raves," he told his hostel-mate.

Brenton chose to speak for his sister. "Juliet's not into blues and parties. She's into her soul and t'ing."

"Your sister can speak for herself."

The foursome settled down to dinner, Floyd's wit in sparkling form as he described to his hosts the achievements of his and Brenton's cooking.

Juliet was sitting next to Floyd, listening to him and occasionally glancing into his eyes. Floyd thought maybe he tickled

Juliet's fancy, which launched him into a very talkative mood. He resurfaced the topic of Brenton's cooking.

"You wanna see Brenton's dumpling? Oh my God, you ever seen white paste? And when they're cooked, dem tough like bouncy ball, that can bounce into third-floor balcony if a crusty bwai has a strong arm. You try to eat the dumpling and your teet' jus' vibrate like Shaka speaker box. And his spaghetti bolognese, kiss me granny belly button. Brenton's spaghetti's tough like hay to blouse an' skirt. An' I can't tell you 'bout his pilchards an' rice, cos dat's a horror story an' might make you run an' go 'long to the toilet. He tries, but his head will never wear dat funny, funny weird hat what dem big-time chef wear. He's good around the yard though, better than me. It's sort of weird though, he keeps the rest of the yard more sheened than his own bedroom."

Juliet rocked back in her chair with laughter, while Cynthia managed a smile. Brenton shook his head sadly, willing Floyd to jail his tongue.

As the three teenagers ate more rice and peas, Ms Massey sensed her confidence rise. "I was on the phone to my sister in Jamaica today. She was telling me dat her next-door neighbour 'ave 'im goat stolen. The man strip it an' lef' it 'anging from ah tree branch, an' 'im gone inside to look some drink. When 'im come back, somebody tek the goat. Dat's a t'ree-day dinner, man."

Floyd and Juliet laughed heartily, but Brenton had a sort of smug smile on his face, thinking of the family rifts his birth had caused.

Cynthia poured herself some red wine. "You know, my sister tell me of a t'ing which 'appen in her area. Dis man, who is a pastor, y'know, one of dem church minister, the police arres' 'im 'cos he was troubling 'im daughter. It mus' 'ave been a big shame an' scandal, for a man like dat in the parish to trouble his own daughter. I tell you, you can't trus' anybody."

Floyd pinned down an elusive chicken leg and remarked, "That's true."

Brenton grabbed the wine bottle and filled his glass as if he was drinking Cherryade. "Serve him bloody right. I always thought them vicars and priestman were a bit dodgy. I hope he gets beat up in prison. That's what happens to them sort of man; other prisoners jook them up."

Brenton discerned how quiet Juliet was during the meal; perhaps she was tired. She only picked at her food. "I dunno why," she told her mother, "but I'm never too sweet on my own cooking."

Floyd gazed at the chicken leg on Juliet's plate like it was a sentimental possession. "I'll control your chicken."

Juliet stood up and scraped the meat onto Floyd's plate.

A couple of hours later, Brenton and Floyd prepared to leave.

Floyd thanked Ms Massey and Juliet for the dinner as Brenton opened the front door. "Bye, Mum."

Cynthia watched her son walk off down the road, then she looked up skywards. "T'ank You, Lord."

Brenton headed for the nearest tobacconist as Floyd dreamt of a date with Juliet. "I think your sister likes me."

"I think my sister was being polite."

"She was clocking me, all right."

"Forget it."

Back at the Massey home, Juliet trudged up the stairs and into her room, flopping down on her pink-coloured quilt. Her reflection stared sombrely at her from her mirror. She recalled the story her mother had told at the dinner-table about the perverted pastor. She closed her eyes, but could not block out the word that drummed in her brain. *Incest.*

CHAPTER TWENTY-TWO

Prodigal Son

15 May, 1980

"**H**ey, Floyd! You kill off the soap?" snapped Brenton, persecuting him with a glare.

"There was only a liccle bit left."

"Then if you used it up, why you never control another bar?"

Floyd emerged onto the landing, grinning as he watched Brenton scrubbing at his face with a drenched flannel. "I forgot, sorry. That soap make your boat too dry anyway. When I did sight you yesterday I felt like taking out white chalk and writing on your forehead, DRY."

"Fuck you, man. I went to borrow your Vaseline but couldn't find the damn jar."

"I hid it under my bed."

"Why?"

"'Cos the last time you used it, you took out a whole 'eap. You're too grabilicious."

Brenton surfaced from the bathroom, beads of water free falling from the nape of his neck. "Who was that in your room last night?"

"Coffin Head and Iggy."

"Who's Iggy? Why the fuck man and man call him Iggy?"

"'Cos he's got rough skin like an iguana," Floyd laughed. "You know, dem scaly lizard dem; like a maaga, tiny croc."

"You lot are wicked, man. He can't help it if he's got eczema or somet'ing."

"Yeah, but Iggy should stop exploding his missile spots inna dance when he can't find no gal to crub."

Brenton could do nothing but laugh, but wondered why Iggy called Floyd a brethren.

Bare-backed, Brenton crossed the small landing and entered his bedroom. Floyd shadowed him.

"Don't you lot have any consideration for someone who's trying to sleep?" Brenton rebuked. "All I heard last night was your spars slamming down domino and cussing each other."

"You're not working today, innit. You got today off. Why didn't you rope-in? Coffin Head had a draw on him; nice herb."

"I was tired."

Floyd plonked himself on the single bed, stealing a glance at Mr Dean; this picture always troubled him. "I buck up on Sceptic the other day. He was telling me he sight Flynn on the line selling herb. It's like a regular runnings for him."

"Yeah? Everyone in Brixton seen Flynn selling his herbs on the line. I'm surprised the beast haven't picked him up."

"So me and Sceptic were t'inking we could come up with some kind of plan. To get your revenge and t'ing."

"Plan? You and Sceptic are thinking of a plan? Sceptic's even 'fraid of schoolgirls to rarted; he's a shaper."

"Nah, he's safe. He's gonna go undercover and check on Flynn's movements."

"You told Sceptic to go undercover? Tell Sceptic to rest himself."

"He wants to help, innit."

Brenton remembered the time Sceptic trod on a bad bwai's crocodile boot inna blues dance. Sceptic apologised and sheeped back home inna hurry.

"I don't want too many man knowing I'm out for revenge," affirmed Brenton. "If we're not careful, news will get out."

"Sceptic won't say nutten."

Brenton donned a white T-shirt while Floyd pastried a spliff of snout butts.

"I sight your sister yesterday in Tescos," informed Brenton.

"Oh yeah; she still dealing wid that idiot church bwai?"

"I dunno. When I see people I don't ask dem 'bout their love-life."

"He's a friggin bounty. I dunno what Jean sees in him. The man's seriously ugly. If I had a face like dat, I'd teach my batty to chat."

"Anyway, she told me that your mum wants to see you."

"What for?"

"I dunno. Probably wants to make sure you're breathing."

Floyd adopted a thoughtful pose, left hand on knee and other hand supporting his jaw. "She didn't fret 'bout me when my paps booted me out."

Brenton studied the way his spar expertly constructed the spliff, wondering why his own joints were never as criss as that.

"Well, I was just told to give you the message."

Floyd torched his tobacco-filled roll-up. "Don't need her."

Later on in the afternoon, Brenton departed the hostel to go for a trod in the park. For some reason, an image of the Job Centre bulldozed into his mind. He recalled earlier on in the year, when he didn't have a turkey hope of even controlling an interview, let alone a job. And those civil servants who worked in the Job Centre always had an 'I'm better than you' vibe, similar to them teacher-arse-kissing prefects at school.

Floyd remained inside the hostel, stewing on his sister's message. He was accompanied by his faithful suitcase, which mirrored his struggles by blaring out Dennis Brown's *Tribulation*.

Maybe his mother did care for him, he thought. Or perhaps she had reached out her hand because of Jean's prompting. Floyd missed Jean's presence in his life. She was forever defending him when accused of badness by their father. Then it dawned on Floyd that no matter what, he would at least be offered something to eat. Since the day he was born, he never had no reason to cuss his mother's cooking.

An hour later, Floyd was stepping across Brockwell Park

towards his mother's flat in Tulse Hill. The park held many memories for him, especially of Uncle Herbie.

Always wearing sticksman clothes, topped off by a black fedora, Herbie seemed to know everybody. He used to have a growlish greeting of: 'Wha'appen, skipper? T'ings irie?' whenever he approached a familiar face.

Herbie would organise junior soccer games in the park, and he always ensured that Floyd was one of the captains. While the game was in progress, he would retire to a park bench and hoover one of his cigar-length roll-ups. Floyd often wondered why his uncle didn't own a tobacco tin like the one his father had.

Following a couple of hours of feverish football, the chiming sounds of an ice-cream van would drown the junior squeals. Herbie would delve into his pocket and his hand would emerge with more shekels than an amusement-arcade kiosk. Floyd and his mates then enjoyed ice-cream cones with a leg of chocolate jutting out of them.

When Floyd was eleven, Herbie mysteriously disappeared from his life. He asked his mother many times what had become of his uncle, but the reply was a repetitive: 'Im gone ah foreign'.

Up to the present day, Floyd looked on Herbie as his real father. His natural father could never find the quality time to spend with his son, while his mother thought it was more important to have her husband's dinner ready by the time he came home from work, rather than see to Floyd's upbringing. Jean, Floyd's sister, gradually took over the parental role in his life. She was the one always attending parents' meetings at school, and she was the one who helped him with his homework.

Floyd reached the housing estate opposite Dick Shepherd School. He looked across the road and grinned as he witnessed a game of netball taking place, wondering if the apprentice sweet bwais still chased the ripening girls in the park during the dinner-break.

Ambling through the estate, he asked himself why his parents had swapped their rum and sugarcane existence in the Caribbean for this grey town in deepest Babylon.

He climbed the stairs of his mother's block, greeting the three youths who were hot-wiring a rusty car below with a respectful nod.

Using his key, he tapped on the window of his mother's kitchen, which overlooked the forecourt of the estate.

"Ah who dat?" demanded a suspicious voice, in the tone a medieval castle-keeper would have used.

"Open the door, man."

The door opened.

"Lord God; me son come to check me, praise the Lord."

Floyd glared accusingly at his mother. He never felt at ease with her Pentecostal church rhetoric.

Mrs Francis was a big woman. Her arms seemed to have stirred the broth for the feeding of the five thousand, her lips appeared to have kissed every Brixtonian pickney, and her bosom could have supplied their milk. She had such a kindly expression, that no one outside her family dared to question her compassion and maternal instincts. Her beach-ball cheeks had long ago learned the art of a permanent smile.

"I always knew you would come back to me," Floyd's mother smiled. "De Lord God 'as never fail' me."

As Floyd entered the hallway, he recognised the imposing crucifix screwed to the wall, and wondered what his mother's reaction would be if he'd grown dreadlocks.

He made his way to the cramped lounge, which was decorated in light colours and framed black and white photographs staring eerily from the four walls. On the mantelpiece above the gas fire stood a framed certificate, awarded to Jean Francis for completing an advanced hairdressing course.

"When did Jean get that?" asked Floyd, pointing at the certificate while collapsing on the settee.

"In March," Mrs Francis answered proudly. "She wan' her own salon one day."

"That's good. Now I hope she will stop giving her wort'less friends free trims."

Mrs Francis parked her bulk in a matching armchair opposite her son.

"So tell me, Floyd. You find work yet?"

"Didn't know you was interested."

"Of course me interested."

"Then how comes since I move to Camberwell, you haven't checked me?"

"'Cos you made it clear dat you never wan' me 'round."

"Doesn't mean I meant it," he said sulkily.

His mother reared up. "You don't t'ink me worry 'bout you when me inna me bed ah night-time?"

"I dunno; do you?"

"Cha! Sometimes you jus' 'ave to be awkward." Mrs Francis glowered.

"Anyway, I haven't got a job, and I probably won't get one until the white bosses decide to give a young black a chance."

"Why you wan' talk you'self down? You 'ave a sharp brain and you was clever wid your drawings dem."

Floyd leaned towards his mother, frustration brewing in his mind. "You know what it feels like to go after jobs and dem boss man say they'll let you know; but you know they ain't gonna take you on 'cos you're black? And to keep going to that blasted Job Centre where the saps working there recognise you and hail you by your first name; and come wid plastic smiles and say to you somet'ing will turn up if you keep looking?"

Mrs Francis dropped her eyes to the floor. Floyd continued his rant. "Do you know that for every job advertised, about fifty sad Giro people like me go for it?"

Floyd's mother was visibly shaken by what her son was saying, and knew in her heart that he was being truthful. The harsh economic climate stretched out its digits to grip everyone she knew. On the news programmes, the jobless totals stacked like early morning supermarkets. Her close friend Edna's dream of retiring to Jamaica had recently been nucleared by her husband's redundancy in the car industry. On her shopping trips to Brixton, she saw the youths of the area bee hiving around the record shops in even greater numbers. She remembered her mother's saying: *Lucifer tek idle 'and, an' mek it stir blood.*

"But your fader has managed to keep a job for twenty-five years now," Mrs Francis finally replied.

"Only because he's doing a job the white man didn't want to do when he first come over."

"Floyd! Dat is disrespectful to your fader."

"It's true; when the white man invite the black man to this damn land after the war, it was because they had no one to do the shit jobs."

Mrs Francis glared at her son, shocked by his vehemence. Why the yout' dem so angry? she thought.

"At least your fader provide fe 'im family. You t'ink it would ah easy inna Jamaica? Back 'ome dem 'ave no social security. If you nuh work out der, you 'ave no money at all. You affe depend on your family dem to mind you."

Floyd put his feet up on the sofa, heedful to kick off his trainers before he did so. He knew his mother was right; and indeed, he was well glad he wasn't living on his Brixtonian wits in Kingston. He nodded thoughtfully. "Can you say you're really happy?" he asked her curiously. "When you left Jamaica, did you have some dream?"

"Well, people used to say de streets ah London were paved in gold," Mrs Francis told him. "But the main t'ing was me and your fader did wan' to give our pickney dem a better chance."

"Some chance."

"You been listening to too much rasta talk," his mother scolded. "When I was a girl, me mudder used to tell me not to go

215

near the blackheart man, the rasta man, who did live inna de gully and mad bush. Dem mad people jus' give up on life, and dem is confusing the yout' dem wid der revolution talk."

"You been listening to too much white man!" Floyd riposted. "When we were slaves, a few used to rebel and run away. So to tame these rebels, they give dem the Bible to read. So they were brainwashed to think that their suffering was all right, and when dem dead they will forward to heaven."

Mrs Francis could hardly believe the talk firing out of her son's mouth. This was not the boy she had taken to church in his formative years.

"As the Gong says," Floyd continued, "you have to look for your heaven on earth; not for the heaven the blasted preacher man chats about."

Floyd's mother hauled herself up from her seat, not wanting to hear any more blasphemous rhetoric. She felt Floyd's words branded her to be a failure, in regards to rearing her son. She thought of his earlier question, and no, she was not content. Memories of signs on lodging houses saying: *No dogs, no blacks, no Irish* humiliated her still.

She made her way to the kitchen, followed by her son's gaze. "You wan' me to mek up a liccle snack fe you, or you staying fe dinner?"

"No, some cheese and bun or somet'ing will be all right, thanks."

Floyd enjoyed his mid-afternoon snack, although he thought the generation gap between his mother and himself had grown the length of the Brixton dole queue. Mrs Francis sat opposite him, busying herself in some dark concern. "So you nuh wait fe your fader to reach 'ome?"

"No! Since when does he listen to me anyway? He cares more about the maaga dogs dem running at Hackney on a Saturday morning."

"Dat's not true, Floyd."

"Then how comes when I used to play some ball for my school on Saturdays, he couldn't drag his miserable self out of the damn bookie shop to watch me play? I wouldn't partial, but he never won a red cent! The damn fool!"

Mrs Francis fell silent, like an accused on trial just hearing some granite, conclusive evidence to sway the jury into a Guilty verdict. The pleasant smile she usually wore struggled to make a return. The truth was hard to accept and wreaked havoc in her tolerant heart. Her husband was a bad father to Floyd, she concluded. But not to his daughters.

Satisfied that he had his mother examining her marriage, Floyd prepared to leave.

"When will you look fe me again?" Mrs Francis asked, her eyes pleading and sorrowful.

"I dunno; maybe when you boot Paps out of the yard and dash his garments all over Brixton Market."

With those last stabbing lyrics, Floyd departed, leaving his mother to search for her smile, while he regretted that he'd forgotten to ask about Uncle Herbie.

CHAPTER TWENTY-THREE

The Killing of Mr Brown

25 May, 1980

Juliet reposed at the foot of her bed, gazing at one particular birthday card, and refusing to allow sleep to claim her. The luminous green hand of her little bedside clock ticked past 1:00 am. Then she picked up the card and read the wording for the eleventh time: *To a special sister on her birthday*.

Juliet had tried to pretend that Brenton didn't share her blood, but the message in the birthday card was like a beacon of fire spelling the truth out in flames. Her love affair with her brother was no dream but very real. 'What have I done?' she whispered.

Despite her pangs of guilt, she knew her love for Brenton had grown strong. Juliet wondered how long she could live a lie in front of her mother. Since her brother had announced himself, on that stormy January night, she had witnessed the once-redundant smile of her mother, gradually etch back into her face. The years of torment Ms Massey had endured were now fading away, like the night making way for the day.

The relationship between mother and son was not ideal, she thought, but it was improving all the time. And here she stood, having a potentially catastrophic and illegal affair with her brother.

How could she stop this secret love affair? Did she want to stop it? Her desire for Brenton had become addictive, and now she recognised her habit and wanted to cure it. Otherwise, where would this affair end? Surely in shame and scandal! They could never marry. Even if they lived together, they would have to keep a low profile, and be careful at all times. If only they didn't share the same mother. Then Juliet could introduce Brenton to Hilary and other friends. They could rave together and do the things normal couples did.

She tried to push back down the slipping lid on her emotions and wondered how her friends would react if they knew the truth. She imagined Hilary saying, 'Here's virginal Juliet, who's always choosy on what man she goes out with, and she's screwing her brother.'

By contrast, Brenton was at ease with the situation. One night, he even suggested they should tell all to their mother! Juliet totally dismissed the suggestion, thinking Brenton was a bit high after a serious lovemaking session. Supporting her head in her hands, she peered through her nail-varnished fingers and stared at the birthday card once more. Then she closed her eyes and relived the evening's events.

Brenton had invited her to the hostel, where he gave her, along with the card, a gold chain with a heart-shaped gold locket hanging from one of the links. Juliet had carefully pressed the spring and the locket opened. Inside was a small piece of paper. She unfolded it and read: *Love you always*. Shortly afterwards, they made sweet, beautiful love. One look into her lover's eyes told her he meant every word he wrote.

When she was alone with Brenton, Juliet felt God blessed her life. She always sensed the adrenaline hose through her body when she gazed at him. His face possessed an encyclopaedia of pain, torment and joy, etched into every pore. He would find it simply impossible to hide any emotion he felt, and she found that irresistible.

Sighing, she rose to turn off her bedroom light and thought about ending the relationship. Easier thought than done. How could she face Brenton and tell him it was all over? Maybe she could go away for a while? Perhaps she could apply for a transfer to another branch for work? Or would that be running away from her problems?

Juliet lay in bed, racking her brains to find a solution. Finally, she decided to take the next day off from work, and use the time to think things through properly. The stress had been making her feel sick and dizzy, so she would visit her GP for a routine check-up, which would provide an ideal excuse for her day off.

The next morning, Brenton awoke in a bubbling mood. He rose early, giving himself plenty of time to get to work. But the familiar sight of snarling traffic on the Walworth Road frustrated him.

The bus snailed towards the Elephant and Castle as the fortunate ones, who lived in the concrete jungle, set off to work.

Brenton idly watched a young mother, carrying a wailing child and pushchair, struggle to board the bus. Only after the number 45 had crawled another half-mile did he realise that the parent was Sharon's sister.

From his vantage point on the upper deck, Brenton observed the East Street marketers prepare their stalls. While stuck at the traffic lights he watched a council roadsweeper. Dressed in dull blue overalls, the ageing black man pushed his trolley, containing an over-used black plastic dustbin, alongside the kerb, sweeping all litter before him as he pondered his day ahead. By some sort of sixth sense, the old man realised he was being watched from above, and glanced up at Brenton with Caribbean-longing eyes.

Brenton wondered what was wrong with the world. It was a glorious, sunny day, he had work to do, which was no mean feat in the present economic climate, and he was well deep in love. He had never bought anyone a birthday present before, so he felt proud of the gift he had given to Juliet.

The site Brenton had worked on for the past week was a short two-minute step from Elephant and Castle Tube station. Three- and four-storey houses there were being converted into flats. As Brenton approached the site, he was greeted by the foreman.

Dressed in a grubby white T-shirt and cement-stained, fading blue jeans, Keith looked troubled as he pulled on an almost extinct snout. "All right, mate? 'Ere, Brenton, got some bad news, like. You know, it's sort of out of my hands."

Brenton halted within a few feet of his boss. The foreman threw his fag on the pavement, then trod on it, not lifting his foot off until he'd extinguished all the smoke. "I always get the dirty work. I've been told to tell you we have to let you go after today. There ain't a lot of work about. I mean, after this job, there's not much else."

Brenton stood absolutely still with shock, only his eyes displaying any sign of animation. Keith continued, "Sorry to do this to you, mate. As you know, I always try and do my best for blacks like you. You know, offering a bit of work here and there. So it ain't because of your colour. It's just the way it is. Sorry, mate."

The feel-good factor Brenton had been experiencing evaporated into a mood of dejection. He dropped himself onto a small wall just in front of the site, not believing what he'd just heard.

"Look, er, we'll give you two weeks' money and I'll make sure to call you myself when work picks up a bit, all right? So you never know, maybe in a month's time, you'll be working for us again."

Brenton didn't appear to be listening. Obviously disappointed, he stood up with head bowed, walked into the half-constructed building. "Oh Keith, when you were talking about you do the best for blacks, well, I've got a white paps," he said tonelessly.

"Oh, I never knew. I guessed you was, you know . . . Er, sorry if I caused offence, I didn't realise."

Brenton turned his back on his foreman and began work on his last day of employment for the foreseeable future. Keith read his watch - a quarter past eight.

8:15 am it read on Juliet's watch. Feeling queasy and not wanting to travel on the Underground network, she had gone to work by bus. A conversation with her mother earlier in the morning was still fresh in her mind. Noticing how quiet and withdrawn Juliet had become, Ms Massey had wondered aloud whether anything was wrong. Juliet could sense her mother tuning into her tension, which made her feel very uncomfortable.

"You would tell me if somet'ing was wrong?" Cynthia fretted.

"Of course."

Now, on the bus, she suffered the tremendous guilt of that lie. She had changed her mind about taking the day off, not wanting time to brood on her worries. But work proved difficult in her present frame of mind. She was irritable and unusually quick-tempered with her work colleagues. Even Tessa noticed the 'don't joke with me' mood. But rather than ask what was troubling her, Tessa guessed it was the time of the month thing.

Juliet sat at her desk, trying to bury herself in her work, but there was no escaping the turmoil. Might as well have stayed at home, she thought. Peace only came when she decided to call on Brenton later that evening.

Brenton arrived home from work in time for afternoon tea, or usually, in his case, a packet of crisps and a Special Brew. He slapped on Mr Lewis's door, but there was no response, so he trundled off towards the kitchen to make a cup of tea.

As he switched on the kettle, he heard Floyd bounding down the stairs. "I'll have two sugars in mine, thanks."

His spar didn't answer. Instead, Brenton simply took out another mug from the cupboard. Floyd, who for once was not at his most well-dressed, wondered why his brethren was back from work so early. "What-a-gwarn? How comes you reach home so early?"

Pouring the boiling water into the mugs, Brenton had a temper warning alarm in his eyes. "I was laid off today. They don't need me for a while. The foreman told me there's not a lot of work about."

Floyd took a seat at the kitchen table. "A couple of my brethren had the same t'ing happen to dem. Y'know, they were doing the same t'ing as you. Then one day, they turned up for work and got the Wellington boot."

"Is it?"

"I was chatting to Sharon the other day, and she says this is the start of a recession. Seems like nuff people are gonna cork up the dole house."

Brenton stirred his drink furiously, spilling some on the table. "No matter how you try, t'ings just don't work out. I'll never get another job. If I had the chance, I'd shoot the saps who run this country."

Floyd witnessed a dangerous emotion buttering over his friend's face, and then he watched him trudge slowly into the hallway and up the stairs. Brenton disappeared into his room, still holding his mug of tea. "I'll have to tell Lewis about dis," Floyd told himself.

Three hours later, Brenton lay stretched out along his bed, half-asleep and half-awake. He was trying to focus on Mr Dean, who stared moodily back at him from the bedroom door. He squinted hard to behold a clear image of the late film star. Then he closed his eyes, feeling utterly exhausted.

A minute later, he was brought out of his doze by a knock on the door. Yawning, he opened it to find a solemn-looking Juliet. Not wanting to appear depressed, Brenton smiled at his sister, but his eyes betrayed him. She raised a half-smile back and sat down on the bed. Placing her handbag on the floor, she nervously inspected her manicured fingernails. "You all right then?" she asked quietly.

"Yeah."

"Look, I have to talk seriously with you."

"What about?"

"About us." She braced herself. "I don't know quite how to say this, and I don't mean to hurt you, but we, er, we can't go on like this. I feel so guilty, and it's tearing me apart. Can you understand that?"

Brenton gazed at his sister, disowning his ears. "What do you mean? We get on great, what are you saying? You haven't told Mum, have you?"

"No, of course not." Juliet tried to control her trembling hands by gripping them together. "For the past few weeks I haven't had any peace of mind. I can't sleep at night. I mean, what does the future hold for the both of us? We can never marry or even live together."

"NO! YOU CAN'T DO THIS!"

"I just hope we can still talk to each other. I still love you and I always will. But I can't go on like this, it's making me ill with worry and guilt."

Looking down at the carpet while clawing his temple, Brenton shook. His redundancy from his job was like a bullet in the arm, but Juliet's announcement felt like a toxic cannon blasting through his skull. He tried hard to remain calm and not show any emotion, but he failed. His sister couldn't control her feelings either, and began weeping.

"How do you expect me to pretend that we are a friggin nice normal brother and sister after what we've done?" Brenton exploded. "You told me yourself, in this very room, that you've never been happier! Why do you want to fuck up something that was so good? Was it all lies, what you said to me in the fucking bed? This ain't no blasted joke, I really liked you. Shit, I still do, and I thought you felt the same. Why all of a sudden you wanna fuck it up?"

"I can't do this to my mother. I can't!"

"What do you mean, you can't? You already have. What the fuck you talking about?"

"Look Brenton, listen to me, please."

Brenton's lips quivered with emotion, his eyes watering.

Juliet stuttered on, "It's true, I have never been happier. But this ain't a dream, it's real. You are my brother. For God's sake, we share the same mother! We can go to jail after what we've done."

"Then let's go away. Let's fuck off somewhere far away where nobody knows us."

"That won't change t'ings. No matter where we go, you are still my brother."

Glaring at his sister, who was crying uncontrollably, Brenton stood up. "SHIT." Then he remembered Biscuit's nickname for him - 'The stepping volcano' - and he thought, Gotta stay cool. Mustn't erupt.

For the next minute, there was total silence as the siblings dwelt on their immediate future. Then Brenton, becalmed, whispered: "Somehow I knew it wouldn't last; it was too good to be true. I suppose it's like one of those nice dreams that has to end." His eyes mirrored death.

Juliet, bitterly upset, embraced her brother in one last gesture of love as Brenton emitted an eerie silence. The emotive face that bewitched her now scared her; she had to get out. For she would either spend the night caressing away his pains, or go insane with guilt. Her heart begged her mind to stay, but her mind refused.

"You'll be all right, won't you?"

Brenton nodded his head unconvincingly. Juliet made a tearful departure, with her brother listening to her footsteps clumping down the stairs. He thought of the beast station cell door as he heard the front door clang.

For the rest of that night, Brenton did not venture outside his room. He tried to make sense of the day's proceedings, but failed. Why had everything sweet to him in life exploded in his face? Should he have pleaded with Juliet to carry on with their relationship? Or would that be selfish? He'd never felt so hurt before and he didn't know how to handle it. Maybe it was Fate. He was not supposed to be happy as far as Fate was concerned. His life was destined to be an endless struggle against the odds. With that thought in his mind, he pondered on taking his own life and ending his tribulation.

If was as if Brenton was driving along a main highway. Many vehicles of all shapes and sizes roared past him and tried to knock him down. Looking out for the most persistent offender, he gazed through the murky windscreen and saw his own reflection. Could he himself be the most reckless driver?

In the surreal chasm between sleep and insomnia, his mind recalled an incident in the past.

He was eight years old, hurrying home from school so he could have his pre-dinner banter with Mr Brown.

Mr Brown was the name of his adopted scarecrow, which he had found in a ditch - his most treasured possession. Over the past few weeks, Brenton had been nursing Mr Brown back to his former glory. A pumpkin, discarded after Halloween night, was the scarecrow's new head. Brenton had pen-knifed out his eyes and mouth, and employed a black crayon to sketch his eyebrows and ears. He glued on half an empty toilet roll for his nose, and his limbs were made out of old, forgotten broomsticks. Mr Brown's torso was a torn-down oak branch, stripped free of its bark. Uncle Georgie, the housefather from next door, had helped Brenton to assemble all the bodily parts that made up Mr Brown, using nails and screws and his carpentry knowledge, but even Georgie didn't known the scarecrow's name. No one did apart from Brenton.

Mr Brown's weather-beaten black mac was decorated with assorted badges, most of them coming from Brenton's good deeds with the Cubs; his Akela had scolded him for not getting the badges sewn onto his Cub pullover. Mr Brown also sported a snazzy pair of strapless sandals, reclaimed from a dusty neglected trunk found up in the attic. Brenton gouged out holes in these sandals so Mr Brown's legs could comfortably fit into them. The scarecrow's headwear was a chequered flat cap, covered in more badges, and his neck was decorated with a daisy flower garland, which Miss Hills had spent a whole Sunday afternoon helping him to create. The Belt adored colourful flowers and she thought it was encouraging that Brenton displayed an interest in constructing something, even though she thought the reassembling of a scarecrow was bizarre to say the least.

Together, Brenton and Georgie had stood the spruced-up Mr Brown in the corner, looming over the damp outhouse like a hellish sentinel.

Today, Brenton reached the outhouse, ready to tell Mr Brown how school had gone that day. But he found Mr Brown's snapped legs on the doorstep, amongst splinters of wood. He stooped down to pick up the fragmented leg and ran a finger over its length. It felt smooth to the touch until he fingered the point of breakage, where it was rough and spiky, almost pricking his thumb.

Brenton inhaled through his nose and smelt the oil, which mingled with the damp aroma that clung to the brick walls. He swivelled round and saw Mr Brown's hideously split head, which gaped from his right eyebrow to his right cheek. The head was precariously balanced on a dusty, paint-cracked windowsill, beside a neglected darts-board. His mac was torn into pieces, scattered like confetti all over the outhouse, and his body was hacked into three parts, which rolled near the biscuit-tin tool-box, lying in the powdery dirt of the concrete floor.

The eight year old screamed a scream to end all horror flicks, and in the apple and pear orchard a hundred yards away, young hide-and-seekers stopped their game and listened, thinking the bogey man was feasting on another victim. Housemothers and housefathers raced to the scene, believing a child had fallen off a drainpipe and cracked its skull. His belly-mangling shrieks only subsided after half an hour or so, when even The Belt's heart was boxed by the wanton brutality of the killing of Mr Brown. The display of Brenton's hysterical emotions moved Georgie himself to tears. Never in his life did he witness such a heart-battering scenario.

Georgie carried Brenton inside his home, as the little boy sobbed his heart out, wondering why somebody had killed his best friend. He never spoke a word for six weeks . . . and he never frequented the outhouse again. The remains of Mr Brown were placed in a corner of it, in a cardboard box, with Georgie keeping an eye on the corpse. To his knowledge, no one ever went near it again.

Social workers, psychiatrists, child experts all tried to unravel the mystery of Brenton's traumatised mind regarding his love for

Mr Brown, telling him gently that the scarecrow was nothing but bits of wood and old clothes. But no one ever understood.

At half-past eight the next morning, Brenton had already been up for an hour; his body had become accustomed to rising at about seven. The only problem was, he had no work to go to.

His mind in turmoil from the events of the previous day, he decided to tidy up his room, putting clothes away in drawers, sweeping the small carpeted area and generally making his room 'Mr Sheened' as never before. Sitting on the bed, his face rippled with a Doomsday pain as he stared at Mr Dean, Brenton found he couldn't look at the poster any more. He had to get out.

So, taking off his work clothes, he donned an old white T-shirt and jeans, and for some strange reason, squeezed on his old tatty trainer shoes.

Not sure of where he was going, he ventured outside. The sun was trying to break through the clouds, making the atmosphere hazy. Instinct told Brenton to head for the park. He thrust his hands in his jeans pockets and discovered some forgotten small change so he stopped off at the newsagents and bought a paper. The owner of the shop, a young Indian man, recognised Brenton and politely asked him if he'd seen the cricket on telly last night. Apparently, Brenton didn't hear him and refused even to glance at the shopkeeper as he handed over the loose change.

The park seemed so peaceful; Brenton only wished its tranquillity could transfer itself to his mind. He rested on his adopted bench and tried to read the sports page of the newspaper, but his tormented thoughts somehow stopped his eyes from focusing clearly. Frustrated, he angrily threw the newspaper over and behind his head.

After a few moments, the slight breeze separated some of the pages, scattering them over the park. He looked at the newspaper and compared his life to it. He wanted to scream out, or even cry. No tears came, and no sound. *Who killed Mr Brown?* he wondered.

Very disturbed, Brenton marched out of the park, and decided to trod to Brixton. Walking down Dulwich Road, he was totally oblivious to what was happening around him. A motorist angrily yelled at him as he strode across the road with head bowed, not bothering to look for the dangers of burning wheels.

An elderly white lady, walking her poodle, studied Brenton and wondered what sort of deep-rooted pain he felt. Brenton didn't even notice her, or her dog, which barked extravagantly.

Turning right into Effra Parade, Brenton hot-stepped his way to Railton Road, the so-called 'front line'. The herb-hustlers and evil-doers watched him suspiciously as the stepping volcano passed them, ignoring the bartering of street drug dealers.

Brixton was vibrant on this summer day. The markets were packed with shoppers who couldn't afford the prices of department stores. Reggae music blared out from the many record shops. Youths were looking in the menswear stores, discussing what clothes would suit them best. Kids who should have been at school were running through the streets, playing tag.

The men's hairdressers were awash with young black men, who all seemed to be talking at the same time. A lone black, dreadlocked skanker, enjoyed himself beside one of the market record stalls. Bopping up and down, adorned only in a white string vest and three-quarter flares, he didn't appear to have a care in the world. The smell of West Indian cuisine mingled with the air, along with the aroma of fresh fruit and vegetables.

Brenton marched to the Tube, where Socialist Worker Party activists were selling their newspapers, and a religious nut condemned all to hell. But Brenton's eye was captured by a white vagrant. The stepping volcano approached him. The tramp's greasy long brown hair matched his complexion.

"Got ten-pence for a cup of tea, mate?"

Brenton ignored him and bounded down the steps. The thought of buying himself a ticket never entered his head. He easily leaped over the ticket barrier and stepped down the escalator. The

229

ticket man watched Brenton disappear and carried on with his job without voicing any objection.

The waiting train had its automatic doors open and Brenton paced into one of the carriages. Choosing not to sit down, he read the many advertisements around him. A white-faced clock could be seen at the end of the platform. Twenty to ten, Brenton noticed.

Various people rushed onto the train, thinking it would depart within seconds, only to feel silly when the train remained stationary. Eventually, the red light at the end of the platform changed to a fading green. Picking up speed quickly, the train accelerated into the blackness.

Brenton remained standing up and attempted to read the advertisements as they flashed by. Then, in a couple of seconds, he stared into the darkness, wondering if death was a similar scenario. Within a minute, the Tube reached Stockwell Station. He jumped out when the doors opened and followed the signs to the Northern Line . . .

On the concourse, a guitarist played a Gong classic, which Brenton instantly recognised. The strains of *No Woman No Cry* echoed along the filthy corridors. He walked by the busker, but halted in his tracks to look into his battered guitar case. He then studied the busker.

Long, straggly ginger hair rested on his shoulders, which were covered by a stained red T-shirt. His legs were clad in dirty army greens, and his feet below it were blistered and blemished.

Brenton fished into his pocket to gather all the remaining shekels he had. He then threw the coins into the musician's guitar case. Not noticing the busker's raised hand in a gesture of thanks, Brenton ambled towards the platform of the Northern Line.

Positioning himself at the end of the platform where the train would appear, Brenton waited patiently. Then after a few moments, he heard the rattling sound echoing from the live rail. He leaned forward and saw two bright lights coming towards him. To Brenton, the train seemed to take an eternity to reach the platform. Just as it was about to enter the station, he steeled himself to fling his body in front of it. As he toked a wailing breath and prepared to leap, the strains of the Gong's classic penetrated his mind. He almost keeled over as he teetered and nearly lost his balance. He felt the rush of wind sheath around him as the train almost ripped off his face. He then backed away from the edge of the platform, sensing his heart accelerate within his chest. Visions of his tormented life flashed through his mind. *Who killed Mr Brown?* he asked himself again.

A woman who had witnessed Brenton's attempted suicide, gaped in horror of what could have been. Brenton stood still with eyes shut. He remembered his time in the beast cell at the end of last year - all had seemed hopeless then. In those days he hovered at the mouth of desolation, dangling from a well-worn rope. Yet he had managed to climb the thinning rope before it snapped. He decided to do the same now. He would not give up on his life yet.

Brenton felt the urge to seek out his sister; confident that Juliet loved him. Maybe he could persuade her not to break off their relationship. Maybe they could elope and leave London. He guessed that if he was persistent, Juliet's steeple of guilt could be climbed. Love can slap down anything.

He would visit her at work. Seeking out a map of the Underground network on the curved wall behind him, he planned his route to the City Tube stop. With renewed optimism, Brenton awaited the train to take him to his destination.

At the same moment as Brenton set off to Juliet's place of work, she was waiting patiently at her doctor's surgery. Feeling sick and groggy after her confrontation with Brenton, she had decided to go ahead with a day off, and had made an appointment to see her GP for a routine check-up, hoping he could give her a tonic to buck her up. Her period was really late, too. Maybe that was why she'd been feeling so low.

But it didn't turn out that way. After a long series of questions, followed by a thorough external examination, she was given an internal by her doctor and had then been told to wait outside. Her face frozen in a panic-stricken dread, Juliet sat fretting in the waiting room, observing the receptionist take calls and write down appointments for patients. What bad news did the doctor have?

Looking back to last night, she felt she'd been cruel to Brenton, and hoped he wouldn't do anything stupid. Maybe she could have spent more time with him after inflicting her blow instead of running off, running away from his pain and her own. Was it selfish of her simply to consider her own guilt? Brenton had been so happy, and she likewise. She fondly visualised his smile and thought of him as a vulnerable man-child who only craved love. Juliet wondered if she had the right to rip away that love. Could she live with her guilt? Maybe she could. Maybe Brenton and she could elope to somewhere far away. With her qualifications, she could always get a job; probably earn enough to keep them both until her brother found a job and learned to stand on his own feet.

A door swung slowly open and a bespectacled man of about fifty years old stuck his head outside. "Juliet Massey, will you please come in?"

Juliet hauled herself up and trudged into the doctor's surgery. She sat down in a chair facing him across a large desk, remembering how kind he had been to her when she suffered from tonsillitis in her childhood. She noticed that the examination couch had a fresh sheet of paper on it now. When she was a youngster, she would jump up and down on that bed, much to the annoyance of her mother. Then, shaking off memories of childhood, she faced up to the present.

In a low, soothing and fatherly tone, the doctor informed her: "My dear, you are pregnant."

Brenton finally arrived at Juliet's place of work, only to be told that his sister had called in sick. He made his way via the Tube to Brixton, planning to go straight to her home and plead with her.

Once he reached Brixton, he bullfrogged up the escalator, feeling he must see Juliet as soon as possible. Halfway up, glancing casually at the downward escalator opposite, he saw someone among the passengers who made his guts tighten. Terry Flynn.

Intoxicated with the toke of revenge, Brenton ran hard, back down the uprising escalator, brushing past astonished commuters. "You bastard!" he roared.

Flynn was just getting off at the bottom; he turned around in alarm. He went for his flick-knife in his back pocket, but before he could reach it, Brenton pounced on him.

"A wha the rass," stammered Flynn.

"You're a dead man!" screamed Brenton.

Springing forward, he wrestled his Nemesis to the ground, his eyes wild, revenge etched in his face. Snarling, he rained in punches. Terry Flynn's flick-knife escaped onto the platform as startled passengers looked on. Flynn managed to evade Brenton's clutches and made for his knife. Brenton rugby-tackled him, causing Flynn's forehead to make an audible scraping sound on the unforgiving platform. With a desperate effort, Flynn sprang up, booting Brenton in the face, smashing his nose and disfiguring his mouth, causing a splattering of blood to spot the ground. Again, Flynn made for the elusive blade. The Gong's *Heathen* suddenly came into Brenton's mind.

Undeterred, Brenton leapt on his prey again, only to be met by an elbow detonating against his jaw. But Brenton managed to grip an ear and almost tore it off, creating a gristly breach at the side of Flynn's head. At that Flynn went absolutely nuts and kneed Brenton in the face, resulting in a pair of teeth skittling along the platform.

The two of them rolled dangerously close to the platform edge, punching and kicking each other. Brenton could smell lager on Flynn's breath, mixed with his BO. The onlookers stood frozen, watching in horror; paralysed by the sight of blood.

Brenton viced Flynn's neck within his hands and squeezed as

hard as his strength allowed. Flynn opened his mouth as wide as he could and guillotined his teeth, ripping flesh off his opponent's shoulder, causing a rush of blood to rapidly swarm over his T-shirt. Flynn spat out something grotesque onto the platform, but Brenton refused to relax his grip, despite experiencing intense pain. The live rail started to crackle. Flynn saw his knife about a foot away from his hand. Blood was pouring from Brenton's nose, cascading onto his gashed lips. And his heartbeat was racing almost fatally. Flynn's head and neck turned crimson, as his ear sagged horribly, dripping a torrent of warm blood. "You're a dead man!" Brenton screamed.

Flynn, panic-stricken, finally heaved his assailant off him and went for the knife again. Brenton saw his enemy's plan and dived onto his back, causing Flynn's right arm to break with a thud on the concrete. The knife skittered over to the platform edge. Brenton had cracked his knees badly on the fall, and now blood drenched his jeans. Suffering excruciating pain, he was forced to relax his grip, and it was then Flynn saw his chance. He lunged for the knife just as a Tube train came hurtling into the station, severing his hand and mutilating his arm. A crystal shattering scream echoed around the station as spectators turned their faces away in shock. Two women fainted.

Brenton sensed he had to get away. Bathed in blood - his own and Flynn's - he struggled to the escalator, using only his adrenaline to keep himself upright, leaving his Nemesis writhing in agony.

This final conflict had lasted no more than a minute.

Underground train guards raced to Flynn's aid. While Brenton made his getaway, bloodying everything he touched.

Oblivious to the shocked eyes that stared at him, Brenton caught a bus to his mother's home. Whilst on the upper deck, ignoring the amazed gawps of passengers, he pulled off his T-shirt, rolled it up and pushed half of it onto his blood-flowing nose, and the other half onto his badly bitten shoulder. Limping off the bus, he somehow made it to his mother's home, only kept going by his determination to see Juliet.

Fresh from her visit to the doctor, she opened the door.

"Oh my God!" she screamed. "Brenton; what has happened? Oh my Lord, oh Jesus!"

Brenton looked as if he was about to join Mr Brown. Juliet quickly supported him, grabbing his arm and helping him inside.

"Juliet, Juliet . . . Jul . . . Jul . . . iet."

He fell on the hallway carpet, blood still pouring from his shoulder, and his knees giving way to shock.

"Brenton! Brenton! What has happened to you? Oh my God, I have to call an ambulance! Oh Jesus. I love you! Love you, with all my heart!"

Brenton prised his eyes half-open, thinking he was going to die. His head swam about in whirlpools, causing his vision to become misty. But he could see an indistinct figure at the top of the stairs. Was it Mr Brown? He'd promised that he would always be there for him, Brenton recalled. Thank God for Mr Brown.

Juliet became hysterical. "Jesus forgive me!"

She laid Brenton on the carpet and picked up the phone, dialling frantically with her blood-drenched fingers. Brenton focused his eyes, and watched his mother coming dreamlike down the stairs. Where's Mr Brown? he dismayed, before slipping into unconsciousness.

After Juliet had called the ambulance, she spun around and tended to Brenton, tearing off her blouse to stem the blood from his shoulder. She was unaware of her mother, standing in acute shock halfway up the stairs, looking as though someone had kidnapped her heart.

"Don't you dare die on me," Juliet whispered. "An ambulance is on its way and you're going to be all right. You've got to be - for your baby. You hear me, Brenton? For your baby!"

CHAPTER TWENTY–FOUR

Mother Of Silence

C ynthia Massey's mind exploded with the thought that perhaps in seven months or so her son would become the father of her daughter's child; if he lived.

Juliet felt a chilling presence behind her. She turned around and beheld her mother.

For a stretched second, the two women looked at each other. Then Ms Massey rushed to her crimsoned son, cradling his head, wiping blood away from his mouth and nose with her experienced nurse's hands.

"Is de ambulance coming?" she asked briskly.

"Yes, yes, Mum. I just called them."

"Run go fetch a towel."

Her face stained by tears, and forgetting the life inside her, Juliet raced upstairs, marking the banisters with Brenton's blood.

Ms Massey managed to turn Brenton onto his side and continued swabbing the blood from his torso, praying that he hadn't gone into shock. He was still breathing; but his body oozed blood, slowly curdling in sickly trickles. She pleasured in Brenton's faint exhales. How she had wanted to mother him when he was a baby; there was so much she regretted.

Juliet bounded down the stairs clutching two bath towels. A strange irony struck her as she took in the sight of her mother tenderly nestling her son's head.

Using one of the towels, Cynthia pressed firmly on Brenton's shoulder wound. His torso convulsed, like a fish that has been freshly caught and thrown down on a ship's deck. His eyes were vacant.

Five minutes later the ambulance arrived, its siren blasting. After the crew were satisfied that the bleeding had ceased, Brenton was stretchered into the van. As Ms Massey climbed in beside him, Juliet followed, hoping her mother would give her a forgiving glance. But Ms Massey turned her back on her and tended to her son, looking him over with such a powerful maternal care that Juliet felt the lurking presence of jealousy embedding itself into her heart. He's mine, he's mine, she thought. I loved him first and I will love him last.

The ambulance hastened its way to Kings College Hospital, where Brenton had made himself a regular visitor. He was wheeled away to receive immediate attention, overlooked by the critical eyes of his mother. Juliet sat brooding in the Casualty foyer, wondering if Brenton would call for her when he regained consciousness.

The doctor informed Ms Massey that Brenton had passed out due to loss of blood and shock. He required many stitches in his shoulder and knees, and his nose would have to be reset. He might well develop sinus problems in the future.

After the doctor had left Brenton's curtained cubicle, Juliet stole inside, unable to keep away from her brother's side any longer. She saw her mother seated by Brenton's bed, gazing at her son, wondering how he had sustained his injuries. He was stirring, tossing his head from side to side, as if reliving a childhood nightmare. His eyes half-open, he mumbled something.

Juliet's gaze searched her brother's eyes, willing for him to see her. "He'll be all right, Mum."

Ms Massey said nothing, and acted as if she heard nothing.

"Do you want a cup of tea or something, Mum? There's a vending machine outside in the foyer."

Ms Massey surveyed her son. "Take time, try and stay still."

Juliet ambled warily to Brenton's bedside.

"Don't touch him!" frosted her mother, feeling a terrible anger.

"He's my brother."

Brenton moaned and his eyes flickered wildly, as if he was dazzled by a myriad of disco lights.

"An' so you jus' realise," whispered Cynthia, her voice echoing a passionate accusation, finally meeting her daughter's eyes.

The tiny life inside Juliet suddenly grew heavier. Her features abruptly appeared drawn as she felt the dawn of her morning sickness.

Ms Massey's eyes returned to the helpless sight of her son. Juliet's gaze dwelled on her stomach as Brenton muttered again.

"We all make mistakes, Mum," Juliet finally replied.

Ms Massey chose to ignore her daughter once again.

For close to an hour, mother and daughter sat in silence, observing Brenton's every fidget, while a nurse entered the cubicle, monitoring his stability. He regained semi-consciousness, but was in too much pain to worry about his mother and sister exchanging silent glares. His shoulder felt as if someone had drilled a hot poker through it. Trust Terry Flynn to fight like a girl, he thought.

Soon, Brenton was wheeled away to a ward, through the hospital corridors. He wondered what Mr Lewis would say about it all. And what had happened to Flynn? he suddenly thought. He might have been brought to the same hospital. Could be interesting if they were parked in adjoining hospital beds.

Ms Massey escorted her son to the ward, while Juliet, sick of her mother's contempt, sought out a pay phone to call Mr Lewis. Floyd received the call. "Hello, is Mr Lewis there?"

"No, it's Floyd."

"This is Juliet. I've got some bad news. It's Brenton, he's in hospital."

"In hospital! Again?"

"Yeah, I think he's been in a fight."

"Oh no . . . Flynn. Is he all right?"

"Who's Flynn? Yeah. He's all right, he just came round. His shoulder is ripped open, his legs are cut, and he's got a broken nose. Who's this Flynn?"

"Er, one of his enemies."

"*One* of his enemies?"

"It's a long story. Don't worry about it now. He's all right now, innit?"

"Yeah, he's at Kings College."

"Where else? I'll tell Mr Lewis as soon as I see him, all right?"

"OK, then. Thanks, bye."

"Bye."

Floyd dropped the phone and raced upstairs to his room, where a smoking Biscuit was studying some newly acquired watches.

"Brenton's in hospital," Floyd blurted out. "Flynn must have catch up wid him. His shoulder is all tear up."

"Shit, they must have had a serious clash. I wonder what happened to Flynn?"

Floyd dropped himself on the bed. "And I wonder where they clashed. Brenton was going on weird yesterday, after he lost his job. He mus' have got all vex and started looking for Flynn."

"Nah," Biscuit disagreed, taking a Mars Bar out of his pocket, "he ain't that mad. They must have clashed on the street, innit."

"And Flynn always carries his blade," added Floyd gravely.

"I hope he's safe and t'ing. Where is he?"

"Kings College. He might as well move in there; doctors probably recognised him when he reach."

"So what – should we forward there and see how he is?"

"Yeah. His sister's there already, and your eyes are gonna think they're having a feast when you look 'pon her."

"Let's step it up then!"

"Hold up. I've got to leave a message for Lewis."

Floyd went downstairs to the kitchen where he found the notepad and pen, and hurriedly scribbled a message for the social worker while Biscuit waited impatiently at the front door.

Two hours later, Juliet returned home, finally satisfied that Brenton was no longer in any immediate danger. Why did I open my big mouth? she chided herself. What was Mum doing at home at that time, anyway? How long had she been waiting on the stairs?

Fate had conspired against her, and was wearing its full battle armour. Her mother would have found out about her pregnancy in due course. But now! She herself could scarcely come to terms with it, let alone coping with the fact that her brother was the father. And now, that bastard Fate had to meddle in her affairs, when it had no right to.

She left her mother at the hospital; Ms Massey was showing everybody how concerned she was about her son. Floyd and Biscuit offered their sorrows, affirming that Brenton had a 'solid body', so his recuperation would be swift. Biscuit was particularly charming, running errands, collecting coffees and generally being the antidote to the gloom with which everybody else was infected.

An hour or so since Floyd and Biscuit made their hurried way to Kings College, Mr Lewis appeared in Brenton's ward. He found Ms Massey stooping over her sleeping son, appearing washed-out and frail. Poor woman, he thought. Only recently she found her son, and now this.

Floyd and Biscuit were standing at the foot of the bed, whispering to each other, with the name Flynn resurfacing from time to time.

"Ms Massey, I believe?" Mr Lewis addressed her.

"Yes. An' you are the social worker?"

"I came as soon as I received Floyd's message. How is he?"

"He's not too bad now. The doctor says he's stabilised but he lost a whole 'eap of blood. He nearly bled to death. He's sleeping now but he's conscious."

Mr Lewis stole a glance at Floyd and Biscuit, still muttering to themselves. "Does anyone know what happened? Was it a fight?"

"It seems so," replied Cynthia. "The doctor say it look like as if someone tek a chunk outta him."

"Someone bit him?" Mr Lewis gazed upon Floyd once more, asking a thousand questions. "Floyd, do you have any idea what happened?"

"No. But I know he was upset yesterday 'cos he did lose his job. He was made redundant, and he was going on weird when he reach home yesterday."

"Did you see him this morning?"

"No. By the time I got up, Brenton lef' the yard."

Mr Lewis's eyes turned to Brenton's mother. "Is there anything I can do? If you want I can drive you home when you're ready."

"T'ank you, dat would be very kind."

An hour later, Mr Lewis drove Cynthia home, accompanied by a subdued Floyd and a crisp-eating Biscuit. The quartet talked little on their journey, all of them shaken by Brenton's near-death.

Mr Lewis saw Ms Massey to her front door, aiding her as she walked. She thanked him, offering an exhausted smile, then went inside, leaving Mr Lewis to ponder if Brenton's assailant was the same one as before.

Juliet heard her mother come in while preparing something to eat in the kitchen. She looked along the hallway and found the carpet still specked with Brenton's dried blood. Ms Massey took off her coat and noticed the hideous sight of a bloody hand print on the banisters. Juliet's hand.

It was as if the bones that had remained hidden under the floorboards for years had now crawled out and were bleeding over everything, reminding everyone of the anguished suffering of their solitary existence.

"You want something to eat, Mum?"

Ms Massey silently trundled along the hallway, towards the kitchen.

"I'm doing a bit of mackerel on 'ard-dough bread," Juliet offered, her heartbeat racing.

Cynthia sat down at the kitchen table, her eyes unforgiving, and her fury obvious. As Juliet nervously buttered the bread, a little dob of margarine dropped onto the floor. Cynthia's eyes followed it.

"The devil himself mus' ah possess you! Wha do yuh, chile? You 'ave destroyed everyt'ing. You're nutten but a leggo-beast. Do you realise what you 'ave done?"

"I'm sorry. I'm sorry, Mum."

The fish and bread suddenly looked unappetising.

"So you sorry. Sorry can't repair the damage. What the Lord God 'ave I done to deserve dis?"

"Sorry."

"Stop say dat 'cos you mek me sick."

Juliet's eyes became sodden. For a fraction of a second, she considered taking the bread-knife and plunging it deep into her stomach. She wanted to tell her mother how she loved Brenton. But how could she?

"My own son," Ms Massey continued, "who I 'ave prayed to see again for years. An' my own daughter is carrying his chile! Haven't I paid enough, Lord? You're a disgrace! A damn disgrace!"

"Well, at least I done it out of love," Juliet retaliated, "which is more than you can say for how you felt for my father!"

"Your fader has not'ing to do wid dis."

"But it's true."

"What do you know what is true! You're carrying my son's chile!"

"Yes, that is true. Your grandson! Are you gonna abandon him like you did your son?"

Cynthia's senses imploded, and a thousand regrets attacked her memories. Juliet would have given anything to take that last statement back. Her mother raised herself deliberately, as if every movement bred a considerable pain. Juliet watched her struggle along the hallway, and realised that nothing would ever be the same. Had her consuming lust caused her family to be torn apart? she asked herself. Whoever dig the ditch, she thought, shall fall in it; a song from the Gong she had heard while in Brenton's bed. And she visioned herself wiping the sweat off her brow as the other hand held the spade.

Coming In From The Cold

30 May, 1980

Mr Lewis drove Brenton to his mother's home from the hospital, escorted by Juliet. Something disquieted him on his journey; he didn't know what, but the tension in the air was tangible. Why didn't Ms Massey come with Juliet to collect her son from the hospital? And what had alarmed the girl? She looked as guilty as an accused burglar in the dock wearing the victim's dress. But what was she guilty of?

Brenton looked like a war casualty. Cotton wool and plaster masked his nose, and the padded dressing on his shoulder made him resemble an American footballer. His knees seemed to be wailing for air under the recently wrapped bandaging. Oblivious to his appearance, Brenton peeked out of the window and saw the late May sun playing hide-and-seek behind a flimsy cloud.

Juliet took note of the road signs, wondering what Brenton's reaction would be when she told him about her pregnancy.

The social worker pulled up outside Ms Massey's home and helped Brenton out of the car.

"All right, I can manage."

"Brave to the last, eh?" Mr Lewis laughed. "Some thanks I get."

"Didn't I thank you at the hospital? What do you want me to do? I can't get down on my knees and say thanks and praises 'cos my knees ain't too good."

Mr Lewis laughed again and returned to his motor. "I have to get to Blue Star House for a meeting. Take care, won't you." His eyes searched for Juliet, who was turning her key in the latch. "Bye, Juliet. Say hello to your mum for me."

"Yes I will, thanks for everything."

The social worker performed an abrupt U-turn, again wondering as he did so if Brenton would ever come back to the hostel again.

Once inside the house, Juliet took Brenton by the arm and helped him into the front room.

"You want something to eat, or a liccle something to drink?"

"Yeah, but later. I wanna hear what you said you have to tell me."

Brenton laid himself gingerly on the sofa, and once comfortable, massaged his right temple. Juliet inhaled sharply, then placed Brenton's bag of clothes in an armchair. Before she could speak, her brother asked, "Where's Mum?"

His sister's eyes flicked towards the ceiling. "She's not well. She's been in bed for the last couple of days, but she wants to see you after I chat to you."

She closed her eyes for a long second, sensing her body temperature warming like a switched-on kettle. "You sure you don't want nothing to eat?"

"No."

"Well, er, this ain't really fair after all what has happened to you."

"What ain't fair?"

"You comfortable?"

"Yes!"

"Promise you won't go all cuckoo?"

"I'm hardly likely to in the state I'm in."

"All right, all right." Her voice dropped. "I'm pregnant."

"You're *what?*"

"Pregnant."

Juliet collapsed beside her brother, as if someone had

kidnapped her legs. Speechless, Brenton looked upon her stomach, thinking dazedly that part of him was now part of her; his cherished sister. But should he skin his teet' or bawl for mercy? He did neither, but wrapped a supportive arm over Juliet's shoulders. "Shit" he breathed. "What you gonna do? You all right?"

"I'm fine. Pregnancy ain't illness."

"Does Mum . . . ?"

"Yes, she knows."

Brenton's throat dried up like a drop of rain in the desert. So this was why Juliet and Cynthia weren't chatting to each other. Then: me a friggin dad! he said to himself. How the fuck will this work out? Poor Juliet, he thought. And I reckoned *I* had problems.

Brenton remembered all those long nights when Floyd and himself would debate about the existence of God. Well, if there is a God, He's having a laugh and joke with my family, he decided.

The couple locked themselves in silence for the next ten minutes, gazing at each other, trying to read each other's thoughts. But somehow, Juliet knew the burden of Brenton's past would now become just a sad memory, and perhaps he could now look to the future. She had accomplished what she set out to do on that cold, dripping night when she first saw him. It had resulted in devastating consequences, yeah; but she felt someone had to pay for her brother's childhood sufferings. And if it was her, then so be it. But no one could convince her to abort her child, or give this baby away. Even Mum and Brenton would understand that. Her career would be derailed, but she thought the life inside her was a gift from God. The flame of her affair with her brother had burned its course, and she could never pick up a match to relight it.

Brenton kissed his sister on her forehead, then laboured up the stairs, feeling burning sensations in his knees. He wondered what had happened to Flynn. Let's see him flash a ratchet now, he thought.

He entered his mother's bedroom and found her lying down, supported by a family of pillows, appearing as if she was tired of living. Her eyes followed her son as he carefully sat down on the bed.

"My son...My son. I know about you and Juliet."

Paralysis crept over Brenton's features as he stared at a framed photograph of Juliet in her school uniform.

Cynthia continued: "Sometimes, t'ings in life work out funny. An' sometimes people don't 'ave no control over dem destiny, y'understand?" Brenton nodded impassively. "It seem like history repeat itself. 'Cos, me fall pregnant to a man my mama did not like. As far as she was concerned, my 'usband was a wort'less layabout who did not want to do nothing for 'imself. I said to my mother at the time dat I really did love 'im. But at the same time, I knew I did wrong."

"I ain't a worthless layabout."

"I never said dat. What I am saying is dis. Juliet an' myself let passion rule over sense. You know what I'm saying? Even wid your fader, de same t'ing 'appen. So, even though 1'm more vex wid your sister, 'cos she should have known better, in a strange way I cry for her an' you."

Brenton fingered his earlobe and studied his mother's face. He finally saw a resemblance between them; it was there, in the eyes.

"I don't want to fight wid you no more, Brenton. Lord God, look upon you, I'm sure you're tired of fighting. When I sit down in the 'ospital beside your bed, I realise der is no time for argue an' cuss, an' no time for t'inking what might 'ave been. We 'ave to deal wid today an' tomorrow."

Brenton's face stirred into a sympathetic expression. She has been through as much pain as I have, he thought.

"I don't know what Juliet is going to do," Cynthia went on. "She need time to t'ink t'ings through. An' I don't t'ink we will help matters if we tell her to do dis an' dat an' t'inking about our own worries."

"I ain't gonna be no burden to her. It'll be up to her what she does."

Ms Massey weakly nodded her head.

"So you don't hate me then?" queried Brenton. "I hated you when I first saw you."

"Lord God, I don't 'ate you Brenton. I could never 'ate my children."

Brenton smiled. "It was worth it."

His mother's heart felt a ray of sunshine, which brought back memories of her beloved Gary. But as she watched her son leaving, she feared for his life in this part of London.

Brenton went downstairs and found Juliet curled up in an armchair. "So how did it go then?" she asked anxiously.

"It went all right; she looks very sick, though."

"Yeah, but she'll be safe. I'll look after her."

It suddenly hit Brenton that his affair with Juliet was over and out. Lying in his hospital bed, he had suspected this. But the realisation was much more painful than the wounds Terry Flynn had inflicted on him. He tried to hide the stabbing sensation he felt in his heart. "So what you gonna do?" he asked.

"Stay here. Look after Mum and our baby when it arrives. After all that's happened I hope you keep in touch."

"Don't worry about that; I will. This family is all I've got."

Juliet smiled. Brenton wished she wouldn't, for when she smiled, she looked so beautiful, and memories of blissful moments flooded through his brain. He felt his eyes dampen and a sickly feeling attacked his tongue. "I'll.... I'll be off now." He collected his bag of clothes.

"Brenton, Brenton. Before you go..."

He halted his tracks towards the front door, and as he turned, Juliet saw the tears moistening the nose bandage.

"I still love you, but I can't."

"I know, I know."

He turned and departed, and wished Mr Brown was still alive. He needed someone to confide in.

Brenton caught a cab to his hostel, then hauled himself up the stairs, where Floyd caught sight of him.

Brenton laid himself on Floyd's bed, observing his spar insert a cassette tape into his suitcase. Floyd looked upon his brethren and knew he wept.

"Everyone is chatting about you," Floyd began, hoping to cheer him up. "Mashing up Terry Flynn has turned you into a celebrity."

"Some celebrity. He mashed me up as well."

Floyd wondered why his spar was still idling in the pit of sorrow. "Is it all over?"

"What's all over?"

"Er, you and your sister, innit."

"How did you know?"

"Brenton, it's me who has a room next to yours; not an idiot."

Embarrassment slapped Brenton's cheeks.

"So what?" Floyd persisted. "Your mudder boot you out of her yard? Saying don't bother come back 'cos you terrorise her daughter?"

"Bwai, you so negative. It didn't go like that. My mudder was understanding."

"Man, what a palaver. Don't worry 'bout nutten, I won't tell nobody what a gwarn. Shit, I won't even tell myself."

"If you do, you will know which side blood run ah pumpkin belly."

Floyd laughed out loud; to hear Brenton quote him felt like a compliment.

In the ashtray, jutting out of the matchsticks and snout butts, was a half-smoked spliff. Floyd arsoned it and reasoned: "You know, what you done weren't so bad."

"Oh yeah? How you work that one out?"

"Well, the Bible say dat Adam was the first man, seen. And Eve was the first woman, right?"

Brenton nodded, wondering what wise words his spar would come out with now.

"So Adam and Eve, the first people in dis world, had Cain and Abel, seen?"

"Yeah. What you getting at?"

"Caine and Abel married, right? But whom did they marry? Adam and Eve must have had two gal as well, 'cos there ain't nobody else about, seen?"

"So what you're saying is that Cain and Abel married their sisters."

"Yes, me brethren. If they didn't, the human race would ah dead innit."

"You're cuckoo."

"Nah, check it out, it must be true."

Brenton took the spliff, hoovered it and laughed until his shoulder pained him.

"You're friggin mad," he gasped.

"What's so funny? It must be true. Read Genesis, man."

"All I know 'bout Genesis is dat Phil Collins is the drummer."

"Cha, man. Can't you be serious for a minute?"

"Look Floyd, man. I ain't in the mood. Turn up the suitcase."

Barrington Levy's *Youthman* blared out from the twin speakers as the brethrens decided on a game of domino.

One Johnny Osbourne cassette later, Brenton departed to his own room. He switched on his battered suitcase, and he found a half-toked spliff under his mattress. The Gong's *Three Little Birds* tweeted out from the distorted speakers.

As he crashed onto his bed, he thought things might work out all right, and he sang in a whisper, "Don't worry, about a thing."

He pulled himself up and stared at Mr Dean, like a painter dwelling over one of his not-so-good portraits. "Why the fuck did I put you on the wall, James?" He went over to the poster and tore it down, screwing the film star into a ball and throwing him into a corner. Then he returned to his bed, closed his eyes, and daydreamed of Mr Brown riding a chariot into town, astride a coffin, with everybody hailing out his name.

THE END.

AFTERWORD

Shortly after the 1981 Brixton riots, I found myself in a police holding cell situated near Lambeth Walk. I was eighteen years old. Reflecting on the stupidity of my petty crime that had led me there, and awaiting a prison van to escort me to Wormwood Scrubs, the very notion of me becoming an author was about as far away from my mind as the planet Pluto. What filled my thoughts was the realisation that my present circumstances had only confirmed the predictions of certain authorities, teachers, career advisors and other naysayers who had observed my tempestuous teenage years. I was way beyond self-loathing, hating the world and its brother. It was only when I had complained bitterly of my unfair life, as I saw it, to a fellow inmate and after he asked me what I had initiated to improve my life, that I began to dream of a better future. Although I was unaware of it, the first seed of what became *Brixton Rock* was planted in an ill-lighted, musty cell in Wormwood Scrubs.

Armed with the advice of the same inmate who had listened patiently to my endless grievances, the first task I had set myself upon my release was to visit Brixton library and read CLR James's *The Black Jacobins*. When I concluded the last page, hope for my own dreams and aspirations began to delicately flicker. I have been stoking the flame ever since.

Brixton in 1980 was a vibrant place. Some have asked me where does the '*Rock*' come from in the title. Well, it's quite a simple explanation: Brixton was *rocking* at the time with reggae music. It could be heard from every tower block, every road and even in Brockwell Park on a Sunday morning where the most determined *rootshead* would strut along the path, burdened by the latest up-to-date *Brixton suitcase*. At the time, for my peers and myself, reggae was the only thing that kept us going through those dark days of early Thatcherism. It spoke of our plight and our struggles and that is why I referred to certain reggae tracks in the text of *Brixton Rock* and even more so in *East of Acre Lane*. My way of paying homage if you like. It was no fluke that *The Specials'* deeply political *Ghost Town*, released in the summer of 1981, was one of the year's biggest selling records.

On most Saturday nights, my friends and I, dressed in our reptile skin shoes, imitation silk shirts and double-breasted jackets, would walk the Brixton streets and council estates, searching for a *blues* party or a rave. We only had to listen out for the bass sounds of the reggae music we so loved to guide us. I cannot remember ever being disappointed and in most instances, we had the choice of nine or ten jump-ups to attend. Indeed, it wasn't rare to discover three or four *blues dances* in the same estate.

None of my friends or myself owned a car back then so after the conclusion of these blues dances, we simply changed into our *trodding* footwear to walk home, chancing arrest from the *Special Patrol Group*, a branch of the police force that we likened to Eastern bloc militia-men. At times we felt we were living in a police state. But there were good times too and I still reflect fondly on the antics, crazy situations and the laughter that friends and myself shared.

Not being as fluent and creative with the English language as most of my friends, I used to listen and observe attentively, unwittingly noting characters in the bank of my brain for use twenty years or so later in the novels *Brixton Rock* and *East of Acre Lane*. The sheer inventiveness of my friends' dialogue was always a fascination to me and although I attempted to 'chat' like a Floyd or a Biscuit, my Croydon childhood betrayed me; I lived in Brixton with my family up to the age of four until I moved away. I returned when I was fourteen.

Urban street dialogue has always been in the ownership of the young and it reinvents itself as swiftly as the passing seasons. I offer a wry grin when I hear the likes of Ali G attempting to mimic street culture. Those of us who know a little something about this realise that the street culture that Ali G presents to the world is totally inaccurate and only barely reflects street talk of the mid-1980s. For example, the term *punanny* that Ali G enjoys employing, was the title of a hit dancehall tune by a DJ called Admiral Bailey in the mid-1980s. Today, a wisened urban youth wouldn't be caught dead using the term. My point is that it seems the establishment wish to sell our own culture back to ourselves in the form of the likes of Ali G, while ignoring what is really happening in street culture. We need to sell our own culture from its original source and I hope my novels redress that balance a little.

One of my many motivations in writing *Brixton Rock* was when I came across a novel written about Brixton, which I will not name here, that critics and reviewers seemed to think was an accurate portrayal of Brixton dialogue and urban culture. It was nothing of the sort. On reading these reviews, I asked myself how would these critics know what was accurate? Although I am only human and rush to see reviews of any books I have written, nothing gives me more delight than when someone from my Brixton past comes up to me and says, 'Yeah, Alex. You got it right, man. Dat's how it was.'

When I perform readings the public continually ask me where does the character, Brenton Brown, come from. They say that a large percentage of first novels are autobiographical and *Brixton Rock* does not wander from that. There is a large part of me in Brenton Brown; his anger, frustration, a yearning to be loved, but I can assure everyone that I have never slept with any of my

253

sisters! There are also character traits I *stole* from people I knew that I infused into Brenton Brown. After all, if Brenton Brown was solely based on me then I would no doubt bore the reader.

Little did I realise in the creating of Brenton Brown that this character resonated throughout the social spectrum. Whether it be a young white man living in an estate in Newcastle relating to Brenton or a retired black man residing in the countryside of Jamaica, Brenton seems to touch the readers in a significant way more than any other character I have created since *Brixton Rock*.

When I was finally content with what seemed the 2,000th draft of *Brixton Rock*, I submitted it to at least 30 publishers and agents. They all turned me down, reasoning that there would be no audience for my first novel. *BlackAmber Books* took a chance on me and I hope they have been rewarded for their enterprise. BlackAmber presented me with an opportunity to create a career for myself in the writing world. But I do dismay when the larger publishing houses turn down novels similar to *Brixton Rock*. Booksellers, fiction directors, marketing personnel and the like love to categorise books and place them in this genre or that genre. The truth is the story of Brenton Brown could be duplicated by a writer who lives in Edinburgh, Lagos or Moscow. *Brixton Rock* is the story of a young man trying to establish his identity, attempting to recover his roots that were cut away from birth, and as long as there are Brenton Browns in this world, it will have resonance and meaning to the reader, for at the end of the day, all of us crave the thing that Brenton needs the most – to be loved.

Oh, one last thing. I have been questioned many times about the very last sentence of *Brixton Rock*. *Then he returned to his bed, closed his eyes, and daydreamed of Mr Brown riding a chariot into town, astride a coffin, with everybody hailing out his name.* It's a reference to a Bob Marley song that he wrote in the late 1960s. Legend has it that on one hot Kingston morning, perched at the back of a courthouse, was a crow dressed smartly in a three-piece suit. Later on that day, this same bird was seen standing on a coffin that was laid upon a horse-drawn cart on its way to a cemetery. These apparent scenarios caused alarm and panic in parts of Kingston, with some people believing they had seen the 'bird of death'. On a whim I decided to end the novel referring to these bizarre incidents. . . Perhaps I was just trying to be too clever.

Those of you who wish to learn more about Brenton's childhood in a children's home should check out my third novel *The Seven Sisters*. Any who aspire to know more about the rising tensions in Brixton that led to the 1981 riots should check out *East of Acre Lane*.

Peace and Guidance.

Alex Wheatle
South London, January 2004

OTHER BLACKAMBER TITLES

From Kitchen Sink to Boardroom Table
Richard Scase and Joan Blaney

The Demented Dance
Mounsi

The Cardamom Club
Jon Stock

Something Black in the Lentil Soup
Reshma S. Ruja

Typhoon
The Holy Woman
Qaisra Shahraz

Ma
All That Blue
Caston-Paul Effa

Paddy Indian
The Uncoupling
Cauvery Madhavan

Foreday Morning
Paul Dash

Ancestors
Paul Crooks

Nothing but the Truth
Mark Wray

Hidden Lights
Joan Blaney

What Goes Around
Sylvester Young

One Bright Child
Patricia Cumper

FROM KITCHEN SINK TO BOARDROOM TABLE

by

Joan Blaney and Richard Scase

This will empower women to release their potential for corporate success and allow them to build on the skills they have developed managing the home and the family. An inspirational book, it demonstrates how women have the power and courage to deal with situations in the face of adversity.

'A remarkable book.' **Baroness Betty Boothroyd, House of Lords**

'The sheer determination of these normal women to turn a raw deal into a good one leaves one humbled and inspired. They remind us all that lateral thinking and courageous endeavour can turn a potential victim into a confident and optimistic survivor. This book delighted me.' **Joanna Lumley**

'A moving and empowering collection of true stories which will inspire women of all ages and backgrounds.' **Juliette Foster, Sky News**

Through real-life accounts that capture the essence of women's flexibility and foresight, *From Kitchen Sink to Boardrooom Table* features women from varied walks of life and shows how their personal and domestic skills can, and have been, harnessed into profitable and valued leading roles in modern-day business. The key skills of financial and time management, team building and negotiation, and the innate strength and courage of women from different backgrounds are revealed through these inspirational stories. These two distinguished authors triumphantly show us that learning can be drawn from the most unexpected places and circumstances.

THE CARDAMOM CLUB
by
Jon Stock

'If Graham Greene were reincarnated in dotcom Delhi this is the novel he would have written. A witty, fast-moving and cleverly plotted espionage romp.' **William Dalrymple**

'If the narrative has the solidity of well-made furniture, it has been decorated in exquisite detail. Stock is as good a travel writer as he is a storyteller.' Sunday Telegraph

'The Cardamom Club is an elegant and assured piece of writing – a powerfully characterised examination of identity and displacement, with a bracing narrative that exerts a quiet but inexorable grip.' Publishing News

'Shades of Greene – in this tense spy thriller with a difference, Jon Stock's Kerala is vividly rendered, and he shows a keen understanding of the complexities of Indian society. Recommended.' **Nicholas Royle**

'Beautiful narratives, a lot of fun but also touches upon deep emotions and at times raises controversial issues.' **Hindustan Times**

The Cardamom Club is a fast-moving spy novel about Raj Nair, a young British Asian doctor at the Foreign Office who is posted to New Delhi. Ambitious and patriotic, he has also agreed to work for MI6 – a decision he soon regrets. The MI6 station head in Delhi does not approve of British Asians working for the intelligence services. In fact, he disapproves of anything to do with the subcontinent – particularly a strong and independent, nuclear India.

Raj, visiting his parents' country of birth for the first time, is soon forced to question his own loyalties, particularly when Special Branch arrest Raj's father back in Britain on trumped-up spying charges. And when the British High Commissioner in Delhi, an indophile and Raj's ally, is mysteriously recalled to London, Raj realises he is up against a secretive, colonial organisation working at the very highest levels of Whitehall: The Cardamom Club.

At its rotten core is Macaulay, our man in Cochin, who used to work for Indian Political Intelligence – the secret service that spied on colonial India. Is the sinister Macaulay responsible for a spate of child sacrifices, suttee and other brutalities at odds with the image of a modern, progressive India? And can Raj, with the help of the beautiful journalist Priyanka, expose The Cardamom Club to the world before it destroys him?

ONE BRIGHT CHILD
by
Patricia Cumper
REVISED EDITION

'*A powerful evocation of the period, an inspiring, heart-warming and loving story.*' **Times Educational Supplement**

'*Poignant, gripping, funny and well-written.*' **Sunday Times**

'*The vivid story of a Jamaican girl's struggle to become a lawyer in the 1950s.*' **Prima**

'*A delight, extremely charming and evocative. An inspiraton. Terrific.*' **Joanna Lumley**

'*Gripping and emotional.*' **Pride Magazine**

'*A beguiling read.*' **The Gleaner**

In 1936, Gloria Carter at thirteen is torn from her island home in Kingston, Jamaica, when her socially ambitious mother decides to give her the best education money can buy. Sent to live in the colonial motherland of England, where she attends an exclusive school for girls, Gloria soon learns that in the mainly white England, she will always need to be twice as good as everyone else in order to be considered half as good. She is forced to adapt to a landscape whose contours are both alien and intriguing. Throwing herself into her studies, Gloria decides to pursue a career in Law and wins a place at Girton College, Cambridge University. Still struggling with prejudice on account of her race and colour, she enters a mixed marriage with a fellow undergrad, a penniless Englishman. However, these hardships, far from dampening her spirits, ignite the fire for her inevitable success. This revised, expanded version of the original highly successful novel based on a true life story is funny, poignant and inspiring!

THE LOCUST HUNTER
by
Po Wah Lam

Western ideals of rationality are pitted against the magic realism of Chinese folklore.

The Locust Hunter is set in the humid and turbulent landscape of 1970s Hong Kong; this coming-of-age tale follows the journey of Sundance and his five friends as they try to avenge the killing of his 200-year-old pet tortoise, Lord Baltimore. Their village, situated between the Big Amber (China) and the looming presence of the British army, teeters precariously between colonial ideals and the teachings of Tao and Chinese customs. At the heart of the story is the contest held every 10 years to find the most proficient locust hunter in Hong Kong. Since time immemorial, the prize has been won by a member of the leading Triad family ... who use every dirty trick in the book. Summoning all his young courage and his belief in life, 9-year-old Sundance takes them on.

RAISE THE LANTERNS HIGH

by

Lakshmi Persaud

A dramatic page-turner, and a rich visual treat full of powerful ideas expressed in equally powerful language. At its heart is the image of burning, which ensures that the intellectual and emotional temperature never drops. It is about the battle between the sexes, the conflict between modernity and long-honoured traditions, beautifully written with a pithy, punchy style.

On the eve of her wedding, Vasti finds her arranged marriage is to the rapist she saw in a sugarcane field years earlier. She can either speak out, defy convention and publicly disgrace her family, or succumb to tradition and submit to her fate. The conflict rages within her and makes her ill; she collapses unconscious and is transported to the Kingdom of Jyotika in North India where, two hundred years before, the three widowed queens of King Paresh are expected to climb onto a burning pyre with their dead husband to perform the suttee or widow burning. *Raise the Lanterns High* explores such cultural violations with compassion and drama, from the perspective of the women asked to make these impossible sacrifices, and shows the bravery required to accept as well as to reject these traditions. This is a story of female emancipation as harrowing as it is beautiful.

A POCKET GUIDE TO BEING AN INDIAN GIRL

by

B. K. Mahal

A touching tale of a rebellious teenager struggling to survive her own culture.

Susham Dillon, born and bred in Dudley in the north of England, talks of her adolescence and observes the differences that set her apart and make an Indian girl's life more than just another arranged marriage. Living in the shadow of her perfect elder sister, Kully, and her 'bhangra chick' sister, Kiz, she suffers agonies about her mentally-ill father; is stressed out by her keeping-up-appearances mother; and suffers agonies from her crush on the dashing Arjun. Susham gives us the full photo album of her chaotic life. Through her talent of making a fool of herself, she is forever crumbling other people's (especially her despairing family's) social expectations of a good Indian girl.

THE DEMENTED DANCE

by

Mounsi

Translated from the French by Lulu Norman

Set in modern-day France, this is the story of the marginal, desolate life of a young boy, Tarik, who exists on the edge of society. His life is so bleak that he is not even sure if he is really alive. His father, an Algerian factory worker and an alcoholic, loses his job, then gradually becomes mentally unbalanced to the point where Tank is taken into care. Shortly after this, Tarik starts to steal, take cars for joyrides and associate with other cast-off children. He and his friend Bako end up in borstal after a raid which culminates in murder. When Tarik is released he tries to go straight, falls in with various hustlers operating in Parisian society, becomes a male escort and falls in love with Lise – who is very different from the other women he meets. Their relationship ends and Tarik moves in with Bako and Fania, who is on the game. When Fania dies of a heroin overdose, Tarik and Bako, accompanied by Fania's cat, drive to the sea to scatter her ashes. This simple incident has fatal consequences.

All BlackAmber Books arte available from your local bookshop.

For a regular update on BlackAmber's latest releases, with extracts, reviews and events, visit:

www.blackamber.com